The Squeeze

LESLEY GLAISTER is the prize-winning author of thirteen
novels, most recently, *Little Egypt*. Her short stories have
been anthologised and broadcast on Radio 4. She has written
drama for radio and stage and published a pamphlet of poetry.
Lesley is a Fellow of the RSL, teaches creative writing at
the University of St Andrews and lives in Edinburgh.

Praise for *Little Egypt*

Winner 2014 Jerwood Fiction Uncovered Prize
Sunday Herald Book of the Year 2014
Longlisted International Dublin Literary Award 2016

'Eerily atmospheric *Little Egypt*, made me shudder; certain passages were read through half-closed eyes, the way you watch grisly scenes in a film — desperate to know what happens, but not wanting to disturbing images imprinted on your mind.'
—ROSEMARY GORING, *The Herald*

'Glaister's greatest success in *Little Egypt* is in her pacing and her use of language to obscure change; through effortless and consistently engaging prose, Isis's transformation, the degradation of the house, the growing panic over her parents' prolonged absence, and the book's more sinister themes, all emerge discreetly.'
—CLARE HAZELTON, *TLS*

'Glaister is very good at creating an atmosphere of rank gloom, and her alternating structure gives her rich opportunities for dramatic tension, which she exploits brilliantly. She slowly ramps up the grotesqueries with just the right amount of dark and light: a gleam of macabre humour leavens the misery, while there is always empathy for Isis, doomed to suffer a horrible life to protect her disturbed and disturbing twin.'
—JANE HOUSHAM, *The Guardian*

LESLEY GLAISTER

THE SQUEEZE

SALT

CROMER

PUBLISHED BY SALT PUBLISHING 2017

2 4 6 8 10 9 7 5 3 1

First published in Great Britain in 2017 by
Salt Publishing Ltd
12 Norwich Road, Cromer, Norfolk NR27 0AX UNITED KINGDOM

www.saltpublishing.com

Salt Publishing Limited Reg. No. 5293401

A CIP catalogue record for this book is available from the British Library

ISBN 978 1 78463 116 1 (Hardback edition)
ISBN 978 1 78463 117 8 (Electronic edition)

Typeset in Neacademia by Salt Publishing

Printed and bound in Great Britain by Clays Ltd, St Ives plc

For Jill Glaister and in memory of Oliver Glaister.

ONE

1989-91

Alis

MAMA'S SALT TIN had a picture of a ballerina balanced on one toe. Her other leg floated up behind her, one finger pointing to heaven. Her dress was made of silver cloud. When I was a little kid, I wanted to be this ballerina.

So stupid.

I am a realist. Of course, I always knew I'd end up like Mama. She worked hard and sometimes the men were bad but not often. Usually there was food for the table, sometimes very good food. And drink. Mama had the need to drink. But when she was not too drunk she was very funny. She made jokes and we'd laugh and laugh at the stupid pricks. We laughed a lot. We did.

Mama died long ago of too much drink.

I don't know what happened to the salt tin.

Mats

WATCHING HISTORY HAPPEN before your eyes, it is amazing. It was on the news, extended news that night: the breaking down of the Berlin Wall. We saw the sudden party it became, people from East and West chipping with hammers and chisels for souvenirs; heavy machinery; cranes swinging blocks through the air; tears and songs and laughter, a kind of ecstasy of destruction.

My wife wasn't a political person, or an emotional person, but she cried. Never had I seen her like this. I was moved too for sure, by what was happening in Berlin, and by Nina's face. In the flicker of the TV light I watched her struggle with her expression – she hates to give anything away. We wanted to be a part of it so we opened a bottle of red though it was a work night. We raised a glass to freedom and then raised several more.

It was seeing Nina in that moment as almost vulnerable that gave me the courage to ask her the question I had not dared to ask before. I'd been offered a transfer from our head office in Oslo, a promotion to Director of Communications and Transformations in our northern UK branch. This would mean a move to Edinburgh, for at least a year, maybe for longer or even for good.

She stood to move away and mute the TV. 'But I have everything here,' she said, sweeping her hand to indicate this. Her back was against the glass wall of our apartment; snowy pine trees behind her showed blue. I could not clearly see her face. Her hair was piled high on her head the way I like, to show her neck, so delicate.

'Why would I want to leave my job? My friends?'

'Not for ever,' I said. 'Maybe a year – and see what you think then?'

She turned her back. So slim in her black clothes. Around her the blue snow glowed. She said nothing; I said nothing. She made coffee. We sat on the sofa across from the window, coffee pot on the table. On TV, silent youths danced on top of the wall, throwing high their fists. We watched for a few minutes more before she switched it off.

Her jaw was pulling little strings in her neck – a bad sign. When she spoke again it was to change the subject. We talked about her work, so much more interesting than mine; her patients, some of them famous. She works with skiers, the Olympic team, sportsmen and women of different kinds, providing physiotherapy. In the early days, if I had a stiff back she used to fix it, her fingers hard and cool, effective. But later, not so much.

Maybe it was stupid of me to bring up the subject of the child at that moment. Next year, she always said, but the years were adding and she was 39. Past time already, I considered. Most of our friends had children by now. My first thought when Kristian offered me the post, had been the child: would this be good or bad news for the prospect? I was excited at the thought of working somewhere new and Edinburgh was a city I had many times promised myself to visit.

Whenever I mentioned a child, Nina's hand would go to her flat stomach. There it went again, onto her thin, black wool sweater. On her white hand the diamond of her ring glinted; two platinum rings, wedding and engagement. Each night she took them off to polish. She'd lay them neatly on the bedside shelf and rub cream into her hands, cream that smelled faintly medicinal.

Her face I could not properly see. I stood to switch on the lamp. She is so fair with slanting eyes, blue like sea glass, even in the light impossible to read.

'You could take a sabbatical,' I suggested. 'Relax, maybe get pregnant. Have the baby there, maybe.'

There we were in the glass, a couple having coffee in the evening. The pine trees had gone now but through our reflections street lamps pricked points of light.

She put down her mug, loud on the glass table. 'I'm certainly not giving birth in a foreign country,' she said. 'What are you thinking, Mats!'

We sat in silence. I stood to fetch a cigarette, switch on music, Garbarek, soft saxophone winding like the smoke. Her hair shone in the lamplight. Her small skull gave me a tender feeling. I bent to kiss her slim neck, downy at the back, fine white strands she has never seen.

'Forget it,' I said. 'It was just an idea.'

She reached up and caught my hand. 'How about the cabin, at the weekend?'

In winter there is nothing at the cabin but fire and snow, the sauna and the bed.

We added brandy to our coffee and went upstairs.

Alis

MAMA TOLD ME not to go near the guy with the flashy car. How do you think he got so rich? And girls did disappear, pretty girls. But in Romania, to disappear was not so strange. An everyday thing.

I took no notice and now I am here.

It is dark and I am alone. I do not like to be alone. I do not like the dark. Please God bring me light.

Marta

POCKED WITH SHELL damage, the bridge was unsafe for traffic, but always busy with pedestrians. On a sultry afternoon, Marta walked Milya home from school. A chemical haze hung in the air – you wouldn't want to breathe too deeply. Milya ran back to talk to a friend and Marta waited, gazing at the posters plastered all over the stonework; not so long ago you'd have gone to prison for that. Or disappeared. Years ago this bridge was lined with statues of saints, but now along the parapet stood only the stumps of feet and shins.

Marta peered down at the riverbank, clogged with rags and rubbish, scum and slime, but in the middle, still deep and bright, swam fish. You'd have to be desperate to eat them, knowing what they swam in. On one side of the river were the flats where the workers lived; on the other the school, shadowed by the chemical plant and the cement works. In the chemical plant lights burned twenty-four hours a day so that the sky never grew properly dark at night, was always stained with orange.

'Come on.' Milya tugged at Marta's hand.

'Five plus seven,' said Marta.

'Twelve. Do me some takeaways.'

Marta wiped her brow, noticed a guy watching her, a stranger in a suit. He had the look of a businessman. Marta began to hurry past but he held his hand up and spoke: 'Excuse me, I'm looking for a place to eat. Is there a restaurant nearby?'

Marta had to fight not to laugh. 'I'm sorry,' she said. 'No, it's just flats that side.' She pointed at the six towering blocks – stained concrete, hanging washing, broken windows, haphazard patchings, hen coops and leggy tomato plants on the balconies. 'You need to go back into town.' In truth there was Yuri's where you could buy tea and onion soup, but it was too close to the stink of the river, not a place for the likes of him.

Milya fidgeted beside her. 'Come *on*, Marta.'

Marta lifted her shoulders at the man, apologetic. He was middle-aged, heavy and well cared for. Though he spoke Romanian, he was dressed as if he came from the west. His suit was beautiful, a sheen to the cloth in the hazy sunshine. His shoes were scuffed, but beneath the dust you could see the gleam of expensive leather. Everything was dusty from the cement works. Even Milya's copper curls looked grey.

'I'm hungry,' Milya insisted, tugging.

'You're not the only one.' The man smiled down at Milya, who stared back at him curiously.

'You can have your dinner with us, can't he Marta?' she said.

'Milya!' Marta flushed. 'Mr . . . the gentleman's looking for a restaurant. Go back across the bridge, take a taxi back to town – there you'll find . . . fine places,' she finished vaguely.

'Of course.' His eyes lingered on her face. 'Good day, *Marta* is it? Antenescu, Pavel.'

She took his moist hand, confused by the look he was giving her, just like those from the factory boys. She knew where such looks led and did not want that, no thank you, not a flat full of babies before she was twenty.

'And you live?'

'There.' Milya pointed. 'Flat 67, block 1. It's the bestest block.'

'And what's your family name?' he asked.

'Sala,' said Milya. 'Come *on*, Marta!'

Before he turned away, Mr Antenescu squeezed Marta's hand tight in his own, leaving an imprint in her fingers.

'Don't be so free to tell people things,' Marta scolded.

'Why?' Milya tore her hand away and ran ahead.

For a change, the lift was working; as it creaked and grunted upwards they held their breaths against the stench. When she entered the flat, Marta tried seeing the apartment from a stranger's point of view, noticing afresh the grease and urine smell that, scrub as they might, she and Mama could never overcome. Nor could they overcome the sadness that had clung to the furniture and deepened the shadows since Tata's death.

Marta began to peel potatoes, cutting away the green bits, the bad bits, the sprouting eyes. The memory of Pavel's warm, smooth squeeze stayed in her hand and she stopped to gaze at it, considering.

Alis

NEVER DID I trust a guy before, but this one, he said he loved me and I believed him! What happened to my brain that day? He said I was his girlfriend, the special one, and then I remember nothing for a while. Maybe a drug in my wine or my coffee. How do I know? I woke up in the dark with a pain in my head. There was noise. Something soft nearby. I could not see, but I could feel long hair, thick hair.

It was a girl and I was so glad there was another girl so I was not alone in the dark.

The trip was rough. I only knew it was a ship when we started to tip. We were hidden behind boxes with dishwashers inside. We did not see this till the container doors were opened and there was light. The girl was small, only up to my shoulder, very pretty, thin but with big tits.

As soon as I saw her I thought she'd never stand whatever was coming next.

Mats

I T TOOK AN hour or two to heat the cabin that had been empty for weeks, to light the sticks and get the logs to burn. There is no electricity in the cabin. We had a routine. Nina likes routine. She is an efficient person. If she says a thing will work, it works. At first I used to argue and find my own way to do things, but she turned out always to be right.

While I worked on the fire, Nina lit the candles and lamps, bringing the place back to life. I set the sauna stove going too, ready for the morning. It was late before we had the place the way we liked it, warm enough to remove our sweaters as we ate bread and cheese and sipped red wine heated on the stove. Snowflakes fell through the darkness against the windows like big hands stroking. Later, we climbed the stairs to the bed on the platform above the main room, made each other hot, watched flame shadows playing on the timber above us. Our shadows were enormous when we sat up, the ski slope shadows of her breasts, the nipples peaked, the mazy patterns of her hair.

We made love so much that weekend I was afraid I'd let her down if she wanted more. We sweated in the sauna; she rolled in the snow, though that extreme is not for me. So tender we were, raw and open. We would have made a baby for sure if she hadn't been on the pill. I wondered if she might have stopped taking it, the way she kept her legs around my waist, keeping me deep inside her even when we were done.

Our best times were always at the cabin, our most natural times. I mean that is where we were our simple selves. It was so good, but curiously I found it a relief when we packed up to leave on Sunday afternoon, the passion, how can I say it? almost too much. I wanted to be back at our apartment in the hot reliable shower, in the flatter, firmer bed.

The way you sank into the feather mattress of the cabin bed, sometimes it was as if you might never climb out. I thought how different it would be if we had a child; there would be purpose other than just our own physical gratification, a responsibility. We had driven all that way basically to eat and drink and fuck. I was tired when we left, after the Sunday routine: clean the stove, strip the sheets to take in the car with empty bottles, wipe up the butter smears, sweep the floor.

The last part of the routine: 'Bye bye, cabin,' Nina said, winding her scarf around her neck. The cabin had been in her family since she was a little girl, and she kept this childish habit, the only one. I found it incredibly touching. And then she turned to look at me.

'Take the job,' she said as she stepped out of the door.

Alis

THIS I HAVE never told a living soul.

It is too sad to tell.

I was twelve the first time. Big money for a virgin. And then many more men paid big money for a virgin. I was small and they believed. Stupid pricks. Mama said I was too young to have a baby. I got bigger round my stomach and tits. Of course, I was growing up. But one day my belly started to jump.

When Mama saw this she cried and said, Sorry, so sorry, so sorry, my baby to have baby. She said, God forgive me and she prayed to God to ask Him what to do. My Mama was not a bad person, only a poor person who needed to drink.

Maybe sometimes she was bad.

But God forgives.

It was a good time for me when I was pregnant. Mama said I did not have to work any more till the baby came. Mama helped me when he was born. My little boy. I held him for one hour. He had dark hair and a sweet wrinkled face. My little monkey. His fingers were strong. He held my thumb very, very tight with his tiny fingers. Nobody else has ever held me so tight – except to get something from me. I can still feel his fingers on my thumb. They squeezed so tight.

But Mama pulled his fingers away and took him to an orphanage for a better life. There was a box in the door for new babies in the night. It was the only way, she said. I cried terribly. My heart was bust right open, never to mend. But I did believe he'd be looked after well in the orphanage and maybe adopted by kind people.

After that I never cried again.

Marta

THE WORKERS ON Marta's shift, 6pm to midnight, were
the young and the old and the feeble. Everyone else – including Mama – worked a full-length day or night shift. On Sundays
– the only day she saw her mother for more than a few minutes
– Marta noticed the grey skin, the harsh lines that dragged from
nose to chin, and knew that soon she must offer to swap shifts.
Although Mama was only forty she seemed an old woman already,
the way she stooped, and sighed.

Not that Marta found the twilight shift and the queueing for
food, the housework and minding Milya *easy*, but at least it meant
she could find an hour most days to study her English books.
Once she'd swapped with Mama there'd be no more time for that.
Giving up her English now would feel like giving up on Tata –
giving up on *herself* – altogether.

You couldn't speak at work. Each side of the conveyor belts
was a line of blanked faces. The heavy canvas masks, which looped
behind the ears, obscured the nose and mouth. Each time she
put one on, Marta wondered how much good it did – the canvas
heavily saturated with the chemical dust that hung in the air and
made the unprotected eyes smart – and so *hot*. The packers were
meant to wear goggles, but the lenses were so scratched and dusty
it was impossible to see through them, so the foreman ignored
their flouting of the rules and was generous with eye drops when

the chemicals were particularly noxious. The work – grading and packing industrial chemicals – was simple, unpleasant, tedious and Marta soon lost any curiosity about the use or destination of the chemicals.

After Tata died she'd had no choice but to offer to leave school and earn money, hoping, *hoping* that Mama would say no. But Mama said yes. Tata would have been so *angry*. Marta struggled not to feel bitter at the irony that by dying in the name of freedom, Tata had left her trapped, any hope of university gone. She'd hoped at least for an office job, sometimes one came up, but at that time there'd been no such vacancies. So here she was, packing chemicals as Tata had promised she'd never have to do. But at least it was part-time; at least she could still study. Until she had to go full time. That day was looming. Still, she hadn't given up hope, not yet, that something better might come along. Some *chance*.

She nodded across at Sig. Her yellow scarf struggled to contain her springy curls, and above the mask, plucked black brows arched above her reddened eyes. Raising her eyebrows, Sig looked across at the clock. Involuntarily, Marta checked too, annoyed with herself for giving in: she tried not to look; the more you did, the more time dawdled, seeming sometimes actually to stop. You might look at the clock several times and see no movement of the hands at all.

Now it was nearly 10, two thirds of the shift done, just the hardest, weariest third to go. If only we could talk, Marta thought, as she did each night, but the machinery that drove the conveyor belt drowned speech and the canvas masks prevented lip-reading. She continued to scoop blue crystals into plastic pots. This chemical was not bad, only a little stinging of the eyes and a sharp clean smell, on the edge of pleasant. There was an itch at the nape of her neck, but she could not scratch it with her contaminated glove so had to bear the itch that bloomed like a sparkly flower. Shrugging her shoulder blades together she concentrated on her dream – to go to England. To travel past Big Ben each day on a red London bus, to send home so much money that Mama wouldn't have to work.

It was how she bore the itchy, eye-stinging hours at work, practising her English verbs or dreaming of the UK and embroidering on the dreams. Sometimes she concentrated on the effect at home of the money she would send: Mama's face smoothed out and smiling; a new carpet, no more smell of pee; Milya with a leather satchel and fresh school blouse – now *she* would go to university.

But tonight Marta had something else to think about. All day she'd fended off the thought but now she let it come. This morning a letter arrived, a letter in a smart blue envelope addressed to Miss Marta Sala. It was from Mr Antenescu, inviting her to meet him for tea on Sunday in the Hotel Bucaresti. The Bucaresti! This was a swanky place in the town – not the sort of place for the likes of Marta. Her first impulse was to tear the letter into shreds and throw it away: this was the sort of thing you were warned about. Strangers making promises. But he'd made no promises. And what if this was her big chance? What if she ignored it and the chance went by? She'd rescued the scraps from the bin and pieced them together. The handwriting was small, neat, educated. *I wish to compliment you on your natural beauty and grace*, he had written. *Natural beauty and grace!* It was nonsense, of course. Just the sort of flattery you must not fall for. But still, no one had ever said such words about her.

Of course, she would not meet him. How could it lead to any good? She wasn't naive. She knew what happened to girls who fell for such men. But still, *natural beauty and grace*. She tucked the scrap of letter that bore these words inside her bra where it made her feel beautiful. Tata used to say she was, but that was a father's biased opinion. Tata used to say – but *no*.

Eight months since he'd gone and she was getting better at bearing it; had learned to shrink the grief into a bean that she could swallow down.

At last the hour hand dragged itself to 12 and the hooter blew. The workers filed out, dropping gloves and masks into barrels by the door ready for the next shift. Sig took off her yellow scarf and her bleached curls blossomed out. Marta shook loose her long, dark hair. The girls walked arm in arm across the bridge. The sour river smell smogged around them making the other figures frail and dreamlike in the lit-up dark. Sig, the same age as Marta, was already engaged to Gustav from the cement works and was chattering about him, as she always did, recounting every conversation, revealing who said what, how many kisses and where she'd let him put his hands.

'It'll be you next, Marta,' she said, 'then you'll know the meaning of "turned on". It's like your belly melting and wanting to slide out between your legs.'

Marta said nothing. There was a boy, Virgil, who'd made her feel the beginnings of something like that. She used to meet him on a dump of wrecked cars, a dangerous place, a place where gypsies hung out, but still she'd go there and sit in a smashed-up car with him. They never did more than hold hands, though surely soon he would have kissed her. She'd loved his hands, long fingers, little red hairs flecked on the backs, thick rough knuckles.

Tata forbade her from seeing him, but still she did. In the car they played a game. Virgil in the driver's seat; Marta, looking at his hands on the steering wheel, telling him where to take her, somewhere like the moon or a crazy made-up place, but most often London or Loch Ness or somewhere in the UK.

Suddenly she clambered onto the parapet of the bridge.

Sig squealed. 'You nutcase! Be careful!'

The parapet was wide enough to stand on, but Marta's stomach plummeted at the dim glimmer of the river through the smog. She held out her arms for balance and took a step or two, almost tripping on the broken ankle of a saint.

'I can't look,' wailed Sig.

'Everything all right there?' Some busybody. Marta imagined falling. Not jumping, just letting go, the swoop of space, the splash and the cold plunge and then the death. Or maybe not death, more likely she'd get caught up in the rubbish on the bank, fished out and rescued, mortified, coated in slime and crap.

'Jump down now, no need to be hasty here,' said someone. Marta laughed wildly. Did he think she was a suicide? The donkey! It almost made her want to jump now just to show him, just to *do* it, and with a thrill of adrenalin she looked down again, it would be so easy and so much less embarrassing than being helped down from the parapet.

'It's Mrs Sala's girl,' said someone, 'she's on my shift.'

'It's all right.' Marta jumped down, jarring her knee in her clumsy landing. 'Some people should mind their own business,' she said as she strode away.

Alis

I GAVE MY LITTLE boy the name Marcus. I thought he would grow up with kind people. I wished for him to be happy. I prayed every day for God to care for him.

After he was born, after he was gone, Mama drank too much and drank and drank until she choked to death.

God forgives her.

I was not alone. I stayed with Mama's friends. I was careful and had no more kids. It was a not bad life. But every year on his birthday I thought of Marcus, where he was, was he happy? I sent him love. I prayed to God to keep him safe.

When they shot Ceaușescu and his wife, and showed it on TV, we did not believe our eyes. We screamed, we were so happy. We fucked for free that day. We thought we were free.

But after Ceaușescu was killed, there was news on TV of things that happened in his regime, bad things, secret things the people did not know. He was very wicked man, more wicked even than we thought.

Please God, never forgive that man.

One day I saw a movie about orphanages on TV. The kids were not looked after. There was no love, no toys, the babies were tied up in cots. When I saw the faces of the kids, empty faces, rows of cots, like hundreds of tiny prisoners, I wanted to die. I wanted to stab myself in the heart.

Forgive me.

I wanted to kill God.

Marta

ON SUNDAY MARTA borrowed Sig's blue dress. Although Sig was taller, it fit Marta more snugly round the chest, showing the crease where her breasts were squashed together in her too-small bra. Antoni was home, dressed in a cheap shiny suit. He'd got away from the neighbourhood, so why not she? He was eighteen, but his greased-back hair and spindly moustache made him appear almost middle-aged – until he smiled and then, with his snaggle of teeth, he looked about six.

The Revolution had brought him freedom. He lived and worked in town – it did not do to think too closely about his work – and had made this Sunday visit bearing a joint of beef and a bottle of wine. Mama was flushed with the pleasure of these gifts (she did not ask how he got them) and with having her son back in her kitchen. Every now and then she reached out to touch his arm, to check that he was real.

All this for staying away for months on end, for barely sending any money.

'You can't go out,' Mama said to Marta now, tearing her gaze away from Ant, 'we'll have a feast.'

'You look like a tart,' Ant said, letting his eyes rest on the strained top buttons of Marta's dress.

'You look like a pimp,' she said.

'Marta!' Mama scolded.

'But he said . . .'

'What's a pimp?' said Milya, clambering onto Ant's knee.

'And how would you know?' Ant said. 'Spend a lot of time with pimps?'

'What's a pimp?'

'I'm going.' Marta grabbed her bag.

'Please stay,' Mama called.

'What's a pimp?'

She slammed the door and wobbled down the corridor in Mama's best shoes, high-heeled, mock leather sling-backs. She took it as a good omen that the lift was working and stood within the scratched steel box holding her breath. It was a risk getting inside on a Sunday – once Ant had been stuck between the 2nd and 3rd floors for half a day and had to pee in the corner. But today it worked smoothly and soon she was stepping out into hazy sunshine.

The shoes pinched as she walked to the tram stop. It was two rides to the centre of town. She could have spent the fare on sweets for Milya, or a glossy magazine. It still seemed amazing that you could openly buy magazines from the west. Once that would have been enough to make you disappear. She could spend her money as she liked, though guilt pinched like the shoes.

Quarter to three; she stopped outside the hotel. What did you do in a place like this? Report to a reception desk and explain your business? It's all in your attitude, Sig had told her. 'Walk in there like you own the place, look down your nose at all the flunkies.' Sig was all grand words, but now she was not only engaged to ordinary Gustav but had missed a period. So, she'd settled for this life and this time next year might be a mother. Not me, Marta thought, not me.

Half hidden behind a lamppost, she waited. The polished white marble steps gleamed with silver in the sunshine. They were spotless. Every day someone must have to polish them. She caught sight of a smudge of brown, half a footprint and it pleased her. Nothing can stay that clean.

When Mr Antenescu arrived, she'd step out, bright and breezy, pretend she'd only just rolled up herself. She held her elbows out from her sides to dry the dampness in the armpits of the dress. A doorman in a gold-frogged uniform stepped forward to help people into or out of the taxis that drew up, and to carry their luggage up or down the steps. These days any man with a car could call himself a taxi driver. So many tourists, willing to pay ridiculous prices.

A horse-drawn trap drew up, and a couple of elderly Americans creaked out. They took a photo of each other beside the horse, the driver – in some version of Romanian national dress – grinning and raising his whip.

She watched and waited, aware of suspicious looks from the doorman. 3:05. How long should she wait? Her stomach twisted with the sudden certainty that he wouldn't turn up – but there was also relief. Two trams and she could be back for beef and wine, tomorrow she'd boil the bone for soup . . . her mind ran on to carrots and onions, dried beans, dumplings flavoured with dill.

'Can I help you, Miss?' the doorman said.

'I'm waiting for a friend.'

'Perhaps you could wait inside?' His eyes rested on her bursting buttons, 'or else come back later. Loitering around like this, it doesn't look good.'

Marta flushed. 'I was only enjoying the sun, but if you have a problem with that . . .' With a dignity ruined only by the wobbling shoes, she made her way up the steps, through the revolving door and into the plush of deep blue carpet, muted light, a smell of smoke and polish. It took a moment for her eyesight to adjust to the gleaming wooden reception desk, big as a bed, the pairs of deep sofas facing each other across low tables, the lamps with their respectfully bowed faces. There were people sitting around, some formally, some lounging as if in their own homes, tea trays and liquor bottles. The elderly American couple shared a huge bottle of Coca-Cola from an ice-bucket on a silver tray. A uniformed waiter moved towards her. About to throw her out, she was sure. She saw the sign for the Ladies toilet and fled inside.

It was beautiful in there. Her heart hammered. It was like a temple. The marble walls and floor. The folded pile of paper towels. The cakes of white soap. A red rose in a vase. Her stupid face, blazing in the mirror. Who did she think she was? She locked herself in a cubicle. Her stomach was cramping. She pulled down her pants and sat. It seemed almost sacrilegious to soil the crystal water in the porcelain bowl, but she had no choice and hunched, ashamed of the smell, jumping up quickly to flush the toilet.

She washed her hands with the white soap, webbing her fingers with scented bubbles. In the bright space the mirror lit her cruelly, the way the dress strained across her chest made her look fat and you could see the ridge of the safety pin holding together her bra. Natural beauty and grace, indeed! What a fool she was! Thank goodness he had not come. She would go straight home, take off the dress, eat beef with Mama, make peace with Ant. She slid a cake of soap into her bag, and a wad of paper towels. The only other thing to take was the rose, plastic it turned out and moulded into a clear Perspex vase. Mama would love it. She bent the stem to fit it inside her bag and scuttled out quickly – startled to find Mr Antonescu right outside the door.

He took her hand and smiled down at her. 'I'm sitting there.' He indicated a table tucked away in the farthest recesses of the room. 'I asked a waiter to point you my way, but . . .' He gestured at the Ladies.

Marta looked down at the shoes, noticed a splash of water on her skirt, screwed the material up in her hand to hide it.

'Well. Here we are,' he said. 'Coffee?'

In his corner they sat side by side on a leather sofa. She sank deeper than expected and gave a little gasp. He sat close beside her, trousers tight as sausage skins round his thighs. Breathing in his smell of expensive cologne, she crossed her legs, letting one high-heeled sandal dangle in a way that seemed casual and sophisticated.

'Coffee, cakes and perhaps a brandy?' he said. 'You look as if you could do with it!'

Marta nodded. She supposed that he would be paying – but what if he expected her to pay her way? How much did things cost in such a place as this? Was this a date? Could you call it that? She kept her bag, fat with stolen goods, clenched under her arm.

Pavel beckoned the waiter and made his order. Then he leaned towards her on the sofa. 'I've been thinking about you all week,' he said.

Smiling sideways at him, Marta hid the little thrill that ran through her. He seemed younger close-to – perhaps not much more than thirty. She'd thought 40 at least on the bridge. But look at Ant, how much older the suit and moustache made him appear. Pavel's eyes were small, deep-set, a very pale blue that reminded her of Mama's best tablecloth. And that cloth would surely be unfolded today in honour of Ant, in honour of the beef.

'How old are you?' Pavel asked.

'Seventeen.'

'You look younger . . . and older at the same time,' he said, as if determined to flatter her one way or the other. 'And so pretty, and so . . .' He glanced down at her chest and she vowed never to borrow Sig's dress again, 'well proportioned.' She waited for him to say *Natural beauty and grace* but he did not. The waiter brought a tray with coffee, slices of vanilla torte, a bottle of plum brandy and two glasses. Pavel leant forward and poured a measure of liquor into each glass. 'Let me toast you,' he said, holding up the glass. 'To you. To pretty Marta!' He swallowed the drink in one go.

'Thank you.' Marta took a sip and felt the burn.

'Knock it back,' he said.

'To you then,' she said and forced it down in a gulp that brought tears to her eyes but then a lovely feeling of warmth and comfort, and at once it was as if she'd been born to sit on just such a sofa, in just such a place as this. She revolved her ankle, enjoyed the prettiness of the dangling shoe.

The coffee was strong, the cake soft and meltingly sweet on her tongue. He was a talker and after they'd chatted about the weather he told her about London, *London*, where he did business. He'd even been to Scotland. The brandy loosened her tongue and she quizzed him about the UK, till with a laugh he held up his hand.

'Enough!' he said. 'Now, tell me about yourself.'

Marta shrugged. 'There's nothing much, I'm just a girl who lives across the river, who works the twilight shift at the chemical plant. What else?'

'Well, you have a little sister.'

'And a big brother who works in town.' She paused for another mouthful of cake. Really it was a waste to eat such a delicious thing and have to concentrate on conversation as well.

'Your parents must be proud.' He poured two more shots of brandy.

She took a breath and made the hard feeling come in her throat before she said, 'My Tata's dead.'

'I'm sorry.' He bowed his head for a moment. 'It must be a struggle for your mother.'

'We manage. Mama and I work and Antoni. He contributes.' She fought to keep the edge from her voice.

'Always a struggle, eh?' he said. 'Another drink?'

Marta shook her head. 'I mustn't, I have to be able to walk!' A silly slurred giggle came from her mouth.

'Another brandy, another coffee and how about another slice of cake?' Pavel said. 'I won't take no for an answer!'

How could she could resist? She was expecting, at any moment, that he would make a pass. She looked slyly at his lips, narrow and wet; at the little paunch that strained against his shirt. Could she bear to let him touch her? People did of course; every day people gave part of themselves to get something back. As long as you were sure of getting something back. Something worth getting.

Pavel gestured to the waiter: 'Again,' he said, and the waiter strode off. It was wonderful the authority Pavel had, the confidence. Would there ever be a day when she would be able to click her fingers and say, 'Again,' like that – and have someone take notice?

'Do you come here very much?' she asked.

He waggled his hand. 'Now and again, you know,' he said, 'when it suits.'

'What do you do?' she said. He looked surprised by the question, which, perhaps it wasn't polite to ask. 'I mean what line of business?' she blundered on.

'Exports,' he said. A silence gaped between them. Marta couldn't think of a suitable question to ask; had she offended him? Leaning forward, he topped up their glasses. She picked up hers and went to drink and missed her lips so that the liquor splashed down Sig's dress.

'Oh no, and it's not mine!' she said, stupid, stupid, what did it matter whose dress it was? And now he'd think she'd borrowed it specially. 'We swap clothes all the time,' she added. She opened her bag to take out her handkerchief and the head of the plastic rose popped out. It was identical to the one on the coffee table, so there was no mistaking its origins – and his smile! Her face throbbed, almost burst with a rush of blood. He leant over, tucked the rose back into her bag and fastened the zip.

'There,' he said, patting the bag. 'For Mama?'

The waiter came with the coffee and cake, took a minute clearing the dirty crockery, tilted his head to look at her. Marta held tight to her bag.

'How about I buy her some real roses?' Pavel was saying. He put a finger under her chin and turned his face to hers. 'Your secret is safe,' he said. 'A dozen red roses. I'll have them sent. Would she like that? Would you?' She pulled her face away. He lit another cigarette. She swallowed the brandy.

'Eat your cake,' he said. He leant back and watched her eat, blowing smoke in long thoughtful plumes. The smell of the smoke mixed with his cologne was cloying and spoilt the taste of the cake; if only he would look away so that she could wrap it in a paper towel and take it home for Milya, but to open her bag again would be impossible. She forked in another creamy mouthful. Ash powdered down on Pavel's knee, a flake or two on the blue of the dress. He brushed it off, his hand lingering. She shifted her leg away.

'Relax,' he said. 'There's nothing wrong with wanting pretty things, a girl like you. It's only to be expected.'

She picked up the brandy, to burn away the sickliness in her throat.

'Steady on,' he laughed as she finished her glass, 'why not drink your coffee? Here—' He passed her the cup. 'You want to earn good money?' She caught his eyes on her chest again, the dark brandy splashes on the tight material. She looked into the shallow blue of his eyes and knew that Ant had been right. She did look like a tart and that is exactly what he thought she was. Or could be. Buying her with cake and coffee, getting her drunk in the afternoon, no doubt there was a room waiting upstairs, no doubt the waiter, like the doorman, thought—

He seemed to read her mind. 'You don't think . . .?' There was an appalled silence. The waiter gloated past. She could feel Pavel's eyes burning on the side of her face.

'You think I invited you here for sex?' His voice had turned chilly.

'No,' she said, 'no, only . . .' But her speech was slurred, tongue gone thick with all the sweetness.

He lit another cigarette and blew a cloud of smoke. 'Believe me, if I wanted to buy sex I could buy it more cheaply than this.' He gestured at the debris of cake crumbs and coffee slops.

She didn't know what to say. There was hard silence until she spoke: 'Maybe I should go?'

She moved forward on the sofa and perched foolishly on the high heels, trying to gather the momentum to stand.

'Thank you,' she murmured, 'for the coffee and . . .' but the word cake was too sweet to say and she lurched urgently to her feet, hand over her mouth and staggered back towards the Ladies. Inside, a white-haired lady was winding a sticky red lipstick back into its tube. Marta rushed past and into a cubicle, just in time to throw up. She sank to her knees and rested her cheek against the plastic seat. She threw up again and again, tears running down her face as all the treats hurled themselves out of her stomach.

She heard the woman mutter and tut, and a disapproving clunk as the door closed behind her.

Marta flushed the toilet, sat down on the lid, head in hands, tears leaking from between her fingers. *Natural beauty and grace*, she thought, *natural beauty and grace*. After a while she opened the dress to fish out the slip of paper, damp now with perspiration. The words had transferred themselves in blurry mirror writing onto the white skin of her breast. Standing up, she dropped the scrap into the toilet and flushed. And then she dried her eyes and when she was sure the Ladies was empty, unlocked the cubicle door, washed her hands, splashed her face, rinsed her mouth and opened her bag to take out her comb. The stem of the rose was broken. When she replaced it beside the sink, it stooped in a studious examination of the hot tap. She took another cake of soap, zipping her bag shut just before a cleaner barrelled through the door with a trolley of cloths, brushes and bleach.

'Shutting for a minute, cleaning in progress,' she said. And then she paused and squinted at Marta.

'You all right?' She began to spray the basins with a giant hissing canister. The smell reminded Marta of a chemical she'd packed recently, sweet and nippy, that had made the eyes stream.

'Do you like working here?' Marta asked, hoping to distract the woman from the broken rose, the absence of soap.

Her reply was a snort and a drawing back of her head back as if to ascertain whether Marta was mad or joking.

'It's better than where I work,' Marta said.

'Hmmm.' The woman put down the canister, leant her hips against a basin and crossed her arms, settling in to give a proper answer. Her bare shins were corrugated with swollen veins. 'It's not bad,' she said with a sniff. 'It's an honest day's work.' As Marta pondered the phrase, the woman added. 'I've done worse. There are perks.'

'Perks?'

'You'd be surprised what people leave in here.' She pulled a little pot from her apron pocket and brandished it at Marta, before she leant close to the mirror and smeared a hectic splotch of blush on each cheek. She turned and grinned. Her front teeth were broken, her chin whiskery, her black hair dye had grown half out leaving an inch of scalpish white. 'I could put a word in if you want,' she offered.

'No, it's all right,' said Marta.

'Suit yourself.' The woman lost interest and went into a cubicle, began vigorously to flush and spray.

Marta stepped out into the lobby, gazing round at the reflections of lamps and sofas infinitely receding in the smoky mirrored walls. Each one a stage less real. The taste in her mouth was bitter. She headed towards the exit and stopped; there was Pavel having an altercation with a waiter. When she approached he gestured towards her. 'It is nothing like that,' he was saying. 'See, here she is: my girlfriend.'

'Is this true?' the waiter asked her.

Marta hesitated for just a moment before she nodded.

'Then I apologise for misconstruing the situation.' Sardonically the waiter bowed his head before he turned away.

'Shall we go?' said Pavel. She gazed at him with eyes unpeeled. He wasn't so spectacular, but he was a chance, maybe a stepping stone. She let him take her arm.

Alis

MARTA WAS A virgin before they did her: one, two, three, four, and she cried to lose her virginity this way.

That's her broken in, one said, like he had done something good. Fat prick with bent dick.

We were put in a tiny room, just us, with a mattress on the floor. The cover was new cotton, pretty and bright, red and yellow tulips in rows. The room had a locked door and a small window, very high. I could see out but Marta was too short. Anyway, no point looking out at roofs and aerials.

Instead, Marta lay down and watched the clouds go by.

Look, she said, there's a fish.

I lay down and looked up at the cloud.

What do you see? she asked.

I saw only cloud but I pretended. Potato, I said.

That made her laugh. I looked at her face, white salt dried on her cheeks, sweet mouth, brown eyes very bright with long lashes, hair all puffed out on the pillow, pretty hair that stank of men.

I looked at the cloud again. Hey, now it's a dick, I said and she laughed again. I liked to hear her laugh.

Mats

VIVIENNE'S WAS THE first face I saw when I arrived at the Edinburgh office. The doors were sliding glass, the lobby wide, her desk like an island in the centre; her red hair the only colour. I was too preoccupied with first-day nerves to register her properly. If I thought anything, maybe it was that her hair was too bright to be natural.

Once I'd introduced myself she nodded. 'Mr Brunborg has arrived,' she said into a receiver and then, 'Go right up.' She put down the phone and pressed a button to let me through the security barrier. 'Oh,' she said, 'hang on. Sorry, Mr Brunborg, did no one say? We have a no shoes policy here and Fergus, Mr Walsh, is really on to it. You'd make a better impression, if you don't mind?' She held her hand out for my shoes.

So strange in the workplace. I hesitated, but she kept her hand stretched out. I noticed the red of her nails, brighter even than her hair. I bent to remove my shoes, glad my socks were new and matched, handed her my shoes and walked across the cool marble floor to the lift.

A man, tall, thin and bald, was waiting outside the lift for me when the doors opened on the 3rd Floor. 'Welcome. I'm Fergus,' he said, putting out his hand to shake. He raised his eyebrows as he caught sight of my socks.

'The girl in the lobby . . .' I began to say.

He threw back his head in a laugh. His glasses were smudged, his lips, dry and rough. 'Did you not register the date?' he said. 'She's a wee minx. Don't worry. I'll have a word.'

It was April 1st. I hadn't thought about it at all. I did not know they had *Aprilsnarr* in Britain too. I thought it a Scandinavian tradition only. Mor would always play a joke when I was a kid. 'Look Mats, there's an elk in the garden,' or, 'There's bird poop on your back.'

I took the lift down to retrieve my shoes.

'You got me,' I said to the receptionist.

I noticed that her front teeth crossed a little, giving her a goofy look. Just above the corner of her lipsticked mouth was a dark brown mole, neat and distinct. Her eyes were green, her nose large and fleshy. Not a beauty, and she was heavy – compared to Nina anyway, who never allowed a millimetre of fat.

'Sorry,' she said. 'Couldn't resist.'

Once I'd put my shoes on, I straightened up and looked at her seriously. 'One day I'll get you back,' I said.

She laughed again. No, she was far from beautiful in any standard way, but she was attractive. 'You've scared me now,' she said. And then her phone rang. She waved her pen at me as I went back to the lift and my first meeting.

At the Edinburgh Office, it is traditional to have an after-work drink, especially on Fridays. In Oslo this is not so true – people are glad to get home after work. If Nina had been waiting for me, I would not have gone, or not for more than a quick drink to be polite. The wine bar was busy and smoky, wide wooden tables, blackboards listing food and drinks. Fergus bought me a very large glass of red. It did its work. As soon as I'd taken a few sips, the tension of my first week fell from my shoulders like a heavy coat. Hey, it was the weekend! It was a good tradition, and good too to see colleagues in a different atmosphere, good for working relationships and maybe productivity.

I loosened my tie, went to buy Fergus a drink and found myself beside Vivienne at the bar. I offered her a drink.

'Is this revenge?' she said in a fake American accent. 'You gonna slip me a mickey?'

I shook my head. 'I will be more subtle,' I said.

She widened her eyes. 'Oooh, now I'm petrified!'

'You should be.' I could not prevent the smile. I did not meant to flirt but it felt good, I must say.

As I was buying the wine – huge glasses they served – I saw a tray of food go past: potato chips upright in a little silver bucket, a curl of battered fish.

'Shall we eat?' I shouted to Fergus. He came over to take his glass. 'Och no, I've got to get home to Karen and the wee ones before they go to bed.'

'I wouldn't say no,' Vivienne said.

Fergus told me about his family – four sons including newborn twins. 'Have to be there for bedtime or I'll be in the shite.' In one movement he glanced at his watch and drained his glass. 'I'll leave you in Viv's capable hands,' he said. 'Put it on the company card,' he said to her as he left.

'Thanks Boss,' she said, saluting. Once he'd gone she grinned. 'You don't know how rare this is! Let's go for it.'

And after all there was only a cold and empty flat awaiting me.

We chose food – fish and chips for me, something with prawns for her – and ordered a bottle of Champagne. I vowed to make sure Fergus knew that this extravagance was not my idea. I'd already had enough with two big glasses of the red. It's true what they say; they do drink more in Britain.

And then there were two,' she said, looking round. And I noticed that yes, for sure, all our colleagues had gone.

It was fun. Too much alcohol in my blood to worry about work. Or even think too much about Nina. After our goodbye at the departure gate, I'd caught a glimpse of her expression before she was lost in the crowd. Already her mind was on the next thing. I knew her so well. I loved that she was so practical, not sentimental. She did not like to talk of love or 'sloppy stuff'. I admired it. But it would have been nice if she'd looked back just once, or seemed a small amount sad at this parting.

Vivienne was entertaining, gossiping about my new colleagues, telling jokes I didn't really understand, though I laughed as if I did. We drank the Champagne, shared a pack of cigarettes between us. She wanted to order brandy but I could not take any more. Since we lived in the same quarter, we shared a cab, her knee warm against mine, and when we arrived at her door, she invited me in for coffee. At first I declined.

'Oh come on . . .' she said.

'My wife would not appreciate it,' I said. 'Besides I'm tired.'

'Wife?' she said. 'I thought you lived alone.'

'Nina is in Oslo,' I said.

'Well, I'm only offering coffee. Sober you up before you go home. Horrible to go back alone, half cut. Come on . . .'

I did not know that expression. Half cut. My apartment in the New Town was cold and I had not yet made it comfortable to be in. There were boxes to unpack, things to buy, nothing much in the fridge.

Her place was only two blocks from mine, a ground floor tenement apartment with big rooms and high ceilings. It was the same style, but warm and cheerful, cluttered with colourful things. And something else – there was a babysitter, Rita, who I was to learn was Vivienne's best friend. A babysitter – therefore a child.

I was surprised she hadn't mentioned that she had a child.

'You didn't say you had a wife,' she pointed out. 'Come.' She led me down the hall and opened a door to show me a narrow room lit by a glow-worm night light, a little head on a pillow, face turned away. Toys and crumpled clothes on the floor, the smell of sleeping child.

I saw her differently as she made coffee. Clumsy from the drink maybe, but still, a mother. She was built like a woman in an old movie: forties or fifties, waist and hips and breasts, curves and hollows that Nina just did not have. I was relieved that Rita also stayed for coffee; she was a small woman, intense, her skin lined, her cheeks red, her eyes bright. When she got up to leave, I pulled myself upright too.

'Don't let me break up the party,' she said, but I knew I must drag myself away from the warmth and the big rumpled sofas before something happened that I would regret.

Alis

WE LAY ON the tulips cover listening to voices in the house below us, and a toilet flushing many times very loudly and water rushing down a pipe as if it would come right into our room.

Marta said she needed the toilet.

I got up and knocked on the door. I needed toilet too. I shouted this but no one came so I lay down again.

Marta put her hand on her pussy and cried because she was broken.

How did they get you? I asked her.

For a long time she said nothing and I thought she was asleep but then she whispered. She told me about a man who bought roses for her Mama. Her Mama, she believed in this man, believed that he was good, that Marta could go with him to the UK and make a better life, send money home. They believed she would be a teacher in the UK and maybe marry a British citizen.

But then one day Marta's Mama she saw sense, maybe, and she told Marta, No, you must not go. First, Marta's Mama wanted to find out more about this man, this Pavel. When Marta told him this he took her out for coffee to talk about it and next thing she woke up on the ship.

Tears ran into her mouth when she told me this.

I told her she must be realistic. She must learn to hide behind her face and make it smile. It's only your body, I said to her, as

Mama said to me. It's not your heart and not your soul. These will not break.

I prayed and asked her to pray with me and she did but she doesn't believe. Her Tata said there was no god.

I never knew my father. Maybe he was a good man. Maybe he was a motherfucking pimp.

Only God knows this.

Mats

THREE WEEKS LATER, Nina visited for the weekend. I met her at the airport. When she came through the arrivals gate she looked so *good*. I was proud she was my wife. Her smart black coat and boots, the pale shine on her lips, her slanting ice-blue eyes searching for me. She looked so fresh among the crumpled travellers. I kissed her and she tasted of peppermint – she always sucked a candy on a flight to equalise the pressure in her ears. I love the way you get to know these things about a person, small details like this.

Back at my apartment, she walked round examining things.

'You need more lamps,' she said. 'And cushions. It's cold in here.'

Nina was right. Compared to our apartment in Oslo it was draughty, and the cold was damp, hard to dispel. The big central lights cast a flat and gloomy light. In the kitchen she unpacked *marsipankake*, *brunost* and home-baked cookies sent by Mor. Our families were always close, spending Christmas and holidays together. My folks were so happy when we got married, so happy to call Nina their daughter-in-law. Mor told me she had wished for this since we were children.

Nina and Mor played tennis together each week. Sometimes we played doubles: Mor and me against Far and Nina; quite an even match. My parents were upset with me for moving away.

They thought I was leaving Nina behind, though they must have known this was not the case. I knew they were impatient for a baby to come; though they would never have put this pressure on us.

Once she'd made a list of stuff for me to buy, we went out to eat. I'd been researching the right place and had asked Fergus for suggestions, but he'd just laughed. 'Can't remember, pal. So long since we went out on the town.' His twins were bad sleepers and his eyes baggy and shadowed. When I asked Vivienne, she suggested a wine bar called Valentine's. It had a good reputation for food and was nearby. *Handy*, she said, a nice English expression.

I thought we might make love first – three whole weeks – but Nina would not even take off her coat.

'You need a better mirror,' she told me, coming out of the bathroom. And, 'Later,' she said, turning her head when I tried to kiss her.

The place was filled with colour from the bottles of spirits, the cocktail menus, stained glass and shiny brass. It was packed with Friday-night people and almost too noisy to talk. Not a good choice, but I could see why Vivienne would like it. 'Somewhere else?' I suggested, but Nina shook her head. It was late already, she pointed out, and she had worked all day, driven to the airport, and then flown to Edinburgh. She was tired and hungry – I should have realised that. I should have known to take her somewhere quiet; it was my mistake. She did not say it; she did not have to.

There were tables on a mezzanine overlooking the bar and at last we were seated with our menus. Nina was tense and answered my questions briefly, but once our food and wine had come – chicken salads, chips, white wine – she relaxed and at last she smiled.

'I'm sorry,' she said. 'I don't feel so good.' She had her period and a cold coming.

'I will look after you,' I said. 'Lots of sleep.'

'No, we should see the city,' she said. 'I've got a list.'

I smiled and took her hand. That was my Nina!

'I wish we were at the cabin now,' I said. Remembering something Fergus often said, I looked up at the ceiling. 'Beam us up, Scotty!'

She nodded. 'I was there last weekend,' she told me. With her fork, she picked up a piece of avocado and studied it before putting it in her mouth.

'You didn't say.' I was surprised. We had talked on Friday and on Sunday nights and she had mentioned nothing of this.

'On your own?' I said.

'The roof needs work,' she said. 'It's an early thaw. Very drippy.'

'Far will fix it,' I said. 'Ring him. They could go down for the weekend. And you with them.' I had never known her to go on her own.

She nodded.

'Maybe I'll fly back next weekend,' I said. 'If I leave lunchtime we could go together.'

I wanted nothing more in that noisy place with drunken Scottish voices yelling all around us, I wanted nothing more than a quiet weekend at the cabin with the snow sliding from the roof. I love the *shush* of this; the sound that tells us spring is on the way.

'Not next weekend,' she said. 'We must stick to the schedule.' We had a timetable of visits once every three weeks, taking turns to travel. When we'd arranged it, three weeks had not sounded so very long, but that first three weeks alone in Edinburgh had felt like months.

She had been treating a footballer with a knee injury and she told me about the difficulties. And there was a skier, a champion, taking up her time. She had played tennis with Mor and two other women. She had lost a kilo and decided to repaint the bathroom floor.

'And what about you?' she said. 'Have you made friends?'

I told her about Fergus and his family – boys of four and two, as well as the new twins and an exhausted ghost of a wife. They had invited me to a welcome dinner at their house, but it had been a mistake. The dinner was late, the other guests had not come and at least one of the babies was crying for the whole evening so that Karen was in a frantic state. She was burning and dropping things and snapping at Fergus, who poured drinks too fast, then almost fell asleep during the dessert.

'Come back in five years,' Karen called after me as I left. I think it was not a joke. On the doorstep, Fergus, full of whisky, pulled a face, clapped me on the shoulder, said, 'Sorry pal,' and tried to shut the door before I was properly outside.

'If that doesn't put you off breeding, nothing will,' he'd said to me on the Monday. But it had not. Of course I did not want four children close together like this. And Nina would manage better than Karen, she would not allow such chaos or such mess. She would not come apart. And I would do so much. She could work and I could stay at home if she preferred, for a few months at least.

'The contract is only a year,' I said to Nina, over coffee. 'Maybe we could start trying for a baby in a few months? Then I'll be home for the birth.'

She said nothing. I felt a tap on my shoulder, saw Nina's eyes widen, and there was Vivienne. She was wearing a fur jacket, a strange netted hat with a veil across her eyes, her big curvy lips painted crimson. 'Fancy dress,' she shouted. 'Who am I?'

She jutted one hip forward, and puffed on a cigarette with her head tilted back. I had no idea but—

'Betty Grable?' Nina guessed.

'You got it!' Vivienne peered at her for a moment through her netted veil. 'We're off to a party.' She waved vaguely in the direction of the bar. 'Just stopped off for a bevvy on the way. Hey, why don't you come?'

I shook my head. 'Nina's tired.'

'Thank you but no,' Nina said.

'See you on Monday then,' Vivienne said and was gone. Nina watched her push herself into the crowd.

'The receptionist,' I explained.

'Not a friend?'

'Not really.'

'Mats, you should get out and meet people,' she said. 'Join a tennis club maybe?'

'There's a squash court at work,' I said.

She smiled and squeezed my arm. 'I don't want you to be lonely.'

⁂

On Sunday evening at the departure gates, I held her tight. 'I'll miss you,' I said. She returned my hug, then pulled away.

'Listen, Mats. While you're here, I want you to be free.'

I stared at her pale face, nose a little red from her cold, eyes clear and with no colour.

'Excuse us.' A large couple with an enormous flotilla of wheeled suitcases trundled between us.

'It's not fair,' Nina said. 'They will pay the same price for their ticket as I pay for mine and they must each weigh twice as much as me.'

'What do you mean, "free"?'

'To do what you want.' Her eyes were narrow, reflecting nothing.

'You mean sex? But I don't want . . .'

'I must go through.' She was looking at the gate now.

'You mean *you* want,' I said.

We stood in silence as people barged and hefted and edged their luggage round us.

'I must go,' she said again. Her flight was called and maybe I caught a flicker of relief in her expression.

She started to move away. I grabbed her wrist. Thin wrist in black leather.

'The cabin,' I said, 'who was with you?'

Her face flinched.

I let her go.

I let her go.

She looked back once. I hadn't moved. After she'd gone I waited in the airport till her flight had taken off. I went outside and tilted my head back and listened for the engine's roar. Above the airport lights you could not make out the stars.

Alis

I N THE MORNING a woman unlocked the door and put her head into the tulip room. She had a big face and big, big, black hair. She let us use the toilet and the shower with gel that smelled of oranges. We sat in the kitchen and she gave us bags of chips all warm and wet with vinegar. The woman spoke nicely about the weather and made us coffee. Her hands were puffy with gold rings on every finger, digging in. She smelled of hair spray. The radio was giving taxi numbers and traffic jams and weather between the music.

She said we must be good and not let Auntie Deirdre down.

Yes, of course, I said. I kicked Marta under the table and she said yes too. But then she cried and said it was all a big mistake. She thought she was coming to the UK to teach Romanian to English children.

Auntie Deirdre laughed and laughed. What a good joke! Why would English children want to learn Romanian? She had purple lipstick on her big yellow teeth.

I wanted to laugh too at stupid Marta.

Auntie Deirdre said that Dr Hari was coming soon to check us over and give us contraceptive implants. We don't want any little accidents, do we? She told us to make sure punters wear condoms or else pay a bonus. Auntie Deirdre smiled nicely at us.

She offered us cigarettes. That day I thought it was not so bad there; she was not so bad.

Even I thought that!

Dr Hari was thin and young with brown skin, Indian maybe. He didn't smile or talk to us. He made us lie on a bed in a cold room. He put his cold fingers inside with glove on. He took swabs and he put implants in our arms. For me it was quick but Marta tried to keep her knees shut. Dr Hari and Deirdre held them open and Marta fought and cried till Auntie Deirdre slapped her.

Marta said to the doctor to please help her get away and go home to her Mama, this is all a big mistake.

So stupid I could not bear to look.

Of course she was punished for this, and me too. This was not fair. Four filthy pigs. Marta cried all the time and got hit in the back and belly and arm twisted behind her back till I thought it would break. By making this silly fuss she was putting her family in danger, Auntie Deirdre said. She must think of their safety and behave.

When we were back in our room she put her hands between her legs and curled up like an animal and sob, sob, sobbed.

I tried to hug her but she didn't want.

Even I was sore. One of the men was very rough.

Then she slept and I slept. When we woke we lay together under the tulips. It was still dark. I do not like the dark but it is not so bad when someone is there. We held hands tight. I could see the bright of her eyes staring upwards. Tiny dots of stars through glass.

TWO

1992

Vivienne

click

OK. HERE WE go. This is weird. Record yourself, she said. Actually she said I should write it, but I don't like writing. So I'll record. Same difference. Sue said OK. Said it would have the same therapeutic benefit. Where to start . . . Just start. Just talk. Just start.

click

Shouldn't have listened to that. Can anyone stand the sound of their own voice?

click

OK. Went to Sue the Counsellor because of the toad. Because Mats made me. That or else. Else what I don't know.

Anyway. OK.

Mats.

Mats is my husband but . . . How can I describe him? You know that game: if someone was a dog what kind of dog would they be? Well, he'd be a Labrador, a really soft one, one that would never bite, not to save his life. He's your original tall, dark, handsome type. Black hair longish, pushed back, cheekbones, jawline. He's got it all going on. Tall, rangy is the word – looks great in a suit – not fat at all but big, big all over if you get my drift. Fit. Yup, a catch. And sweet with it – flowers, treats for Artie, you name it. When he started work with us all the girls fancied him right off. Rita too, eyes goggling like marbles, like they were going to roll right out of her head. He was a catch all right. And if I hadn't caught him someone else would have. It was like there was a row of fielders behind me, hands cupped, all set, but I wasn't letting him past. Oh no.

He was in Edinburgh to do a temporary job for the company, fancy free, I thought. I think I thought.

click

Told Sue this wasn't working, hadn't made any difference to my mood levels. She said, *persevere*.

click

Anyway, at first we were happy. It was, well it was brilliant, like a dream. Whirlwind romance, quickie wedding in Mexico – talk about romantic! – *and* a new house in Morningside near a good school. Morningside! Me! Mats was fantastic with Artie, who was five when we got together. It was almost as if he was *hungry* for a kid. Nothing funny about it, I don't mean like that. Not Mats, he's straight as they come. Straight as a die whatever a die is.

He just wanted to be a dad. And what a good one he is.

Arthur's dad, well. OK, quick detour. Is this relevant? Dunno. Anyway, decided to go it alone, biological clock going bonkers, no one on the horizon. Didn't want or need a man, then anyway. Did it all unofficially - you wouldn't believe the hurdles you have to jump to do it through the proper channels. The proper channels! Well, my channels were functioning all right; bull's eye first time. Of course, I do wonder about the dad. What I do know - he's 5'11", brown hair, blue eyes, a university professor, some kind of ology.

Arthur's got my eyes, greenish, and fairish, nondescript hair, which mine would be if I left off the Nice'n Easy. He definitely looks like my child. £500 I paid for him basically, for the makings of him. Anyway it worked. To cut a long story short, Artie was born; five years went by, and Mats came on the scene.

Soon Artie was asking if he could call Mats 'Daddy'. And Mats was so delighted, he took him to Legoland, just the two of them on a boys' weekend and they came back very bonded. I sometimes wonder if Artie prefers Mats to me. We're good cop/bad cop parents, and guess which is which?

Of course, it wasn't long before Mats wanted a baby of his own. You know when your guts say no? Well mine were printing it in neon lights against the sky. But Mats, he wouldn't let up. Partly for Artie, he said, so he didn't grow up an only child. Mats had always wanted a brother or sister. I was an only child too, but it never bothered me. My folks were great. Dad died when I was fifteen and Mum five years ago. Cancer. She did get to meet Arthur before she went and though she didn't approve of my method, fell madly in love with him. She would have been such a brilliant granny.

I did string Mats along, I suppose, you could put it like that, hoping he'd get over it. When we made love he stayed in me for ages, so I couldn't get up and wash. Once I couldn't find my diaphragm and found it pushed right to the back of the bathroom cabinet. I'm sure I didn't put it there. And he knew my cycle better than I did, red crosses on the year planner.

No way he was going to forget it; I could see that.

click

Alis

MANY WEEKS AND many tricks later we were moved. Sunshine woke us that day, hot through the window. Auntie Deirdre's hair was bigger and blacker than ever. There was so much hair spray in the kitchen it made me cough. She gave us new work clothes and told us to make up then she walked round us, saying, hmmm, hmmm. My tits spilled over my bra and Marta wobbled on her high platforms. Auntie Deirdre moved my bra straps and put more lipstick on Marta. Bubblegum pink. Marta hates lipstick but she said nothing. She was learning.

Auntie Deirdre gave us new names. Lola for me, Rosa for Marta.

I'll be sorry to see you go, Auntie Deirdre said. Good girls after all. Even you. She smiled at Marta and Marta made a smile but her brows were pulled down, dark.

Where are we to go? I asked.

I saw the flash in Marta's eyes and I knew she was thinking of home, but I was not so stupid.

That's for me to know and you to find out, Auntie Deirdre said. She made Pop-Tarts with burning red jam inside and strong coffee with as much sugar as we wanted. The radio said it would rain in London after a bright start. I asked her when we would get cash. She laughed and shook her head. We heard footsteps on the stairs and she said, Heels on, quick, quick, look sharp.

Two guys came into the kitchen and Auntie Deirdre smiled and fluffed her hair. One guy was skinny and ginger, the other tall with a hat and shades. Mr Chapman and Mr Smith. Mr Smith never spoke a word.

Aye, Mr Chapman said when he saw us. He was the ginger runt man. They both walked round looking. Mr Chapman patted my butt; he poked Marta's tit.

The long and the short of it, he said. He laughed so hard spit shot out and landed on Marta's cheek like a bit of silver.

Aye?

Mr Smith nodded. No expression on his face.

This one's fine. Mr Chapman pointed to me then looked at Marta. She lifted her hand to rub the spit off. The wee one's got great tits but a face like a slapped arse, he said. Can you no make her cheer up? Or we'll just take blondie here.

Marta switched a smile on her face but there was fright in her eyes.

Hope she's no gonnae be trouble, said Mr Chapman.

She's shy, Auntie Deirdre said, but she's a goer.

Mr Chapman laughed and rubbed his hands. 'Look forward to finding that out for myself.'

Deal, he said to Mr Smith.

Mr Smith nodded.

They drove out of London in a minibus with about ten girls, some to be dropped in cities on the way north. Marta and me, we stayed in the minibus all the way to Edinburgh.

Vivienne

click

I DON'T KNOW if this is helping. It's getting like a habit. Or a hobby.

I dreaded meeting Mats' folks, but in the end it had to happen. Rita minded Artie and we flew out for the weekend. It was March and still winter there. We stayed in a hotel right on the water, a honey coloured room overlooking the harbour, the iced-up boats. It made you feel so cosy, romantic, it *was*.

We arrived on Friday, saw the sights on Saturday - Munch Museum, Viking Museum, Vigeland Park with hundreds of statues - nearly walked my feet off. Then came the big moment - dinner with his folks. It was more like clog dancers than butter-flies in my guts that night. Sneaked a couple of vodkas from the minibar to get my nerve up.

Their house, half an hour's drive out of the city, is typical Scandi - sleek and modern, pale fabrics, wooden floorboards, tasteful lighting, tall, slim Bang & Olufson speakers in the corners of the room. Don't know why I noticed them! I'm not bothered about techno stuff like that. It was all so perfect, like something from a Sunday supplement. Too perfect maybe. Kept looking for a crack in something or a dead plant or fleck of toothpaste on a mirror. But nah. It was only one evening so I went with it, relaxed. Lovely music came through the lovely speakers, some sort of Norwegian Jazz, like Mats plays sometimes.

And they were nice. Put me at my ease. Mrs Brunborg, Mette, was teeny weeny. How could Mats have come out of something that size? And so perfectly dinky in her tiny tasteful clothes and swept up fair hair. Her face was wrinkled but in a sophisticated way, not ravaged. How do some women manage that? It wasn't till his Dad, Jan, came lumbering into the room that I saw where Mats got his looks from, and his size. Jan was a vision of how Mats will look in twenty years: very nice too.

'So lovely to meet you,' he said and squeezed my hands in his enormous ones.

Mette said, 'Welcome to the family,' and kissed my cheek, and to my relief offered drinks. (Mats is not a big drinker, and nor am I, but it does help break the ice.) I knew they'd been upset not to come to the wedding, not even to meet me before, but before I couldn't. Now I could see I'd been silly. Just like Mats said, there was nothing to worry about.

Though it still felt as if I was at an interview. How could I possibly be good enough for the job?

The table was set like it was Christmas and the main course was actual reindeer in some sort of berry sauce. Plenty of red wine and aquavit went down – at least in my case! Well I was nervous. They asked me question after question about myself till Mats had to call them off. But no, it was OK.

click

I knew they loved Mats' ex – who was some sort of family friend. They'd been terribly upset about the split. I did notice and pretended not to, a photo of her and Mats on the wall. You'd think they take it down, wouldn't you? I saw her once in Edinburgh. (Of course she had to be thin as a rake and blonde as . . . I dunno . . . Shredded Wheat or something.) I thought the Brunsborgs might see me as some sort of scarlet woman or husband stealer. (It turned out he wasn't quite as fancy free as he'd said when we met, or else I'd got it wrong. He now claims I seduced *him*. I don't bother correcting him. What's the point? The past is the past.)

Anyway, the Brunsborg's couldn't have been nicer to me (apart from that photo). They wanted us to give up our hotel room and stay with them; but that would've been too much – having to face them at breakfast as well. And it was more romantic. How romantic can you be in the in-laws spare bedroom?

I'm pretty sure it was that night, in that hotel room, that Tommy was conceived. I was so relieved about the evening, maybe a little woozy from the aquavit, and let Mats persuade me not to use my diaphragm.

I should have listened to my gut feeling. I should have thought harder. I should have admitted to myself that though I loved Mats for his kindness, looks, for taking Artie on, giving us a lovely home, for bringing money in (with our two salaries we were pretty well off for a while there), I wasn't actually *in love* with him anymore. Does that make sense? Or is it even true? Don't know if I ever was properly. What is *in love* anyway?

As soon as I was pregnant though I started to feel kind of . . . just off. I can't put it in words. It was like I just wanted to crawl inside myself and not be touched, not let him in.

A tiny glass of wine, I think.

click

Alis

MARTA GAVE CHAPMAN the name Ratman and we laughed at the little runt. Ratman likes us to be scared. But he was more scared of Mr Smith. Mr Smith never said one word on the drive to Edinburgh or took his shades off even when it got dark. Stupid prick.

Ratman pretends that he likes girls but he is gay. I can tell. I have the gaydar. Dario is Ratman's boyfriend, he is only idiot boy from Bucharest, but he helps Ratman manage his girls. Dario is beautiful like a girl but he has no soul. I told Marta never trust him.

We worked every day but we got no cash. When I complained, Ratman said we must work to pay for our keep. He said, You are illegal immigrants and if the police get you they will put you in jail and throw away the key. He said, If you are not good girls your family at home will suffer.

I have no one but this scared Marta so much. Her face was the colour of bad milk.

Ratman's girls were not allowed to mix with the other girls, so we stayed upstairs in kitchen to wait for tricks. Other girls came in sometimes but Marta and me, we didn't really talk to them; we stuck together. We watched each other's backs.

Now I can't watch Marta's back. Please God keep her safe.

Mats

I DREAMED I was cupped in the palm of a hand and felt so safe. But then came a sound like a saw, a danger, a snickering; the palm was too hot, and started to tighten like a fist. I began to struggle and woke sweating. Vivienne was asleep on her back, breath catching in her throat. She was not supposed to lie that way, the weight of the baby pressing on her spine. Her belly pushed the duvet up in a mound. Seven months pregnant. The child in there – she thought girl – but we didn't know for sure was almost ready. Almost cooked, as she said it. I'd read that even if it were born now, it would be OK; thin, for sure, the last few weeks are when the fat accumulates, but otherwise OK. The baby was made. *My* child was made.

Very slowly and too lightly for her to feel it, I rested my hand on her belly. Whenever I tried to touch her when she was awake she withdrew, sometimes she actually flinched. Maybe it's normal behaviour for a pregnant woman; how would I know? It's my child in there, I wanted to say but I did not allow it, this petulance, which would sound so childish.

Even before she got big enough to make it necessary, she dressed in baggy shirts and sweaters, her waist gone, her style gone, as if she was trying to hide the pregnancy. It turned out she had kept her father's bathrobe, a massive grey felt thing that smelled of mice. She unpacked it from one of her many boxes, and hid herself inside it, never allowing me to see her. She was not one for walking about naked, as my family do at home – in Norway it is the normal thing – but now she seemed afraid for me to see her body. When I saw a pregnant woman in the street I found my eyes following, watching her curves, her movement. Some women seem proud to display their shape, and that is how it should be. This was crazy! My own wife pregnant, my own baby growing inside her, and I was not allowed access.

We had not had sex for weeks and I was trying to be patient. I attempted to ask Ferg about it at one of our Friday evening drinks, but he misunderstood what I meant and laughed, claiming that Karen was insatiable when pregnant. 'One of the perks of all those hormones,' he said. 'But you pay for it when the bairn's born. Make the most of it,' he advised me. 'Once it's here you won't get a sniff for months.' What could I do but nod and grin? I was ashamed to admit I'd stopped getting it already. Ashamed of Vivienne. A little angry maybe. Why didn't her hormones work like that?

Always I'd looked forward to my wife's pregnancy (though of course, I thought it would be Nina). I thought lovemaking at this time would bring a new kind of intimacy; it would feel a privilege to touch the growing belly, come close to the child, like being granted access to the process of creation.

Now Vivienne shifted and swallowed and I removed my hand. She began to snore. I had to talk to her about the sleeping position. Lying on the side with a pillow to support the bump was the best way, they said at the class. Tonight I would insist, but for now . . .

I knelt and lifted the duvet away. The light was poor through the curtains, but enough to see by. She was wearing a big T-shirt with Marge Simpson on the front. When we'd first got together she dressed up for bed in beautiful silk and lace nightgowns, she'd called them that herself, that she found in vintage shops, but since the pregnancy not at all. The T-shirt was rucked up showing a mess of pale brown pubic hair. Holding my breath I picked up the hem of the T-shirt and lifted it further to expose her belly. I admit I was shocked by the way the hair grew in a line, spiky as barbed wire, from her pubis to her navel. The skin was streaked with shiny red marks as if she'd been clawed by some kind of beast. What had I been expecting? A pure white dome? I forced myself to stare, to confront this truth. This was the animal thing that pregnancy was. That she was, that we all are. My stomach roiled with a kind of revulsion but also with compassion for this animal, my wife, and with the first painful throttle of love for my child. The mound shifted. My heart beat fast and I was dizzy. Gently I put my fingertips to the movement and felt a slide of hand or foot or knee or elbow.

My child, my responsibility, as was Vivienne, as was Artie, of course.

'What the hell!' She woke suddenly and jerked away from my hand, pulled the T-shirt down, the duvet up. 'What the hell?' she said again, frowning at me as if I was a stranger. 'Jesus, Mats, I was fast asleep.'

'I'll get you some tea.' I stepped away.

'Mats?'

'I wanted to see,' I said.

'But that was *weird*. You don't want sex do you?'

I went into the kitchen to fill the kettle. My reflection in its smudged chrome side was warped and tiny. The way she said it! As if wanting sex was strange, or a weakness. Last time I tried she said: 'Do you really like the idea of ramming your penis right up against the baby?'

And since she put it like that, I found the answer was no.

I showered and made coffee. She got up, came in and sat at the table flicking through a magazine. She'd been off work two months already with high blood pressure and headaches, and in the mornings, while I got ready, she sat among the scattered Coco-pops and dirty plates, drinking tea, flicking through baby magazines.

Of course, she needed to rest. It was good for her to rest, good for the baby. I was better in the mornings than she. I was a lark while she was an owl. Neither of us could help it, she said, it was biorhythms. Since watching a documentary about biorhythms, she used them as an excuse for everything.

'I think I'll knit this,' she said now, showing me a picture of a baby in stripy jumper.

'I didn't know you could knit.'

'Can't be that hard, can it?' she said. 'Oh, would you take Artie? Save me getting dressed.'

'For sure.'

In this new house (on which the mortgage was immense) the kitchen was dim, the wrong side for the morning sun. Because the flicker of the fluorescent light - the tube needed replacing - brought on Vivienne's headaches, we had to breakfast in the gloom.

Arthur grinned up at me, small elf face with big specs, a rim of milk on his upper lip.

'Marmite or jam?' said Vivienne.

'Peanut butter.'

'We're haven't got any.'

'Peanut butter!' Arthur folded his arms and stuck out his bottom lip.

Vivienne slathered jam on the toast and put it in front of him.

Arthur sighed and shrugged and gave me such an adult look it made me smile. Though Arthur wasn't mine, I cared for him *almost* as if he was.

'Dad,' Arthur said, and I sighed inwardly knowing what was about to come. This was his favourite game. 'Would you rather be run over by a truck or eaten by a lion?'

'Truck,' I said. It was best to play along and wait for him to get tired of it.

'Would you rather cut off your hand or your foot?'

'Foot.'

'Obviously!' Vivienne smiled at Arthur and I saw how it softened her face, the way her front teeth were a little crooked. I'd almost forgotten that. Relieved at this feeling of tenderness towards her, I looked at her lips, at the lovely distinct mole. I had to love her; she was my wife. My palm remembered the sensation of the squirm of my child squeezed in there now, waiting, nearly cooked.

I topped up my coffee, the Vinyl flooring sticky against my soles. I'd offered to pay for a cleaner but Vivienne had been hurt. She hated the idea of *help*, which meant that I'd taken on most of the housework. Not that I minded. Of course, I'm not that kind of guy. I'm a feminist, for sure, trained by Nina, no question about it. But I did work long hours and cleaning the house was not my preferred activity at weekends. Was that so wrong?

The post flapped through the front door and I went to pick it up. Junk mostly, but one letter addressed to me, a letter from Norway. The handwriting, small, neat, precise: Nina's. Here the sun shone in wavy greenish patterns through a narrow stained-glass window. I stared at the envelope, watched the green light wobble across it before folding it and shoving it in the breast pocket of my jacket.

'Might join the boys for a drink tonight,' I said as I went back into the dim kitchen. There was a strange deep feeling in my stomach, as if the ground beneath me was hollow, as if I could easily fall through.

'Go for it,' said Vivienne. She stretched and yawned and her dressing gown fell open to reveal a white, swollen breast, veined with blue. It made me think of Stilton. I looked away.

'Could you pick up a fluorescent tube?' she said.

'Drown or burn, Dad?'

'That's enough,' Vivienne said, pulling a wry face at me.

'And peanut butter?' Arthur added.

'Bathroom now,' I told him. It was as if I was looking down at the boy from a vertiginous height. 'Teeth, toilet, face,' I heard my voice say. 'And clean your glasses.' Arthur got down obediently and trotted off.

I bent to kiss Vivienne's head. Her hair was messy, the red growing out leaving a finger-width the same colour as Arthur's. Also they both had similar greenish eyes. Mother and son. What would my child look like?

'Sorry about earlier,' I said.

'Weirdo!' She wrinkled her nose and laughed.

***

'Dad?' Arthur was saying. '*Dad?*'

I blinked, disorientated, found we were parked outside the school. I had no memory of the drive at all.

'Which one, Dad?'

'What?'

'Would you rather eat a worm or a dog poo?' the boy repeated. The playground, with its red and blue snakes and ladders, its hopscotch squares, was empty of other children.

'Worm.'

'Me too.'

I got out of the car and stretched. I opened the door for Arthur, made sure he'd got all his stuff, watched him walk through the playground, dwarfed by his rucksack packed with swimming things, lunch box, reading book – and my heart contracted at the frailty of the boy, my stepson, at his trust in me, at his spindly little legs.

Back in the car, I took the letter from my pocket. I knew already what it would say. It was tempting not to read it at all, not to know for sure. But I had to know. Imagine Nina's scorn at such ostrich-like behaviour. Taking a deep breath, I slid my finger under the flap, opened and unfolded the paper all in one, and made myself read to the end before I breathed out. Nina was getting married. I'd guessed already from something Mor had said. But still, to see it in her own familiar writing.

I know you'll be pleased for me Mats, as I was for you. With love always, Nina.

My hands went into fists and I shut my eyes to a wash of red, a shocking surge of jealousy and anger. But these emotions are futile and uncivilised. In any case, who was I angry with? I sat and breathed until it was under my control.

Before I started the car I tore the letter in half, and then in quarters and tore and tore until there was nothing but confetti scattered on my lap, my thighs, the floor.

Vivienne

click

SO. TOMMY. SAILED through the pregnancy. Mats was with me for the birth. I'd missed a 'hubby' as the midwives put it, to 'hold my hand' when Arthur was born. On that day, as I writhed about in my hospital bed, I thought about Mr Professor and what he was doing and whether he'd feel some sort of twang in the ether when his son was born. Maybe he'd stop work, look up from his microscope, feeling *something*. And then shrug, look down, forget it.

Of course he might have hundreds of sprogs. That's a thought.

click

Anyway, with Mats it was different. Perfect. He booked time off work to come to antenatal classes with me. Actually, it started to really get to me, how the other mums and even the nursing staff played up to this big handsome male in the room. He could have gone on *Mastermind* about pregnancy and birth, the amount of books he read.

And when it started he left work the moment he got the call. We were booked in for a water birth. While I was being checked, he lit scented candles, rigged up speakers to play some classical stuff I'd once pretended to like. Thomas came quickly, swam out, loads of dark hair plastered down, face red and scrunched as he bobbed to the surface. Mats cut the cord. I couldn't watch. All eyes in the room went to Mats, bare chested ready for skin-to-skin bonding, holding his tiny, new, wet son, such love in his eyes, I had look away.

click

Thomas is a mini version of Mats; just as Mats is of Jan. Strong Viking genes (the dark version of Viking). He was small at birth but soon piled on weight. A big healthy boy, handsome from the start. He was like a catalogue baby, looks and everything. He slept through the night nearly straight away and as soon as he learnt to smile, smiled and smiled.

So what was wrong?

click

Hate the sound of my own voice. Shouldn't listen. Don't listen till you're ready, Sue said. And you might not ever need to listen. The therapy is in the speaking. Getting it out there. Getting it out where?

click

Sometimes I don't know if I'm really depressed or if I'm putting it on; bringing it on myself. If mind is matter then my mind is the matter. At first it was normal baby blues, they said, but it didn't lift. It did the opposite, clamped down like a lid. A toad, the toad squatting over me, damp and warty, blocking out all the light.

It was partly the house's fault. The toad was waiting when we moved in.

Mats loved Thomas; Arthur loved him; the Brunburgs, who flew over as soon as he was born, loved him; Rita loved him and blablablablablabla. It was easy for them. I don't know why it was so hard for me, but it seemed as if there was no need, no *room* for me to love him. He hoovered milk from me until I started on the medication and then he went onto formula with hardly a squeak of protest.

click

If he'd cared it might have helped.

If he'd screamed for me and only me.

click

I'd knitted him a jumper, red and white stripes, nearly killed me. But it wouldn't go over his head. His big, handsome head.

Apathy, was the word. I couldn't be bothered with him. Sounds awful. I am trying to be truthful.

Nobody need ever listen.

I need never listen.

It is therapy.

Supposedly.

click

Alis

GEORDIE IS MR Smith's friend. I think he is a rich, important man. Maybe he is famous even. He is a man who looks kind, who speaks soft. Marta said he looks like a grandpa or a nice doctor but I know he is a psycho nut.

He likes to hurt girls big time; he liked to hurt me. He sticks things in, not just his prick.

Sometimes it is hard to hide behind your face.

What he did to me, it got worse.

I told Ratman but he was no help, too scared of Mr Smith.

Geordie gets free rein, lassie, Ratman said.

No one to help me.

I did not tell Marta too much, I did not want to scare her.

I should have warned her.

Please God do not let him move onto Marta.

I cannot help her now.

Ratman, Mr Smith, I do not think they could know Geordie would go as far as this. He put something sharp inside me, maybe it was broken bottle, and I am broken and now I bleed and bleed. I think it will stop but when I move it starts again. Blood is a warm thing in the cold.

They put me down here in the cellar. It's dark and I am alone. I do not like to be alone. I do not like the dark. Please God bring me light.

Mats

FRIDAY EVENING IN the wine bar. After red wine and tapas, most colleagues had gone and I was left with Fergus, and Frank, a consultant from the New York office.

Frank was a big guy in every way: loud, thick-necked, beer-bellied, and Fergus was on a long leash for once, wife and kids away for the weekend. The three of us stood in the crammed and noisy bar, leaning into a high round table. In Norway, I'd rarely drunk like this, as much as this. The three of us pouring it down as if there was something, some kind of answer, that just another glass might help us reach.

Tomorrow was Nina's wedding day.

'You're quiet,' said Fergus. 'Surprised you're allowed out.' Frank had gone to the 'john' as he called it and it became apparent that he's been doing most of the talking. 'Everything OK? How's Viv? How's the bairn?' Fergus lit a cigarette, offered one to me. On the next table a crowd of girls screeched with laughter.

'Thomas is fine,' I said, resisting taking the photo from my wallet. He'd already seen it. 'But Vivienne's not . . . oh I don't know.'

'Getting any sleep?' Fergus asked.

'Tom's a pretty good sleeper.' I was proud of this. As soon as he'd been weaned from the breast, I let Vivienne sleep and got up at night with him. Though it was tiring, I loved those moments, the most tender of my life, soothing and feeding my son while, it seemed, the rest of the world was asleep. I almost missed those moments when he started sleeping through.

'You mean you're getting *sleep?* Fergus looked at me incredulously. 'You lucky fucker. Right enough, you look OK.'

'But Vivienne, she's . . .'

'Haven't had a full night's sleep for years,' Fergus spoke through a yawn. 'It's a good night if only one of them's up. Sometimes it's all fucking four of the wee fuckers.'

'How was Karen after?' I asked.

'Oh you mean that?' Fergus snorted. 'Nothing doing. Mind you,' he added, 'I'd rather have a good night's sleep than get my leg over. Never thought I'd hear myself say that!' He was propping his head on his hand, slurring. 'But Karen's away at her mum's with the kids for three whole nights, the house to myself, peace and fucking quiet.'

'Nina's getting married tomorrow.' I had not meant to say this. I splashed the last of the wine into my glass and swallowed it down. What was the matter with me? I was married, for God's sake. I had married only months after splitting with Nina. When I told her I was going to marry Vivienne, I hoped she'd change her mind about me, about us. I hoped she'd want to see me, beg me to take her back – but she only sent congratulations. It must have hurt her though. Of course it did. But Nina would never let this show.

How did any of this happen? This life in Edinburgh; it didn't feel real. It was like a branch line from reality. Real life was back in Oslo with Nina, whom I'd know all my life, loved since I was twenty.

'Aye?' Fergus raised his eyebrows, drained his glass. 'What's the problem?'

'No problem.' I stared at the shiny surface of the table, scattered with ash and salt and drips of wine.

'Jeez,' Fergus clutched his head. 'I'm away home. Get myself on the sofa with a lager and a DVD.' He paused, swaying. 'Want to come?'

I shook my head and clapped him on the shoulder. 'Enjoy your sleep.'

'Aye, if I can remember how to do it.'

Frank came surging through the crowd towards us, with another bottle. 'You cannot be serious,' he shouted, as Fergus pulled on his coat. 'The night is young.'

'Wish I was, pal,' said Fergus. 'See you Monday.'

'Party pooper,' Frank remarked to Fergus' retreating back. He shrugged and grinned. His grin like a teenager's on his paunchy middle-aged face. 'We'll just have to sink this between us.'

'I need to go too,' I said. 'Wife waiting.'

'Pussy whipped? Jesus, what is it with you Brits?'

'I'm not a Brit.'

'Swede then.'

'Norwegian.'

'Whoa, Scandi chicks! Blonde and gorgeous, eh? Legs up to here,' Frank indicated his armpit, 'that's how I like them.' He sloshed out two glasses of wine. I put my hand across the top of my glass, but it was too late and wine splashed over my fingers.

'You married?' I asked.

Frank shook his head. 'Not now.' Below his pale crew cut his shiny forehead crumpled and his small eyes filled – did they fill? – with tears. Maybe it was just the smoke or maybe just the drink.

'Wife, Pammie, wanted to do a history class. I paid out, anything to make the little lady happy, I was crazy about her. What do they call it? A fool for love? Then what did she do?'

I shook my head.

'Took off with her professor, would you believe? Holy shit, I don't mind admitting I was cut up at first.' He was silent for a moment, then took a swig of wine, wiped his lips with his fist and there was that grin again. 'Then the compensations started to kick in, plenty of mercy fucks coming my way. Yessir!'

I looked at my watch.

'Mighty unfriendly to leave a visitor drinking alone in a strange town.' Frank pulled a sad clown's face.

I sighed. 'A few minutes,' I said. Maybe it wouldn't be such a bad thing to be late. The rule was that if Vivienne was in bed when I came in, I slept on the sofa. Waiting there ready for me would be the single duvet in a *Star Wars* cover, with my pillow and bathrobe. Or I could sleep on Thomas's floor, be right there ready when he stirred.

'Use my cellphone to check on the little lady?' Frank took his telephone from his pocket. I turned it over in my hands – I hadn't got one yet, wasn't sure if I'd bother.

'Better go outside,' Frank said, 'and don't forget the area code.'

The wind was whipping icy rain about. I keyed the home number into the phone, imagined it ringing, imagined Vivienne sighing, hauling herself off the sofa, or stretching out across the bed, her grumpy voice. 'Ye-es?' she'd say. How much venom she was able to pack into that one word. Venom that was undeserved. I did everything I could for her, for Thomas, of course, for Arthur. What more could I do? I stood with my eyes shut, the wind wet on my face till my cheeks were frozen. There was no point disturbing her. And besides, the phone might wake Thomas. I took a last breath of freshness, swung open the door, shouldered back into the crowd.

Yet another bottle appeared at some time and we were both leaning on the table, conversation about work had veered to sport and back to women. I found myself talking about Nina, about her neck, her hands, her neatness. How she could solve any problem, make everything all right. How she made me feel safe. I hadn't felt safe since I'd left her, I realized this, and now it made me blink.

'But hang on, *Vivienne's* your wife, right?' Frank was frowning.

'Yes.' I shrugged. 'I know.'

Frank raised his eyebrows but refrained from comment. He rolled back his cuff to look at the flashy gold face of his watch. He seemed to be taking more from it than just the time. He looked up: 'Reckon the little lady'll be asleep now?'

As I nodded, I knew I should have said no, should have said that she never liked to sleep till I was in, that she would be cranky if I was late, that the baby might wake, that I really must go home. Maybe that was the moment of choice?

'Hey,' said Frank, grinning like a naughty kid. 'I know just the thing to cheer you up.'

'What?'

Frank tapped one side of his nose. 'Trust your Uncle Frank.'

We went out into a swirl of coldness, a painful fling of hail. Frank, with surprising speed for a man so big and so drunk, leapt forward to intercept a cab. 'Get in out of this,' he said, and, hatless, icy pellets scouring my face, I obeyed.

'You can drop me at the bottom of the hill.'

'Yeah, yeah.' Frank leant forward to speak to the driver, then sat back, slapped me so heartily on the leg that it hurt.

'First,' he said, 'a little detour.'

'I should get home.'

'You've rung Nina.'

'Vivienne.'

Frank laughed. 'Whoever. Look, cut yourself a bit of slack, that's what I say, that's what I do.'

Squinting through the taxi window, I could see no more than smears of light through the rain, coming so hard the windscreen wipers could only just cope. It was not the direction of home though. *Cut yourself a bit of slack.* What does that mean? Something like a bubble travelled in my blood, a giggle; here was I, half abducted, prevented from going home when home was – in any case – somewhere I really didn't want to be. I was almost enjoying the unaccustomed feeling of helplessness. Of course it was not real helplessness. I could insist on the taxi stopping and get out whenever I wanted.

Yes, I could have.

But then we'd reached our destination. Frank paid the driver and we stepped out into the pelting rain. We were in a narrow cobbled street shining, tenements towering on each side. There was the dim throb of music from somewhere and the sound of water cascading from a broken gutter. The windows of the corner building we stood in front of glowed pink. Over the door was a red neon sign: Massage City.

Still I could have walked away. If I had turned my back and gone home, so much would have been so different.

Why didn't I walk?

⁂

Frank pressed his finger against the bell, the door opened with a jangle and a skinny, long-haired boy stood there.

'You wish massage?'

'You betcha,' said Frank. He grabbed my arm and propelled me into a reception area with a pile of towels on a counter, and a list of therapeutic massage treatments – Swedish, Sports, Shiatsu.

'This kind of massage?' asked the boy.

Frank just laughed. The boy led us through a hall and into a lounge, hot and airless and thick with the smell of scented oil and incense. It was like a sleazy dentist's waiting room. Gold and pink fabric smothered everything that could be smothered. Pink shaded lamps cast light on soft chairs and sofas, a pile of magazines on a low table. High on a wall in one corner a silent TV showed a Western and Sinatra's voice came from a speaker.

'My treat.' Pink light flashed on Frank's teeth.

The boy indicated that we should sit. He was wearing a skimpy, muscle-revealing vest, loose grey sweat pants and his long-toed feet were bare.

'Which way you want?' he said.

'The usual,' Frank said. We had sat down on the same sofa, too close, and he nudged me in the ribs. 'Assuming you don't want a change of scene?'

'What?'

'Desert rather than swamp?'

'Sorry?'

'Only kidding!' Frank threw back his head and laughed, Adam's apple surfacing amongst his neck-fat. I put my hand to my own throat. Of course, it was a brothel; of course, I had known this. The right thing to do: stand up and walk right out. But then the girls, *women*, were there. And they were just ordinary, attractive women. By then Sinatra was crooning – appropriately – 'Strangers in the Night'.

'Now we're cooking,' said Frank, rubbing his hands. 'Take your pick.'

I could not look at the girls' faces. Or I should say the women's faces. If I met any eyes I knew I wouldn't be able to do it and now, drunk and with all that flesh close to my face, the perfumes, the swish of thighs and wraps, I did want to do it. It almost didn't matter which one. I pointed to a girl, slighter than the rest, much slighter than Vivienne. Her hair was dark and waved right down to her tiny waist. As I followed her through a bamboo beaded curtain and up some stairs, along a corridor and into a small room, I watched her small high buttocks moving under her white silk slip, her ankles delicate above tall platform shoes.

There were Indian bedspreads pinned on the walls, the smell of incense, a neat bed, with sheet and pillows but no duvet.

'What you want?' she said, smiling. Her voice wasn't English. She came up close to me, fingering my jacket buttons. 'Standard?' she said. 'You want to fuck?'

She turned away to light a joss stick, stick it in a little holder shaped like an elephant.

I took off my jacket. I couldn't speak, didn't want to speak, didn't want the reality of that. I wanted it to be a dream. She undid my belt, small hands quick, she helped me out. And then we were on the bed and under her firm springy body it was over before it began, release hardly three thrusts away. If it had been real sex I would have felt guilty. But it wasn't real. And she, unconcerned, pleased even, jumped off and left me to dress.

❧

I waited for Frank in the sofa area, tingling and buzzing, feeling sick, a headache starting, a hangover before the night was even over: it was still not quite midnight, I saw with surprise. Frank came out, a grin on his face, paid the guy and we were seen out, back up the steps to the cobbled street.

'How was it?' said Frank, scanning the street for a taxi.

'Satisfaction achieved? Attaboy!'

I said nothing. Yes, was the answer. I gasped in the fresh, cold air. The rain had stopped and as we turned onto the wide main road, I saw the moon, three quarters waxed, smudged behind a ragged cloud.

Never again, of course, never ever again, but still . . .

I felt light and childish, as if I had got away with something; I felt like a dog; I felt like putting back my head and howling at the moon.

Alis

Dear God,

Please forgive my sins.

Please take care of my little boy wherever he may be. Make him a good man.

Please forgive Mama. Take care of her soul and give her peace.

Please God protect Marta.

Please keep her safe.

Please God take me home.

Amen.

THREE

1992

Mats

HE DRAGGED HIMSELF into work, thinking it would be OK. Managed to avoid Frank. But it was not OK. He'd only been working for a few minutes before the screen began to swim. He persevered with work for another thirty minutes but it was no good and he had to go to the bathroom and throw up. He hadn't been sick since he was a boy, found it frightening, the helplessness to stop it. No question of staying at work. He rinsed his mouth, splashed his face, dried it on a paper towel and went to tell Christine he was going home.

'Och, you poor wee sausage,' she said and he saw her eyeing his vomit-splashed tie. 'Give it here,' she reached out her hand. 'It's likely a bug. Go home and get your head down. I'll sort things here.' She patted his arm and his throat hollowed. Sympathy destroyed him, though he overflowed with it himself. All give no take, Nina told him once, you need to toughen up.

In the lift his stomach lurched at the sinking sensation. You could never describe Nina as sympathetic. Rather she was helpful, but that was different; she was clear and logical. Never would she have looked at him so kindly – and nor would Vivienne. A shame he didn't fancy Christine, a woman who'd sponge your vomity tie, who'd call you poor wee sausage and, no doubt, tuck you up in the bed. Such a woman would be a treasure. Why had he never chosen such a one?

As the lift opened and he hurried out of the building, he tried to remember whether Nina had ever needed his sympathy. Once she'd broken her wrist, skiing, and needed him to drive her about, but she had not needed – had put up a barrier against – anything you might call sympathy. He gasped in the cold, damp air. Was it a bug or a hangover? Or was it a punishment?

Nina had never said, 'I love you,' not unprompted anyway. Only once he'd been craven enough to ask her.

'Of course,' she'd said in that clipped voice, raising one of her fair eyebrows.

'But you never say.' He'd felt so vulnerable then that now, years later, a tear ran down his cheek. Why can he not get Nina out of his mind?

But, 'Can't you tell?' she'd said, genuinely puzzled. 'All the things I do for you? We're married aren't we?'

And she'd been right, of course, always right and it was weak of him to need to hear the words when she was there. Unmanly?

The front door was unlocked, but the house was empty. Vivienne must have taken Thomas out, good, doubly good: quiet for him and she was doing something with the baby, using her own initiative. Though she should have locked the door. Lately she'd been careless like that. It had been nagging him, how she was, not right, not how a new mother should be surely? She showed no joy.

He got to the toilet just in time but there was nothing to vomit but spit. He flushed and rinsed and washed his hands, cleaned his teeth, comforted by the smell of soap, the taste of toothpaste. In the bedroom, the bed was unmade, the curtains closed, the bedside light still on. He dropped his clothes on a chair and fell onto the bed.

How long he slept he didn't know, a shred of Thomas's cry

insinuated into a messy dream in which a girl in silk *no, no, no,* what had he done? Half awake, he tried to think of other things as he waited for Vivienne but fell back asleep into another horribly arousing dream and was woken again by the baby crying steadily. He waited for Vivienne to do something about it; how could she leave him wailing like that? At last Mats pulled himself up, head throbbing, weakness in his legs, a raging thirst.

'Hey Thomas.' When he picked him up, he was hot and struggling, almost in convulsions of rage and tears. He carried the boy into the bathroom, took off the Babygro, peeled off the heavy, filthy nappy. So heavy and filthy, it must be last night's. Yes, he recognized it. There was a tear where the tab had come off and he'd mended it with tape. That was after he'd got in, about midnight, and now it was . . . he looked at his watch; past noon. Thomas screamed as he dabbed at the shiny inflamed skin. Too sore for wipes. He turned the taps off, filled the baby bath. Thomas stopped crying to listen to the running taps and shuddering fixed Mats with outraged eyes.

As he lifted Thomas and lowered him gently into the warm bath, he heard the front door open and Vivienne come in, running upstairs calling 'Tommy?' anxiety in her voice. She must have seen the empty cot, before she realized Mats was there.

'In here,' Mats called and she came and leant against the door frame.

'Thank God. I thought, I thought . . .'

Mats said nothing, hand cupped under Thomas' head, watching the kicking of the froggy legs.

'What are you doing home?' she asked.

'There you go,' he said, 'all better now.'

Children should not be exposed to tension, keep smiling, keep calm. His hands shook, his head banged.

'Be like that then,' she said. 'I'm putting the kettle on.'

'You could make up a bottle,' he called after her.

He dried Thomas and dabbed Sudocrem on his sore skin, dressed him in a fresh nappy and Babygro.

In the kitchen Vivienne sat at the table pretending to read a magazine, drinking tea, crunching Doritos. She'd made up one eye, heavily, with mascara or whatever it was, but not the other. Had she gone out like that? He said nothing, cooled the bottle under the tap, holding struggling Thomas against his shoulder. Once the milk was the right temperature Thomas latched on desperately and gulped too fast, gave himself wind, began to writhe and cry again.

'I'll take him.' Vivienne pushed her tea away and reached out. Mats filled a glass with milk, swallowed a couple of paracetamol.

'Silent treatment eh?' she said, putting Tommy against her shoulder and rubbing his back.

Mats' head was slamming. He needed to lie down. 'Going back to bed,' he said.

'You sick?'

'Bug, I think.'

'Not a hangover then?' she shouted after him as he went upstairs. Back in the bedroom he fell into a half sleep this time, aware of his watch ticking close to his ear, aware of sounds: Vivienne's voice, the TV going on, Thomas wailing, eventually of Vivienne coming into the room.

'How are you feeling?' she said.

He felt the tipping of the mattress as she sat on the edge of the bed.

'Bad,' he mumbled into his pillow.

'Can I get you anything?'

'No.'

'Poor you,' she said, as she left the room, and she did sound sympathetic, but sympathy from her, at this moment, filled him with fury.

In the evening, after an afternoon of semi-sleep, the headache lifted and he experienced a first wisp of hunger. She was in the kitchen, stirring a pan of spaghetti hoops.

'Hi Dad,' said Arthur. He was kneeling on the floor with all his cars lined up, using the grid of squares on the Vinyl as roads and car parks.

Thomas was in his bouncy chair kicking his feet. Mats jiggled him the way he liked and was rewarded with a crooked smile. He put a slice of bread in the toaster. Dry toast was what Mor would give him if ever he were sick.

'Are you OK, Dad?' said Arthur, looking up. 'Have you actually sicked up?'

Mats nodded.

'Cool. Lucy sicked up at school and it went on Dominic's shoes.'

'Poor Dominic,' said Vivienne at the same time as Mats said, 'Poor Lucy,' and they almost smiled at each other, snatched their expressions back.

Mats took his toast and water back to the bedroom, lay listening to her try and cope with the kids. He couldn't leave it. What would Nina advise? Be straight; come out with it. For Nina this would be obvious. He stopped himself getting out of bed to help when he heard Arthur searching for his reading book, Thomas crying – he guessed it was a nappy change, hoped she'd remember to be gentle, remember the ointment – Arthur calling out for water, needing a pee. But he lay and let her cope and eventually it was quiet, and he fell asleep.

She woke him, coming in smelling of wine and smoke and

climbing into bed beside him with a sort of exaggerated care. Having slept half the day he was suddenly wide awake and zinging with anger.

He sat up, back against the headboard, pillow on his lap. 'So, you went out and left Thomas?' he said, managing to keep his voice low and even.

'Oh God, I knew you'd have to go on about it. We're not all as perfect as you, Mats.' She was lying on her back, staring at the ceiling. Her face looked young like that, smoothed of lines, her wine-stained lips were slack.

His fists clenched and his stomach rumbled, roared almost, the way some men would roar now, the way he had a right to roar. He swallowed, continued evenly: 'You left the door unlocked. Thomas, wet and dirty and alone. And hungry. Anyone could have come in.'

'But it was you,' she said childishly. 'You came in and saved the day. As usual,' she mumbled.

Is that what she said?

'Pardon?'

There was an inscrutable smile on her face. 'I mean you always come to the rescue. My knight in shining armour.'

He thumped his fist down on the pillow. 'This is not a fairy story,' he said, voice rising now. 'Where *were* you?'

'It was the toad,' she said. 'It's in the house.'

Silence, while he tried to make sense. *Toad?*

'I came on,' she said. 'No tampons. Baby asleep. Didn't want to wake him and get him dressed and all that palaver.'

'But he still had last night's nappy on!'

'Thought I'd only be ten minutes. Anyway nothing could happen to him in his cot.'

'You cannot do that! You cannot leave him!'

'Don't shout.'

I'm not shouting, he thought, *if you think this is shouting . . .* He breathed steadily, tried to unlock the tension in his hands. How satisfying it would be to swing his fist. But violence is not the way. It cannot be the way.

'Why were you so long then?' he said carefully.

'I don't know,' she said. 'It was kind of sparkling.'

'What?'

He watched her expression harden as she manoeuvred herself from wrong to right. 'What was I meant to do? It's all right for you, you don't have periods. Anyway, you can talk. You were out till all hours last night. What were you up to?' She rolled onto her side, facing away from him and righteously clicked off the lamp. 'Everything's OK isn't it?' she added. 'We're all still breathing.' She pulled the duvet across, leaving his leg exposed. He tugged it back, more forcefully than necessary. 'It's his skin, Mats,' she murmured, 'it's damp. He presses out the light.'

'What?'

'Don't you feel it?'

He was silenced, eyes wide open in the darkness. Not quite dark. Street light fell between the curtains, making the white paper lampshade glow like a too-close moon. 'Toad?' he said at last.

But she said nothing more.

Vivienne

click

click

Damn thing. Is this right? Are you working?

click

Testing. Testing?

click

It was after Thomas that the toad showed up. Well, didn't show up, more came out. Even when we viewed the house there was something. I'd rather have stayed in the flat, right in town, friendly flat that knew me. In this house, it's a good house, three bedrooms, attic room, even a garden, but there was this heavy feeling like a smell. I thought it would go when we moved in, when we opened the windows.

But then I found out what that smell was: toad. The smell got stronger and closer and then I woke one morning and it was squatting over me, damp and heavy and I can't explain but *in* me, blocking things out.

click

All fuzzy now what came next and next. Some kind of problem, can't remember, and Mats reckoned I needed help. Rita helped, but it wasn't fair, Mats said, when she had her own life. Pills from the doctor and counselling. Sue with her clipboard, long plait and fluffy lip.

Without even asking me, Mats hired a Norland nanny. It was like we were suddenly back in the 1950s or something. She was about fifty and wore a beige uniform. Beige! It was all about 'routine' and I wasn't meant to interfere with 'Baby's this' or 'Baby's that'. She must have looked after Arthur too.

I always picked him up from school, well sometimes.

It was the wallpaper in the hall. One day I twigged. It wasn't paper but toad skin, bumpy, greenish and I started to pick it off. When it was all off the toad would be gone. Nobody said, there were no voices or anything, I'm not mad, but I just knew. I broke my fingernails and bits of plaster came off and trickled on the floor. Mats said stop it stop it and Artie helped until the nanny said it was unhygienic and look at all the dust.

One morning, maybe a month after she arrived, I woke late and went into the kitchen in my dressing gown. There she was, the nanny mixing up Tommy's feed. The toad was watching from behind the fridge. He was weakened by the skinning, thinner, I knew it, but still there was the stink of him, pond slime, rust, bad breath.

'Hello, Mummy,' the nanny said. I filled the kettle. 'Please Mummy, wash your hands before you touch the kettle,' she said. Yes! She actually said that to me, in my own kitchen!

I swivelled to face her. 'Sorree?' I mean, was that even sane? I couldn't look at her. I made coffee without washing my hands. I didn't even look at Tommy. I know that's bad but she had this way of parting his hair on one side so he looked like a cabinet minister.

I left the room and went into the hall to keep on with the wallpaper. I wanted it all to be white. There were layers of old wallpaper, roses on a trellis, and something yellow under the thick green warty skin. My blood on the plaster from broken nails but it was nearly done. Mats said stop he'd get a decorator but I didn't want a decorator. I don't like people in. So he bought lining paper and Polyfilla and white paint and said he'd do it at the weekend.

Since the nanny had come he'd been out a lot. Working late. But he did help a bit with the peeling. He got a steamer and it was gorgeous when the skin went soft and came off all live and fleshy so you could feel the shudder of the toad. You could feel the weakening. It was something Mats and I were doing together and I loved him in the hiss of the steam.

After that morning with the kettle the nanny had to go. Rather than helping me bond with Thomas she was cutting me off from him. And Artie. And my own kitchen. Wash your hands! Before I would at least know vaguely what was in the fridge. And Arthur had taken to parroting her sometimes, calling me 'Mummy' in that irritating way. 'Would Mummy like to see my painting?' Ha!

My throat is dry.

click

OK. That night – I think it was that night or it was some night anyway – I stood in the hall and waited for the toad but he was not there and the walls were bare, the plaster the colour of skin under a scab and patched with white where there were wires threading underneath and holes where maybe pictures and mirrors had been. My nails were in such a state I thought about a manicure.

Sue said it was a good sign to take an interest in my appearance; a good sign that I had even thought of it and I felt dead proud. Now the toad was dead I could take an interest, I would. The mirror reflected back a skank. How could Mats even look at me? I wanted to tell him how much better I was and that I would be better and that I was sorry; but he didn't come home when I thought he would and all my positive feelings soaked away.

Focus on the positive, Sue said, and I tried and tried but it was hours and too hard. I waited and waited drinking Rioja, watching whatever was on the telly after the news. He came in at midnight, an enormous, stubbly version of Thomas.

'Thought you'd be in bed,' he said.

The room was hot, the realistic flames fluttering on the realistic coals, the radiators cranking out their heat. The TV was blethering on about the election. I saw him scan the room. All right there was a dirty dish or two and I might have had a cigarette. The nanny went upstairs after 'kiddies' bedtimes' and I didn't see her again till morning. There may have been some chocolate wrappers or something. Artie likes those Babybels, and so do I, and the rinds do get everywhere.

Matts took off his jacket and undid a button of his shirt to make the point that it was too hot, and sat down on the opposite sofa.

'Watching this?' he asked.

'Half.' I gazed at the screen where a grey-haired man's chin was wagging up and down.

'Mind if I?' He muted it. 'So, how was your day?' He was eyeing the bottle. I probably shrugged. 'Thomas?' I shrugged again. How was I supposed to know? That was the nanny's job. I remembered that she had to go. 'Arthur?'

'Asleep.' He must have been picked up from school, had his tea, played, been bathed, gone to bed. I must have been on automatic. So pleased about the hall. No smell of toad, or only a lingering whiff in the corners.

'Did you notice?' I said. 'It's finished. Ready for the weekend.'

He reached down for a Babybel that had rolled under the table. It sat in his palm like a little planet and made my mouth water.

'I think you should see the doctor again. I'll make an appointment,' he said. 'I'll come with you. And you shouldn't be drinking wine with your medication, you know that.'

'But it's gone now.'

He gave me wary look.

'Toad?' I said though he knew what I meant.

He put the cheese on the table and took the bottle as he'd been itching to do since he'd walked in. I didn't mind. It was nearly empty anyway. I picked up the cheese, split the red wax with my thumbnails, pulled away the halves and bit into the bland fat, shut my eyes until it was gone. When I opened them he was staring at me.

'What?' I said.

'I want to talk about something,' he said.

I ran my tongue round my teeth and smiled. 'Me too!'

Now he looked surprised and waited to hear.

'You first,' I said.

He paused before he spoke, pressing his lips together in this way he has that makes them disappear. 'I've been thinking,' he said. 'There's an opportunity at work. I could transfer back to Oslo. How do you think about that?'

'*What* do you think,' I corrected him. I wondered if *he'd* been drinking; usually his English is perfect. Better than mine. He was flushed, his eyes all slidy. I wondered where he'd been all evening, but couldn't be bothered to ask.

'We could get a house on the water,' he was saying, 'more floor-space; my folks nearby to help with the boys.'

'But what about the hall?' I said.

'I'll have it to finish it anyway.'

He waited for my response.

'We have to sack the nanny,' I said.

He looked down at the bottle. 'I think we need her for now.'

'I can manage. She stops me managing.' I was trying to think of the word, there's a good word for it.

click

Disempowering. I wanted to say, I feel disempowered; she's deskilling me as a mother, but I couldn't think of the words then.

The cheese wax had gone soft in my hands and I began to squeeze it, shape it into fingernails, lovely red. I would ask for a Babybel colour when I had them done. I almost forgot that he was there. 'I'm going to check on Thomas,' he said, and left the room, swinging the bottle like a club.

click

Marta

LUNCHTIME AND IT'S busy down there. She used to be surprised that men would pay for sex in their lunch hour, but nothing surprises her now. Nothing about men. No one has chosen her today and she knows why and Dario knows why. It's because of the darkness on her face. When they run their eyes over her, she scowls. But she has to stop it. She has to force herself to smile. Ratman will be mad if he hears she's had no punters; he'll blame her. Maybe he'll punish her. But how can she smile? With no Alis?

Last night Geordie asked for Marta – Rosa. Never has he asked for her before. Before it was always Alis, but Alis has gone.

Marta's guts contract remembering thick, panting, alcoholic breath, the way he whispered, as he hurt her, *This is just for starters, pet.*

You can see sunshine out there but this kitchen is not a room for sunshine. Always it's cold. Lily has been busy this morning but now she sits curled up on a chair, wrapped in the big brown cardigan everyone borrows, twirling her hair and sucking her thumb; the tiny wet noises make Marta want to scream.

Dario comes up and she and Lily rise to their feet, but he shakes his head. Lily curls up again. Dario goes to look out of the window. 'You must to do some or Ratman, he will be mad with me,' he says.

'Where's Alis?' she says.

He shrugs his thin shoulders. His eyes are bright and slippery. 'Hey, smile,' he says, grinning exaggeratedly as he squelches his chewing gum.

But she won't, she can't.

'What you want from me?' he says. 'I can do nothing.'

He turns away, stretches out to touch the window. His finger leaves a smear on the glass. She comes to the window and looks down at the street, the roofs of cars shining.

'Sunshine,' she finds herself saying.

'You want sun?' For a moment he stops chewing. 'OK.' Marta's heart jumps. He moves towards the door. 'Come then?'

Marta looks at Lily but she is sucking and twirling her hair, eyes quite blank. Marta follows Dario upstairs to a room she's never seen before. It has a narrow rusted balcony, where they can perch on rickety iron seats. The view is a blank wall stained green, a garden down below with a broken bedstead buried in ivy, rubbish, rubbish, rubbish. In the corner of the balcony, a pigeon's wing, dried and trapped between the rails, splays as if still soaring.

Dario fetches bottles of Coke. They sit in the full blare of the sun. Leaning back against the wall, he props his feet on the hot rusty rail. She studies his long monkey toes, the one black painted toenail on his right foot, the silver ring on the second toe of his left.

They sit in a silence she can't gauge. Is it awkward or companionable? The Coke is invigorating; cold bubbles prickle in her throat. 'I hate that guy, Geordie,' she says after a while. 'What he does. It's not normal.'

Dario swigs his Coke, dabs his lips with a neat fist.

'Who is he?' she asks.

'Special man. Important,' Dario says.

'Important? Why?'

Dario shrugs.

'I wish I could ask Alis.' She swallows with a painful click.

'Ratman say not to let him in no more, but if Ratman is not here, how I can stop him?'

Marta stares. This is the most she's ever heard him say. He closes his eyes against the sun. There's a pink glow through her eyelids as she does the same. If she makes a friend of Dario, then maybe he will help her. She asks about his life; but his answers are brief. He's from Bucharest. He knew what he was getting into when he came to the UK. That's all.

'You don't hate Ratman?' she asks.

He shrugs. 'I hate no one. No point.'

'Can you ask him about Alis for me, please?' she says. 'Where she's gone?'

Dario lights one Mr Ratman's panatellas, spits a fleck of tobacco from his lip.

'What about your family?' Marta asks.

But he has no family. She stares at him, this is so sad. I'll be your family, she thinks of saying, but does not. Blue smoke drifts from his pretty, girlish lips but he gives her a hard look. *Enough.* They sit in silence; the smell of smoke makes her feel sick. Ratman's smell. Pigeons scrabble on the opposite roof, cock their heads, eyes like fruit pips.

'I haven't seen her for two days,' she dares.

Dario shrugs, leans over the balcony, hawks and spits, watching it splatter on the ivy. And then he relaxes back again. Another silence. From an open window somewhere there's a sudden burst of laughter. A slim grey cat balances along a wall, stops to sit and lick one paw.

'Hey,' Dario says, 'this is secret, you say nothing?'

She nods.

'This place is shut down soon, all go. Not just Alis.'

'Why?'

'Don't know. I hear word "Council" or maybe is police.'

She stares at him as he tilts back his head to mouth a smoke-ring. 'Dario?'

'All girls to move is all I know.'

'And me?'

'You are girl, I think!' He smiles sideways, so pretty.

Inside a tiny leap of hope, but there is nowhere to land; how should she feel?

'Where?'

He shrugs.

'What about Alis?'

He's absorbed with blowing smoke rings, watching them rise and dissolve. She gulps the rest of her Coke, chucks the bottle down into the garden. The cat darts away, the ivy shifts, the bottle vanishes.

'Wish I could go out now. Properly out. In the street,' she says without any hope at all, but he finishes his cigar, flicks the butt over the balcony, turns to her, and grins so that she can see his bad teeth. 'Ratman's away,' he says. 'Business in London.'

'So?'

'Hey, how about we take walk, eh?'

The whole balcony lurches with the surprise of it. She hasn't been out in the streets since home. Not really *walked* except up-stairs and down.

☙

So strange to be out on the hot, busy street, bag heavy on her shoulder, knotted strap digging in. To be among ordinary people with the traffic roaring, the smell of exhaust, sun lancing off glass. Some people are still bundled in heavy coats, some stripped down to their winter white limbs. Like a creature just crawled from a crevice, she blinks, shrinks in the brightness.

People give them odd looks, eyes resting on Dario's bare feet and he stares boldly back. In a corner shop he chooses gum and sweets – strawberry shoelaces, white mice, pink shrimps. She wanders into the back of the shop. On a stand are plastic dolls and water pistols, toy cars, crayons and colouring books; and also pads of blue airmail paper, the sort you fold up to make an envelope. An idea shafts through her. She looks around but no one's taking any notice.

Dario's still queueing; the woman in front arguing with the Indian man behind the counter, waving a packet of biscuits in his face. The airmail paper slides into Marta's bag and she tenses, waiting for something to happen. But nothing does. The argument goes on. The man behind the counter shakes his head, arms folded. Dario jiggles from foot to foot, darts Marta an anxious look. He's losing his nerve, she can tell; they must go back, he's going to say that. Pens on the same display, different colours with a scribbled tester card. She picks one and scribbles. No one's taking any notice. It joins the paper in her bag.

'I'll wait outside.' She passes him to step out into the sun, rigid, expecting a hand on her shoulder or a shouting voice. But there's nothing, just sun in her eyes and the tooth-rattling vibration of a bus idling at the traffic lights. Quick, quick she must plan. Write letter, get it posted but how? Go back with Dario and write her letter – but how to post it? And if it's found?

For Ratman's girls nothing's private. Under the mattress, their pockets, their bags, everything is searched, even her crappy plastic satchel. She's heard that a girl took a watch, a present from a punter and hid it – but it was found and taken and soon after, she too disappeared.

Girls do that sometimes, disappear and you never know anything.

Like home.

Like Alis.

She watches a girl, no older than herself, slot her card into a cash machine and the fresh money sliding out. A beggar also watches, a guy with a thin face, a sturdy dog curled beside him, twitching. In his cap is a scattering of copper and silver.

'Spare a pound?' he says to the rich girl.

She shakes her head as she puts the money in her purse and walks away.

'Have a nice day,' he calls. He ruffles the dog's ears and it beats its stringy tail against the pavement.

The guy catches her looking. 'It's OK darling,' he says, 'I don't bite. Spare something for me dinner?'

His voice is a bit like Geordie's; she steps away, eyes skimming the street. Geordie could be back tonight. She edges away, sees the guy shrug, fondle his dog's ears, look up at the next passer-by with little hope. Marta peers into the dim interior of the shop. Dario's paying now.

She takes off, pelts along the main road to the traffic lights, across a big street full of shiny shops and onwards. Nothing in her mind, except to run. Such a long time since she's run, or even walked very far, it burns the muscles in her thighs and the soles of her feet; her lungs feel like they'll burst. Past men and women and bicycles and babies and dogs on leads she runs, not daring to look over her shoulder. She crosses a road and hurries on until, forced to stop for breath, she leans against a wall, sweat trickling down her neck. She's on a steep and wide grey street with clean and haughty buildings, fancy shops with leather coats, and paintings, swirly gold writing above the doors.

No sign of Dario. No sign of the police or anyone taking any notice of her at all.

So what now? She dithers, must not look suspicious, stops to gaze into a shop window, sees only her own reflection, hair wild, eyes wilder. *Think, think, think.* She will write her letter. Maybe beg money for a stamp? How much is a stamp? Is there a post office?

And then what? Where will she go? What can she do?

She walks downhill to the gardens opposite the busy shopping street and recognizes where she is; she ran this way. Above the park there's a castle built on a cliff, a statue of man with pigeon shit on his face.

Other people beg here. She could beg.

But what if Ratman sees her, or Geordie or Mr Smith? If she doesn't go back they will look and if they find her . . . she cannot bear to think. And if they don't, and even if they do, they'll go after Milya and break Mama's heart.

And if she goes to the police . . . then it will be the same.

Down the steps into the park, a deep valley in the middle of the city. On an empty bench she sits. In the flowerbeds are tiny daffodils and knotty little blue flowers, the earth around them rich and wet, gleaming like pudding in the sun. She wriggles her toes, waits for the throbbing in her feet to ease, before taking out the pen and paper. Leaning on her bag, she clicks the pen, open, shut, open, shut thinking of what to write. This pen will write in blue or green or red. How Milya would love such a pen as this.

She tries to picture Mama's face when she finds the letter in the mailbox, pictures the rows of tin mailboxes in the dim lobby, the musty smell, the sound of the creaking lift, the crackling of the faulty lights. Remembering such ordinary things takes her breath away. Never would she have dreamed she could long for that crappy place; to be there, just to be *there*.

Write.

Mama will cry out at the sight of her writing and crumple the letter to her chest. And then smooth it and . . . maybe read it to Milya in the kitchen. The thought of that kitchen – *no*. Or Milya will snatch it away and read it. Ant will come home, Mama will look to him, the man of the family now, the so-called man, for advice. Ant will have guessed what happened to her. Mama will know. She said not to go with Pavel, she said to wait.

Marta swallows hard.

But still, they'll be glad to know she is alive. They have to know that.

What can she write? What can she tell them? Only a short note, saying she's fine and do not worry, saying she'll be back soon – hoping this is not a lie. When she's home, she says, she'll explain. She tells them sorry, sorry, so sorry. She says keep safe; keep Milya safe.

Of course she cannot give them a return address.

How will she know if they even get it?

Once she's licked and sealed the flap she hides her face in her hands and lets the tears come.

Mats

HE SAW HER in the street and followed. Not a decision. He rarely left work at lunchtime but he had a headache, too much wine the night before - getting to be a habit. Anyway he was avoiding a corporate lunch. And more particularly, avoiding Frank. He'd taken to walking this way lately, a way that took him near Massage City. Not that he had any intention of going in, of course not. But somehow that was the way his feet would take him. There was a good sandwich shop just around the corner, and he enjoyed the leg stretch.

The heat took him by surprise. It was only March, a freakishly hot day. He loosened his tie, undid the top button of his shirt as he gazed at the list of sandwiches. Chicken salad or cheese and ham? A girl ran by, a little thing with long hair . . .

He stared after her. Something about her. He began to walk fast; she was disappearing. He began to run.

Was it *the* girl?

People stared. Maybe they thought he was chasing her. He felt absurd jogging along behind her, only fast enough to keep her in sight, trying to keep his expression pleasant and unthreatening as he ran. He wasn't even sure it was she. Maybe it was not? What did it matter? One piece of bad judgment weeks ago. A dirty secret. Do not repeat. Forget it. Move on. Stop running. But he could not. Sweat trickled under his shirt. His leather shoes were tight, no cushioning, he felt the jolting in his knees.

They ran all the way to Princes St. She only stopped when she got to the road, waiting for the crossing, and he almost caught up. She crossed the road and, panting, resting his hands on his thighs, he watched the way she went, no longer running, but she was getting lost among the crowds. He could not wait for the next green man but dashed across the road, a cyclist swerving, a bus blaring its horn.

It *was* the same girl, he was pretty sure now. His shirt was soaked. He took off his jacket, slung it over his shoulder as he threaded through the crush. She was small, her shoulders, her hips, her long hair bunched up messily, revealing a slim nape. She was wearing a knee-length skirt, a loose T-shirt, flat canvas shoes; not whorish at all, you'd take her for a student. Maybe she was a student?

She turned off and he followed her along, she was slower now, he had to walk slowly behind her, she was dragging her feet. She stopped outside a shop and he walked past her to the top of the hill where, looking north, you could see distant hills, and a frill of coastal villages across the blue neck of the Forth. Maybe, he thought, they might drive across the bridge at the weekend; Arthur would love it, maybe it would cheer Vivienne up, a change of scene—

Casually he looked back. Yes, it *was* the same girl; that was established. So what? Now he should let her walk right out of his life. Now he should go back, pick up a sandwich, return to work. She was staring into the shop window but as he watched she turned away, began to walk back the way she'd come, but slowly, wearily. Something hopeless in her gait, pulled a string in his heart. He began to follow her back down the hill – it was the way he had to go anyway. He paused to look in the shop window. There were some bad splashy paintings of hills and boats and below them a display of art materials – his eyes were drawn to a wooden box of pastels, graduating through every nuance of every colour. Beautiful. Although he wasn't artistic in any way they made his fingers itch. Maybe she was an artist, an art student? Of course, a poor student turning tricks to pay her way, not really a whore at all.

He followed, gaining on her. Her hands were in the pockets of her skirt, on one shoulder hung a heavy bag, pulling it down. For the sake of her spine she should wear a bag on her back, or at least across her body. Nina always did, and Nina knew.

He looked at his watch: 1:40. No time for a sandwich now, he must go right back. As he passed a café, the smell of pizza made him hungry. She reached Princes St and crossed the road. He had to wait and once he was across, she was lost to him. OK. Good. Leave it. Go. But there was a gap in the railings, steps down to the gardens, maybe . . . just a quick look. What did he hope to gain from this? It was crazy. But it was where his feet took him.

And there she was, sitting on a bench in the shade of a tree. He had no choice now but to walk past her. He could not look over his shoulder, could not stare, what a creep he would seem. Was he a creep? This might qualify as creepy behaviour. But no, it was just interest. It was just . . . he recognized the sensation, ridiculous in this case; it was *responsibility*. Having used her in that shameful way he felt responsible. And that was dangerous for him; responsibility was irresistible.

He tried to walk away, focus his mind on work; must make the meeting. He turned back decisively, hoping she'd be gone – that would have been a relief. But no, she was still there and the bench next to hers was empty like an invitation.

Accepting, he sat down.

Why wouldn't a man want to sit down on such a hot day, a man with a headache, yes it was still there, he pressed his fingers to his throbbing temples. The bench was half in the shade. Twiggy shade, no leaves yet. The wooden slats were sticky with spilt juice or a melted lolly. He moved across to the sun, let his head hang back, feeling and seeing through his closed eyelids a glare of gold. His sunglasses were in the office, on his desk beside the papers he needed for his meeting with, among others, the American delegate. Frank. Without Frank he would never have used a prostitute. Never dreamed of it. He gave a sudden snort, the irony occurring to him; in avoiding Frank, he'd seen the girl again.

The girl. He stayed in the same position, soothing for his head, but opened his eyes slightly and manoeuvred himself so he could watch her. She'd taken something out of her bag, a book? No paper, she was drawing, no writing. A writer then? A young writer, subsidizing her meagre earnings? Or maybe she was applying for a grant, or for Art School?

He watched her bend over her knees and write, pause, gaze into the distance, write a few more words, pause. A poem? A story? An essay? 1.55. Christine would be getting twitchy about the meeting. She would be *having kittens*, as she always put it. He should eat something. Get up, go, grab a sandwich and an Irn Bru on the way. Christine always had Nurofen in her bag; she'd give him a couple.

The girl licked the flap of an envelope, flimsy blue airmail; he glimpsed the dart of her pink tongue. And then she buried her face in her hands, shoulders convulsing.

Go.

Get up and go. Forget her.

He walked as far as her bench but could not pass. He sat beside her. At her feet was a scatter of broken bottle glass, glittering green. Her gym shoes were childish and worn out, her ankle bones frail and sharp.

'Excuse me,' he said. 'Are you all right? Can I help?'

She sat up, face shining wet, and scowled from under dark brows.

'You're upset,' he added.

Her skin was a pale olive, sickly in the sunshine and the lines between her brows were deep already, odd on her young face. Did she recognize him? She gave no sign of it. So strange to think that he had had her, in that way, and she didn't know. Or maybe she did? She inched her hips away from him on the bench, put the letter in her bag.

'Well,' he said. He had to stand, it was clear she wanted him to go. 'If I can help?'

'Money for stamp,' she muttered without looking up at him. The line of her jaw was very pure; her little ears nestled among dark, messy curls.

'Stamp? Sure.' He put his hand in his pocket, jingled his change. 'Where are you from?'

'Why?' Her face turned up to his, a small, fierce wedge.

'Just wondered.'

'Why do you wonder? What do you want?'

'Nothing.'

'Where are *you* from?'

'Oslo. Norway.'

Silence stretched between them. 'OK,' he said at last. 'I'll take your letter and get it franked at work.'

'Franked, what's this?'

'Posted.'

'Airmail. Quick way?'

'Yes.'

'Sure?'

'I'll put it right in the post.'

She stood up, hesitated, then with a quick movement, shoved the letter into his hand. She was so small, her head did not quite reach his shoulder, he'd forgotten how very petite she was, but curvy too, fabulous breasts, though he should not notice, should not think it. He had a flash, a migrainous glimpse of rosy light, white silk, then only the true silk of her bare skin.

She replaced her bag on her shoulder and walked away. He fell into step beside her, though it was the wrong direction. An emergency at home, he improvised, they all knew Vivienne, they all knew the situation; no one would disbelieve him.

She stopped. 'You walk this way?' she pointed. He nodded.

'OK,' she said, and turned and walked in the opposite direction. He watched the quick swapping of her feet, the bob of shadow behind her and he followed. She looked over her shoulder, saw him, stopped and turned, hands on her hips.

'What do you want?' Round her lips was a tight white line. Her lashes were still wet.

'Sorry. I just . . . you're upset.'

'So?' Frowning, she narrowed her eyes. Such a warm, almost flowery brown. 'OK. Thank you for posting the letter. Now I am going. OK?'

'What's your name?' he said.

'Why?'

'Just tell me and I'll go. Promise.'

She blew through her lips. 'Marta,' she said. 'OK?'

He watched her walk away and noticed someone else running towards her. It was the boy, the long haired boy, running bare footed! He grabbed her arm. Did she recoil? Did he imagine this? They were too far away to see. Not his business, not his business, oh his head.

Marta.

He looked at his watch. 2:30. He would not be back till nearly three; Christine would have had kittens already, with maybe another litter due. A laugh surprised him as he climbed the steps back to Princes St where buses roared and tourists toured. Crossing the road, he started back towards work, passed a bar where a couple sat drinking cold lager and walked into the dim interior where, as if he was someone else entirely, he ordered a Heineken and a steak sandwich. He sat in the flicker of a gambling machine, numbly sipping and chewing, aware of the ticking on his wrist, gleeful, aghast. In the Gents he stared in the mirror, half expecting to see a stranger's reflection.

Had the boy grabbed her? Was he coercing her?

Not your business, Mats.

Back in the office air con, it felt icy. As he stepped out of the lift, Christine came hurrying. She was a tall, quiet, clumsy woman with a mass of almost colourless frizzy hair. 'Are you all right? What happened? Fergus is having kittens.'

'So many kittens!' He put his hand to his brow, pretending to look for them.

'You know fair well what I mean,' she said stiffly.

He straightened his stupid rubbery face, which was trying to stretch into a grin. Had he actually lost it?

'Sorry Chrissie,' he said, 'problem with Vivienne, had to pop home.'

'If you'd only said . . . phoned . . .' She gazed at him, head to one side and he felt a qualm: did she know about the girl, about that night? Did Frank blurt something at lunch, though secretaries didn't get invited to work lunches, he was being paranoid. Christine was a nice, loyal, beautifully ordinary woman, very, very good at her job.

'Sorry Chrissie,' he said. 'I really appreciate . . .' He waved his hand vaguely. 'I'm sorry.' And he was sorry, very sorry for everything. Sorry and puzzled. He was a straightforward guy; he always knew what he was doing. Always did the right thing.

She softened, her neck flushing. 'Don't worry about it,' she said. 'Fergus ended up postponing till the morning. You look knackered. I'll bring you some tea.'

'Thanks Chrissie.'

He shut his office door and put his head in his hands, the headache still there, but faintly now, threads of steak caught in his teeth. He fished the letter from his pocket. The handwriting was neat. It was addressed to *Doamna Sala*, at a place he'd never heard of in Romania. Christine came in with the tea and shortbread.

'Thought you could do with a wee lift,' she said.

'Thank you. Perfect. Could you get Fergus for me. In five.'

She nodded. 'Take ten. Drink your tea.'

'Oh,' he added, 'found this on the street – could you drop it in the post?'

She took the letter. 'Nice of you.'

Once she'd gone and shut the door behind her, he sipped the strong and sobering tea.

Vivienne

click

NEXT DAY, WAS it? Anyway around then I woke to a tray with orange juice, coffee, toast with marmalade, sun in my eyes as the blind rolled up. Like something in an advert. My handsome husband, wet haired in a fresh white T-shirt and jeans. Ah yes, Saturday. It was the weekend and he was going to paper the hall and I would get a manicure and then we would be safe.

'Morning,' he said and as I sat up he bent over and kissed my head. And then he left me to it. I sipped the coffee feeling beautifully blank. Artie crept into bed beside me with his Action Man.

'How would you like to live in Norway, Arthur?' Mats asked, suddenly back in the room with Tommy in his arms, red cheeked in a banana-coloured sleepsuit, curly hair wild, reaching towards something. Surely not me!

'What's in Norway?' Artie asked, making Action Man do the splits on the hills of his knees.

'Grandma and Grandpa Brunborg of course,' Mats said. 'Skiing, the mountains. You know this.'

'Do you want to, Mum?' Arthur looked up at me, green eyes – he hadn't got his specs on yet – sleep in the corners, a scaly patch of skin beside his nose. He needed E45 on that. Nanny was remiss!

'Mum's thinking about it,' Mats said. He sat down, sinking us all to an angle. 'Careful of the coffee.' Mats reached over and removed the tray before Tommy could reach for it; he'd just worked out what his hands were for. He sat propped against my knees, staring at my face, doing his hundred-watt smile.

'Hello,' I said. I could see I needed to show willing, especially if I wanted the nanny to go. I was better, loads better – but it was still like they were separate from me, like maybe they were real and I was someone on TV. Or the other way round. It turned out the nanny wanted to leave anyway for some reason. Maybe we weren't posh enough? But if I didn't want another nanny, which I did not, I had to pull myself together. The toad was gone. I only needed someone to help a bit around the house. In the mornings I could think like this, think positive.

click

OK. This is hard. Really hard. I don't have to do it. I don't have to say it. I don't have to listen to it ever. I could pull all the tape off the spools, I could burn it, I could throw it in the river. I'll have to open another bottle. Don't know why they call it Dutch courage. What's Dutch about it? Anyway, this is Australian.

The hall is white now.

The toad has gone.

click

So there I was in bed that morning that was nearly like an advert.

But then it went back into real life. Artie moved his Action Man across to show me something and Tommy tried to grab it.

'Get off!' Artie shouted.

I tried to help and somehow Tommy got knocked off the bed. I think Mats thinks it was me; my fault anyway. How could it have been? I don't know. I don't remember. All I remember is yellow legs disappearing over the edge of the bed and a clunk as he landed on the floorboards on his head. We waited for the scream but there was no scream, only silence. Mats' face went grey, his eyes black as he looked at me. He reached down and picked Tommy up.

He was silent and floppy.

'Is he deaded?' said Artie.

I slid down flat in the bed, the sheets felt wet. I felt cold and hard as a fish in ice. Time did a big dangerous warp and then Tommy let out a cry. Not his usual yell, more of a mew, but thank God thank God thank God thank God.

We took him to A&E where he was X-rayed and kept in overnight for observation. It was nothing but concussion, no lasting damage they said. But it marked a turn. As if the dynamics had been shifted. Mats never blamed me, not out loud at least. He never said it. If he'd said, 'I blame you,' I could have defended myself, but he never said it. He was different from then on though, he never looked at me with love again.

And Tommy, the concussion seemed to make him crankier. Not such an easy baby any more. And I don't know but . . . I can see that this does sound mad. He was checked over at the hospital and they said no damage. But I am his mother and I think that he *was* damaged. And that is when he started to need me. He looked so vulnerable in the hospital cot, now that he was broken. My love for him came suddenly awake. He had seemed huge now he shrank to normal baby size. He's not an easy baby any more. He's hard to manage and Mats . . .

I miss how he was.

He's here and he does all the right things. He did the hall for me.

All white and fresh.

click

Marta

A S SHE RATTLES through the curtain she sees him rise from the sofa. It's the man who took her letter to post, the Norwegian, standing awkwardly, briefcase in his hand. He smiles but she does not.

'Come then.' She leads him up the stairs. When they're in the room, she shuts the door, turns to face him. 'How did you know I'm here?'

He looks down. Must be a punter then. No memory of him. At least he was no trouble. You only remember trouble.

He fidgets on his feet, reluctant to meet her eyes.

'Did you post my letter?'

He nods, clears his throat, fiddles with the end of his tie.

'Really?'

'Of course.'

She imagines the relief. 'She's all right!' Mama will cry and she and Milya will hug, and there might be tears. But once they're over the relief – what will they think then? Maybe they'll hate her stupid guts.

She crosses her arms waiting for him to speak. But he just stands like a big donkey, shifting from foot to foot. 'What do you want?' Her stomach gurgles, the taste of coffee in her gullet.

'To talk,' he says, trying her with the smile again. 'Only to talk.'

She sighs. 'Dirty talk?' Sometimes that's what they want, to say the things they'd like to do to her, without doing them. Fuck, cunt, tits, cum, arse - only sounds. She could get an Oscar for pretending to get turned on. Men are so easy to fool, eager to believe they're such big studs.

But he shakes his head. 'Can I sit here?' He indicates the bed. There's nowhere else except the rickety chair for putting clothes on. She shrugs and he sits down. He's a big man but not fat, clean. At home you do not often see men as tall as this, as strongly built, not with such strong white teeth. What does she know of Norway? - fjords, snow, the aurora borealis and probably fish, lots of fish.

He puts his briefcase on the floor. His jacket's undone, blue shirt open at the neck, tie pulled down low. The tie is dark red with pattern of brighter red Vs that make her think of flying birds.

'OK,' she says after a while. 'Talk.' He does not seem to expect her to join him on the bed so she lowers herself carefully onto the chair. One of the legs is loose and she has to brace her feet against the floor to help it to stay up. But still he says nothing. Is he some kind of nut?

They sit wordless for a few moments more. It's weird but no weirder than many things. Harmless. A rest. The speaker crackles and the music stops. You only notice it when it stops. There's the sound of footsteps hammering down the stairs, Cristal in her boots maybe, and the stupid yell of someone coming. She sees him flinch at that and squashes down a smile as she shifts to release her cramping muscles.

'You know you must still pay,' she says. Music starts again, the cabaret type stuff that melts your brains, women's voices frilly like lingerie.

'Marta,' he says. The name is wrong in his mouth. Not his to use.

'What?'

'Would you, if you could, stop doing this?' He waves his hand.

She gives up on the chair, stands and leans against the wall. He has to pay. Or she'll be in trouble. Other tricks have asked her this, asked her to stop, asked her to come away with them, marry them even, but it's fantasy. It's bullshit.

'I want to help you.'

She forms her lips into a smile.

'Seriously,' he says. He bites the inside of his cheek as he gazes at her, tugging at the lobe of his ear, trying to meet her eyes, but she doesn't let any trick look into her like that.

'You don't know my life,' she says.

'How do you come to be here?'

She does not answer.

'The other day, that boy, did he force you to come back here?'

She gives a mild shrug.

'I feel so bad,' he says.

'Not my problem.'

'Bad that I . . . that I used you like that.'

'You paid,' she says, shrugging. Why do they think they are so important? 'It's fine.'

He meshes his fingers together now, bends them back till they clicked. 'I'm still paying,' he adds, banging his fist against his chest.

It's hard not to laugh. 'I don't remember,' she says.

He nods. Another minute or two tick by. She thinks about toast and jam. Getting the shoes off.

'It's against everything I believe in, men and women, sex it should be free and beautiful.'

Now it's a real fight not to laugh. Idiot man! Donkey! Like someone on TV with a bad script.

He catches her expression and shuts up.

The music swells, sickly harmonies, violins. Her stomach growls.

'Maybe I could help you find another job?' he says.

Now she does laugh. 'Oh so nice,' she says, 'what shall I be? A teacher maybe? A doctor?'

He looks so deflated, so sad, the big crazy guy, that she almost feels sorry. He turns his wrist to glance at his watch. 'I have to go,' he says. 'Can we meet? Somewhere else.' He takes out his wallet; she thinks it will be money, must not take it, must not – but he only hands her a little card with his name and phone number.

'You think I come and go as I like?'

'I don't know.' He shakes his head heavily. 'I don't know anything about it. What to do.'

'If you want to see me you must come here and pay.' Her hand closes round the card, sharp corners digging into her palm.

'Is there a number I can reach you on?'

He's ridiculous, a big, innocent fool. But there's an odd and awful feeling, as if wires are tugging right through her, twisting deep in her belly.

'You're very pretty,' he says, a compliment so stale she hardens against him again and that's a relief. 'I'll come here then,' he goes on. 'Oh, and I have a present for you.'

'I can take nothing.'

'Of course you can.'

He pulls a carrier bag from his briefcase, puts it into her hands before he goes. How Alis would laugh at him, such a baby in his big, clean, handsome body, a rich man with the luxury of a conscience.

She listens to his feet on the stairs before opening the bag, thick slippery polythene, black with gold lettering. Inside there's a wooden box with a metal clasp. What? When she lifts the lid she sees crayons, chalky, in every colour. It looks like hundreds. Hundreds of crayons. Crayons? *Crayons?*

Anger rises in her, sour curds of anger. What does this mean? Why? Crazy prick.

She slams shut the lid. Oh but how Milya would love them. She remembers her little sister's drawings, the ponies, the dancers. If only she could send it. What a useless present! Opening it again, she sniffs the crayons, good things, not for children; for an artist. *Oil pastels*, says the label inside. She snaps shut the box, fastens the clasps, examines the card. Pale blue with his name and firm, his contact number in tiny embossed letters. She can't keep the crayons of course, but she can keep this. Just in case. It will slide inside the lining of her bag.

Marta

How many today? Lost count. Anyway, what's the point of counting? Sore and weary, wrapped in the brown cardigan. Alone in the kitchen, waiting for the kettle, she flicks through a magazine, stares at the hair and heels, at Madonna and Princess Diana. At home this magazine would be a treasure; here it's trash.

Dario comes into the kitchen, hops on the table, swings his legs, chewing juicily. He smells of bubble gum.

'Coffee?' she says.

Since the day they went out together they've been friends. Of course he was pissed off that she'd run away – but she came back with no fuss and he doesn't care enough to stay angry. He'd followed her and watched her talking to Crazy Man. Walking back he'd held her arm so tight he left a ring of finger bruises. Maybe it was a relief that he found her. What else anyway could she have done?

When Crazy brought the pastels, he took them for her. 'Don't tell Ratman,' she said. When he flipped open the box another little blue card dropped out – Crazy making sure she didn't forget him. Dario picked it up and slid it in his back pocket. 'Rosa's got boyfriend,' he teased.

But now he says. 'Bad news. Is Geordie.'

Marta swallows. 'Please *no*.'

Dario raises his hands and lets them fall. 'What can I do?' He goes off down the stairs again. She pushes away her coffee, stands, tugging at the hem of her slip, goose pimples bristling her thighs. She puts a finger in her mouth and bites hard on the nail. Pain is nothing. Only a feeling and it goes.

Physical pain. Not pain in the heart. That is harder to bear.

Alis, Alis.

Geordie looks like a good man. When they first met, she thought that. Round face, thick grey eyebrows, soft grey beard, eyes like a dog's, soft and kind and brown. You might think him a doctor or teacher. You can't tell by looking at a person. You can't trust your eyes to know. His kind face is a lie.

He opens his trousers and stands behind her, but he does not put himself into her, he puts a bottle. And he pushes into the wrong place and she can't help but cry out but he likes this, he likes to know she's in pain, so she tries to make no sound. While he's hurting her she plays a child-song in her mind.

A mouse lives in the clock
and a flea lives on the mouse
and they both live together
in a gingerbread house.
When the boy eats the house,
the flea bites his nose
and the little grey mouse bites
his 1, 2, 3, 4, 5, 6, 7, 8, 9, 10 toes.

In the playground they used to chant and clap it. She bites her two thumbs as he does her and makes the words come quicker through her mind, like you did with the rhyme and the clapping, quicker and quicker until one of you went wrong and sometimes in bending down to touch the toes, crashed your heads together. He puts his hands under her chest and hurts her breasts, squeezing so that *the boy eats the house the flea.*

At last finishes, zips his old-man's trousers, calls her a good wee lassie. He has expensive shoes, kind looking hands, a broad wedding ring. He looks like somebody's grandpa. Probably he is.

He leaves her bleeding. When she washes it hurts so much she almost cries out. Sitting on the toilet dabbing at herself with paper she folds forward on her thighs staring at her *1, 2, 3, 4, 5, 6, 7, 8, 9, 10 toes.* How can she work anymore today? She wads her pants with toilet paper. Her slip is soiled; she must wash it. She prefers the slip to the tacky underwear that is the alternative. At least the slip covers her, if only thinly. Innocent, Ratman calls it, because it's white, some of the punters go for that look, the innocent look. Fresh like a flower. Ha. She puts on grey tracksuit bottoms and sweatshirt. In the bathroom she fills a bucket, shakes in Persil, leaves the slip to soak.

In the kitchen, two new girls are talking fast, smoking, speaking a language she doesn't know. They ignore Marta. Lily sits alone, a tiny frightened doll wearing the cardigan round her shoulders, over the lacy black slip that reveals her copper nipples, shrivelled with cold. Though hot downstairs it's always cold in this kitchen; the window's painted open and a damp wind blows right in.

'Coffee?' Marta says.

Lily regards her blankly. One of other girls, enormous teeth, too much blusher, pulls a face at her friend and they snigger. Ignoring them, Marta points to a mug. Lily nods. Alis reckoned Lily was about thirteen, but maybe Cambodian girls only look young?

A trickle of blood reminds her of when she used to have periods, no more of that now. The implants mean no time wasted with menstruation. Her coffee's still there from before, and not even cold, though it seems hours since she left it. She tips it out and makes fresh coffee for herself and Lily. Her favourite mug, yellow with a smiley face, fits nicely between the hands. Comforting. She shovels sugar into both cups and sits gingerly down.

Lily frowns at her coffee, says something. Marta reaches for the huge plastic tub of Marvel, in case she wants that. When the girl doesn't move she spoons some in and stirs, watching the greasy powder blob the surface. Lily's like a child, used to being looked after by her mother. Mother, daughter, little sister. Clench your mind against these words.

Dario comes up, a punter waiting, they must come down to be selected from. Taking in how she's dressed, he frowns.

'I'm hurt,' she says.

He says nothing, only gestures for Lily and the others to follow him. With no change of expression, Lily gets up, drops the cardigan, puts her feet in the high black shoes that are too big for her tiny feet and follows him down. When the clomp of heels on stairs has died away, Marta picks up the cardigan, still warm, and pulls it round her own shoulders. The coffee cup is hot against her palms, underneath her the wad of paper is lumpy and wet.

Dario's feet patter back up the stairs.

'Geordie hurt me,' she says.

'Ratman's back,' he warns. 'Get ready.'

She stares at him. 'But I'm hurt.'

'Quick,' he says.

Though fear prickles through her, she can't move.

'Think about Alis,' he says. 'You not want same.'

'What do you mean?' She tries to grab his hand.

'Quick,' he says and darts out.

You not want same.

Alis has been moved on, that's all, maybe she's safe; maybe even she's free. Girls get moved about. There are always new girls, not only from Romania, but from other Eastern European countries, from Africa and Asia. You hardly get a chance to get used to people. Alis is a new girl somewhere else. That's all. And maybe when this place is closed, as Dario said, she'll find Alis again in a new place. Maybe a better place.

Ratman steps into the kitchen, bringing the smell of rain. He's wearing a pale raincoat and a trilby and furling an umbrella. 'Having some time off, Rosa?' he says, smiling. 'A nice wee breather?'

It's hard for her to speak. 'He hurt me,' she manages. 'Geordie did. I can't work.'

'Geordie?' He presses his lips together and frowns, as if he doesn't believe her. 'Wait.' His heels hammer down the stairs; gone to ask Dario if it is true, maybe, and maybe Dario will be in trouble too. The coffee is cooling; she takes a sip, closes her eyes. Ratman's footsteps up the stairs.

He hooks his finger. 'Come with me.'

She follows him up a flight of stairs, unlocks a door into a flat and takes her into his small hot office where a gas fire flickers blue and orange. A black leather sofa, a glass topped coffee table, a stink of cigars. Against the dark window glass, rain streams, threaded with orange glitters from a street lamp below. On the sill is a row of cacti, gleaming with health.

'Sit.' He indicates the sofa. She perches on the edge while he removes his raincoat, shakes it meticulously and hangs it on the stand. He strokes his trilby, sets it on his desk.

'Dreich out there,' he remarks. He's smart in a blue suit, a paler blue shirt, a mid-blue tie. He pours whisky, sits behind his desk and lights a thin cigar. 'Disappointing dinner,' he says, 'disappointing day all round.' He puffs out smoke, tilts back his head so that she can see the smooth whiteness of his throat and the way the red whiskers thicken into the point of his beard. And then he sits suddenly upright, fixes his eyes on her. She looks down at her knees, holds them stiff to stop the trembling.

'So he's been back?' he says.

She looks up. 'He hurt me.'

He taps his cigar on an ashtray thoughtfully. 'He shouldnae have come back.'

She finds a shred of courage. 'So how can I work?'

He smiles and there's just a tiny hope in her, just a tiny glint of hope that he might be kind, but above the smile his eyes are frozen. 'Mebbe I should be the judge of that. Stand up. Show me.'

'No. It's OK. I will work.'

'Show me.'

'It's OK.' She gets up and edges towards the door.

'Stop right there,' he says.

She stops with her back to him. Feels him approach.

'Show me.' His breath is hot on her neck. 'Where did he hurt you?' he speaks close to her ear. 'Show me what he did.' She shuts her eyes as he pulls down the tracksuit trousers, pulls down the pants with the paper stuffing. She hears his breath, a blowing out of smoke.

'OK. Enough,' he says.

As she pulls up her pants, the wad of filthy tissue rolls to the floor. She snatches it up. He draws on his cigar, spits smoke. 'Go and flush it.'

He takes her out into the hall, nods towards a door. Inside she pulls the string to click on the light, drops the paper in the toilet and flushes. There's a bar of soap with a little red label. She washes her hands, snatching her eyes away from her scribbled reflection in the mirror.

Back in the office, he's sitting on the sofa now, legs stretched out. Feet small, shoes shiny but splashed with city dirt.

'Where's Alis?' she asks quickly, before she can lose her nerve.

'Who?' He frowns. 'Oh, Lola. You mean Lola. Sit down.' He pats the sofa by his side. She obeys, gathering herself in tight, so that she will not touch him.

'I've got a wee bone to pick with you,' he says. 'I hear you've got yourself a boyfriend.'

She tightens further, heart squashed against her ribs and struggling.

'A wee birdie told me. So? What's the story?'

'No story,' she says. 'It's not true.'

'The Swede?'

'Oh,' she says, carefully, trying to smile. 'You mean crazy Norwegian?'

'Giving you presents. Lovely present, eh? Was it your birthday, eh? Are you a wee artist now?'

His thighs are flattened against the leather, smooth trousers, too close to her thigh. She shrinks herself further from him. 'I did not ask for a present.'

'I think there's a bitty more to it than that,' he says. 'You can tell me.' He puffs on the cigar, making the end glow red. 'I think you know his name.'

She's silent.

'Poor Lola,' he says. 'So bonny, but so stroppy. We don't want you getting hurt now, do we? We don't want you going the same way?'

Against her breastbone her heart peck, pecks, pecks so sharply she thinks it might split.

He gets up and stands looking down at her. She cannot raise her eyes higher than the knees of his trousers, which have a faint crease down the front – has someone ironed them for him? Does he have a wife? There are splashes of wet on the hems, a white hair, like a dog's hair clinging to the shin. Does he have a *dog*? Somehow this thought emboldens her and she looks up.

'Is she dead?' she says.

His beard's a sharp tawny wedge; his eyes are dirty ice.

'Is she?'

He inclines his head in a way that might or might not mean assent. She squeezes shut her eyes till all she can see is sparkling. She hears the creak of the floorboards, the clink of a glass, liquid pouring. When she opens her eyes he's sitting behind his desk swishing a tumbler of whisky.

'So,' he says. 'Tell me about this guy.'

She says nothing.

'Name?' He picks up a pen and taps it on the edge of his desk.

She has no energy for refusal or invention.

'Brunborg,' she says picturing him suddenly, his handsome, sad, romantic face.

'Good lass.' He sounds surprised. He sips his whisky, swills it round his mouth before he swallows. 'We know that. We know all about him. Where he works, where he lives.'

She stares. How? And then she remembers the little blue card that fell from the pastel box, the way Dario slid it in his pocket.

'But why?' she manages. 'He's only a crazy punter.'

'He doesnae want to take you away from all of this?'

She shakes her head.

'That's not what I heard.'

'I'm never going to see him again. I don't want to see him. I never asked to see him.'

'A wee warning is all.'

Marta looks down at her own legs, her fingernails sharp in her palms.

'But listen.' Ratman lights a cigar, rolls it between his fingers. 'Geordie shouldnaie have done that to you.'

She's so startled she almost chokes.

'You won't be seeing him again.' He reaches for the whisky bottle and she sees that his nostrils are pinched.

A little puff of hope, like a breath. 'Really?'

'Go now,' he says.

Vivienne

click

I feel—

click

OK. The nanny left and I got by. Not easy, Tommy grizzly and Artie playing up because I had less time for him, I guess. Never noticed what a sulker he was before. But no one's perfect. But I was managing. I was.

Then one day this weird thing. I was upstairs kneeling on the floor doing Tommy's nappy and right in the middle the doorbell rang. At least it distracted him from his screaming. I stuck him together, hoisted him over my shoulder and took him, Babygro poppers all undone, to the door.

A skinny young guy stood on the step, a black cab was waiting at the kerb.

'Does Mats Brunborg live here?' he asked, his accent foreign. Some sort of Eastern European.

'Why?' I said, 'Who wants to know?'

'No reason.' His face was pretty as a girl's but there was something sleek about him that made me shiver.

Anyway, it was cold with the door open and Tommy's legs were all bare.

'I'm busy,' I said, 'sorry.' I started to shut the door but he put his shoulder in and stared at me, right into my eyes. He might have had mascara on. His teeth were bad and his breath smelled like crappy sweets.

'Excuse me!' I said. 'Shall I call the police?'

'Sorry,' he said, 'is just to ask if you hear of girl called Rosa? Maybe your husband knows this girl?'

'No,' I said,' and anyway my husband is not who you said.' I don't know why I said that; it was an instinct. 'Go or I will call the police.'

I shut the door and leaned there for a minute. *What?* Then I looked out of the little window beside the door and saw the black shape that was the cab drive away.

When the child minder came I went out. I was on a sort of mission. It sounds pathetic but I might as well say. This is going in the bin anyway. I could unspool the tape and . . . I don't know . . . hang myself with it! No only joking. Knit a table mat! Knit Mats a tie!

Anyway, I was on a mission to win him back.

Maybe because my medication had kicked in

Maybe because I'd stopped drinking, just about.

Maybe because I was frightened he would leave me.

I had the works, eyebrows waxed, hair bobbed a la Louise Brooks, roots, lowlights. I had false nails stuck on, red as Babybel. I bought a new top, silky orange flowers, low cut and a diet book.

Also I bought a posh lasagne and the second most expensive Chianti from M&S. I put on lipstick and mascara, rang work to check that he *was* coming home for dinner. Asked Christine to please make sure he wasn't late. Stuck a rose on the table in a tiny vase. My finger bled when I picked it, which I liked, the red of it not so bright as my nails but pretty against the creamy petals. A little smear there, like a secret.

Rita came round after work to help me get the kids in their night things, both clean and sweet at the same time. And when he did come in I was ready with a kiss.

He was amazed, you could see. Maybe a bit shocked. He smelled of sweat and tension. His jaw was dark, a little rough. Once I used to lick that roughness.

He showered and we got the children settled, and sat down at the table like proper people. I'd put a candle there, a tall pink one, it made me think of a spindly penis and I couldn't light it, it would have seemed barbaric. I felt weirdly awkward, like this was a date rather than dinner with my husband. I opened the wine. I would only have one tiny glass.

'Don't,' I said when he went to light the candle.

He gave me a look and lit the wick.

'So,' he said, when at last we were ready with our wine, our food, the rose, the poor pink candle squirming, 'what's all this in aid of?'

I shrugged. 'Just us,' I said. 'I mean you. I mean . . . I want to start again. I want to say thank you . . .' I tailed off. I couldn't read his face.

'Well,' he said, after a bit. He seemed to be struggling with his expression, but then he looked up, reassuring me with a smile. 'That's good. I'm glad you're feeling better.'

'And,' I said; this was my big moment, 'I've been thinking it over. You're right. Let's move to Norway. A fresh start.' I thought of glaciers and fjords and cleanliness, grandparents, Norwegian jazz.

'Too late,' he said.

'Surely there'll be another chance?' I fought gravity to keep my face from smearing down.

'Perhaps,' he said.

I asked him about his day, he asked about mine. It was like we were strangers, until the wine loosened us up a bit, and then I remembered the boy who came to the door.

'What boy?' Now I had his attention.

'He said something about a girl.'

'What girl?'

'I don't know. Rosie or something. Why? He just wanted to know if you know her.'

'What did you say?'

'I said who wants to know and he said me and I said no.'

'You said no.' He looked relieved, maybe impressed.

'So,' I said, 'what's it about?'

The candle was scorching a petal and I shifted it, the jiggle sending hot wax running onto the table.

'No idea,' he said. And he would say no more about it. It was nothing. It had to be nothing. Of course I did go through his pockets like any wife, but there was nothing. And this was Mats, my Mats, the straightest man on earth. We finished our meal and talked about oh I don't know.

The subject of the boy forgotten.

For then.

click

Mats

H E SCANNED THE road before pressing the bell. The barefooted boy opened the door, and Mats stepped in. Behind the reception desk sat a woman in a white coat, filing pointed burgundy talons. She flicked her eyes at him, bored, and returned to her manicure. A *bona fide* masseur? Surely not with such nails?

The boy led him through into the lounge. It was almost familiar now, the oily sweetness of the shuttered air, the velvet music, the weak pink lamps – though outside the light was still hard, bright and clean. Six o'clock, the days were lengthening coldly. Billy Holiday was playing: *Come Rain or Shine*. Silent gymnasts performed backflips on the television. He noticed white knitting on steel needles, looked like leggings for a baby, a handbag, a lip-sticked cup.

'Was it you?' he said.

The boy looked at him eyes blank, jaws going at his bubble gum like a sheep's.

'Do not come to my house again. Understand?'

An insolent shrug.

'I'd like to speak to . . .' Mats hesitated. Was *manager* the right term? 'Whoever's in charge. Whoever sent you.'

'You are friend of Rosa. Yes?'

'I don't know a Rosa. I know Marta.'

'Is same.'

'How did you know my address?' Mats said.

'Wait. I will see if boss is free.' The boy threaded through the bead curtain so smoothly it barely rattled, pattered up the stairs. Uneasily Mats lurked, noticing a Gameboy on the table – Arthur wanted one of those. When all this was over, he should have one. He should have anything he wanted.

A middle-aged woman entered rubbing cream into her hands. She nodded and settled herself down, picked up the knitting. 'You being seen to darling?'

Mats nodded.

'Please to wait,' said the boy, returning. 'Rosa is busy. You want a different girl while you wait?' He cocked a silky eyebrow. 'Plenty other girls, you want to look?'

'Aye. Plenty of lovely ladies,' added the woman.

Mats shook his head. He should just get the hell out, but no, not having gone through all it took to come here, collar turned up like a criminal.

The boy stretched the grey gum, poked his tongue through the skin of it, blew a bubble and took it back inside his mouth, as gently as if it were an egg. Mats tore his eyes away. Smirking, the boy resumed chewing, turned his attention back to his Gameboy. The woman examined her knitting, tutted and began unravelling it.

Mats sat on one of the low pink velvet sofas. *You're going to love me, like nobody's loves me.* Did they have a sense of irony here? There were magazines on the table, his nervous impulse was to reach for one. Spread legs, bum up, cheeks pulled apart to show a pursed little bum hole – he replaced it quickly, glancing at the woman, picked nervously at the scab of a cigarette burn on the velvet.

The doorbell drilled, making Mats almost shed his skin. The woman heaved herself up, patted her hair, went to bring the newcomer through. Five girls rattled through the curtain and stood in their underwear; one was tiny, Asian, looked like a child in a pink mesh nightie, dark nipples glinting through. One had wide pale thighs, silky green knickers, tight and humid against her crack. He looked at his lap, mortified, horrified by the beginnings of an erection *I guess when you met me it was just one of those things.* He could, he actually could, have one of them if he wanted. But not the child. Surely she couldn't really be a child?

The woman chatted away to the man about the weather, the football.

Mats kept his eyes on his knees, sweat beading on his upper lips. The man chose; Mats didn't care to see which one.

The boy spat his gum into the bin, swigged his Coke. From a paper bag he took a strand of red liquorice and began to nibble it slowly into his mouth, propping his bare feet up on the desk displaying black, leathery soles.

A guy rattled out through the beads and paid the woman. Mats stared at his corduroy legs, scuffed brown shoes, tweed jacket. Teacher maybe? Had he been with Marta? Mats stomach roiled at the thought. He cracked his knuckles, stared up at the gymnasts on the TV screen.

Another guy came through the curtain and approached him. 'Mr Brunborg? Mr Chapman.' He was smart, slight with a tidy ginger beard. Mats stood and the man extended his hand. Mats gave it a reluctant shake.

'This way.' Mr Chapman rattled back through the curtain. Mats was seized by a sudden impulse to barge his way out of there and forget it; he looked at the door. It was as if the boy was reading his mind.

'Best to do what Mr Chapman say.'

'I would, darling,' said the woman comfortably, turning her knitting to begin another row.

Mats forced a breath into his lungs. *Man up*, Vivienne said to him sometimes. Man up, he told himself now. He had come to get this mess sorted out and he would do it. Put an end to it.

He pushed through the curtain of beads. Mr Chapman was waiting on the stairs, and once satisfied that Mats was following, continued upwards, past two floors of closed doors behind which the women worked. Was Marta in there now, on top of, underneath a man? He shuddered as he followed Chapman up another staircase; here the warmth and scent of the place were replaced by chill bleakness and the smell of damp, bare bulbs dangling over stained plaster and the frayed remnants of a stair carpet. Mr Chapman unlocked a door and ushered him into an apartment, and through into an office. In here it was hot and reeked of cigar smoke, a smell that reminded Mats of his father, the *last* person he needed on his mind right now.

'Sit, please.' Chapman indicated a black leather sofa. Mats obeyed and regretted it as the springs groaned him into a low, subservient position.

'Drink?'

Mats nodded and the man splashed Bells into two glasses, handed him one and retreated behind his desk. He took out a cigar box. 'You don't? He waved it and Mats agreed. No he didn't. He sipped the drink. Mr Chapman lit himself a cigar and savoured the smoke thoughtfully before he raised his glass. 'Slainte.'

'Slainte,' Mats muttered and took a sip.

Silence followed. Mats knees were higher than his hips. Crossing them had only made it worse. He felt ridiculous.

'So, you wish to see me?' Mr Chapman said. 'You have a complaint?'

'You sent your boy to my house?'

'You are a regular, I understand?' Chapman said.

Mats snorted. 'Hardly!'

As Mr Chapman considered this he popped his lips, fish-like, emitting puffs of smoke. Under his jacket he wore a white roll-neck sweater, above which his beard was sharp and fiercely red. Though Mats was sweating this man looked cool. The gas fire was turned up high. To remove his jacket he'd have to stand, awkward from such a low position. But he wouldn't be here long. Stick it out. Man up. Take the initiative.

'So, you sent the boy to my house? Upsetting my wife. Is this your usual practice?'

Mr Chapman shook his head slightly. He appeared amused.

Mats loosened his tie, tried surreptitiously to undo a button. 'Look,' he said. 'OK. I've been here once or twice. But why—'

Mr Chapman interrupted. 'See, a wee birdie told me that you're interested in . . . how shall we put it . . . poaching one of my lassies.'

Mats frowned.

'You had a "date" with her.'

'No,' Mats said. 'No. I mean yes, I did see her once – it was a coincidence.'

'A coincidence?' Mr Chapman smoked and smirked.

The fire was heating the fabric of Mat's trouser leg; he tried to angle his knees away from the glowing orange bars.

'Aye, all right. A coincidence mebbe. But then you bring her presents, turn her head . . . what's a man to think?' Mr Chapman grasped his beard in one hand and smoothed and smoothed. 'Pastels. Do you think she's a wee artist? I dinnae ken that about her. Makes me think you must ken her pretty well.' He snickered. 'What's a slapper like that gonnae to do with a box of pastels!'

Sweat was trickling down Mats' neck. He wondered if his trouser leg was scorching. Might actually burst into flames. On the windowsill pots and pots of prickly cacti. Through the glass there was the shape of gables and chimneys against the orange-dark of the sky.

'So, what did your missus make of it?' said Mr Chapman.

'Leave her out of it.' Mats put both his hands to his face, pushing the sweat back into his hair. His heart was like something bouncing on elastic.

'Maybe you plan to dump her, take up with Rosa? Bonny wee bint, I'll gi' you that. Beg pardon if that's offensive,' said Chapman, with a narrow smile. 'Another?' he waved the bottle. Mats shook his head. Chapman poured himself a drink, took a sip and smacked his lips. 'Now.' He leant forwards. 'Down to business. You want her, you can have her.'

Surprise opened Mats' mouth.

'Take her away from all of this,' Chapman said. 'Ride off into the sunset. That the kindae thing you have in mind?'

Mats longed to get up, push up the window, shove his face out into the cold, or to punch Mr Chapman's smug bastard face, hammer down the stairs, grab Marta and run. Like a scene from a movie this played out before his eyes. Jump in the taxi that would be conveniently waiting and then . . . then what?

'It's very touching,' Mr Chapman said. 'Lucky wee lassie, eh?'

Mats breathed in. Keep calm, keep calm.

'I'll be sad tae see her go,' Mr Chapman said. 'But if it's true love, who am I to stand in the way?' He paused, smoothed his beard. 'Shall we say a hundred grand?'

Mats stared at him dumbly.

'How much did *you* have in mind?' Mr Chapman said. 'Come on now, I'm willing to bargain.' Silence. He grasped his beard in one hand in a kind of disbelieving glee. 'Dinnae tell me you thought I'd give her away for free!'

'I didn't think anything. I don't have that kind of money.'

Quiet, but for the distant sound of a door slamming, the shrilling of a phone.

Mr Chapman exhaled a plume of purplish smoke. 'What kindae money do you have? See, I'm prepared to bargain. I'll let you into a secret, I'll be glad to see the back of her. One way or another. If you dinnae want her then, well, I cannae say what might happen to her. Just between you and me.'

Mats stared, groping for his line. He thought of Marta's slim neck under the dark cloud of hair, her wet eyelashes as she looked up at him. If he said no now, if he walked away, what would happen to her? Was he to have that on his conscience now? He didn't want her, not in that way, not in any way. But if there was a chance for her to be safe and free and for himself and his family to be safe and free . . .

'I could maybe find twenty grand,' he found himself saying, his tongue in charge, reality spinning free.

Chuckling, Mr Chapman shook his head. 'Seventy,' he said. He opened a drawer in his desk, brought something out. Mats swallowed a lump of panic, half expecting a gun, but it was a pastel. There was quiet for a moment but for the swish of pigment on paper. After a moment Mr Chapman raised his head, sat back, arms folded and regarded Mats. Then he reached his hand out for the phone. 'Mebbe I should call a colleague in,' he said, 'to help with negotiations.'

'No,' Mats said quickly. 'No need.'

'No?'

'I need time to think.' Mats sounded unconvincing even to himself. 'Look over my accounts.'

Mr Chapman shook his head and smiled, lifted a phone. 'I'll call that colleague.'

'Fifty,' said Mats' mouth.

Mr Chapman, put down the phone and nodded, pressing his lips together. 'Fifty grand, eh?'

Mats found his head nodding.

'Tomorrow?'

'Longer.'

'See, I'll be losing money for every day we wait,' said Mr Chapman. He swilled his whisky thoughtfully. 'Tell you what I'll do, pal. I'll wait.'

Matts watched him.

'But you can't have her.'

'Where will she be?'

'Working.'

'But—'

'If you dinnae want her working, that's an extra £500 a day. Only fair recompense. A nice wee holiday for her, eh?'

Mats shifted uneasily. £500 a day? Is that what she earned? If it took him ten days, that would make it £5,000. Maybe she *should* work? But if he assented to that, he might as well be a pimp himself. Fresh air, he needed fresh air. Or cold water. If he just said no? If he just left? God, how simple his life would seem then. What problems had he thought he'd had before?

Chapman sat considering for a moment, and then leaned forward. 'OK. Tuesday. That's the best I can offer. 8pm. The King's Arms, Toll Cross. Know it?'

'I can find it,' Mats said. 'But Tuesday's too soon.'

'Take it or leave it. Best I can offer. Cash in twenties in a Tesco carrier bag. At 8 o'clock you order two drinks, a pint and a . . .' he paused to think, 'a vodka and lime, the lassies like that. You go and sit down, the bag on the floor by your feet. You wait, my colleague will come and sit down, lift the bag and once he sees it's all in order, Rosa will come in and have a wee drink with you. Then it's up to you.'

'How do I know she'll come?'

Chapman shook his head slowly. 'Where I come from, pal, a man's word is his bond.'

Mats swallowed the last of the whisky and hauled himself up from the fleshy clasp of the sofa.

'Go to the police,' Chapman added, 'and not only will your missus know *all* about this, but I cannae vouch for her safety either, nor the bairns. And as for Rosa, well . . .' He shook his head. 'That would be a shame. A waste and a shame.'

He moved towards the door, 'Cheer up, pal. All you need do is make that date and everything will be rosy, ha ha, rosy for you and Rosa. And the wifey at home will be none the wiser.'

Mats shirt was wet against his back. He noticed that Chapman had drawn a horribly convincing portrait of him: taut face, horrified eyes, brow gleaming.

'Want it?'

Mats shook his head.

'I'll see you out.' Smirking, the man extended his hand, but Mats did not take it. His own was dripping and he was afraid of what it might do. Afraid of the satisfaction he might get from smashing his fist into that smirk.

Down the stairs he went, past female voices, Sinatra, through the hot pinky scented murk where sat a couple of men, through the reception, deserted now, and out into the street. And once outside he ran to the main street where there were people about, buses; it wasn't even mid-evening. He went into a pub, ordered a pint, stood and gulped it back almost in one.

'One of those days, eh?' Amused, the barmaid pulled him another. He waited, leaning his weight against the bar, feeling as if he might tip through, tip right through into the abyss where all that money wasn't.

Marta

ALL DAY THERE have been bumps and thumps from downstairs, men's voices, things being moved. In the kitchen, Marta quakes with fear and uncomfortable excitement. Every bang of a door, every shout, shoots a thrill through her veins. What will happen? Where will she go? The electricity's off so it's cold and dim and there's no coffee. She and Lily, Ratman's last girls, sit at the table, not allowed downstairs, Dario said.

Alis is not dead. If she was, Marta would know. Surely something inside you goes cold when a friend dies? And there is still a warm knot like the knot of hands squeezed tight; she can still feel that.

Lily, wrapped in the brown cardigan with her feet pulled up beneath her, coughs and coughs. Dario comes in with bags of chips and cans of Irn-Bru. At least the chips are warm, gritty with salt; the strange sweet drink makes Marta's teeth feel like they're melting.

Ratman puts his head round the door, frowning, checking they're there.

'What's happening?' Marta says without hope of an answer. Of course there is none. He looks as if he hasn't slept for days. 'Are we being moved? Where?' But he's gone, shoes hammering down the stairs.

She goes up to the room where the girls doss on the floor.

There's a blanket nailed over the window in place of a curtain. Before she did not dare but now she tugs until the tacks come out. Cold grey light floods into the room. Outside the twigs at the top of a tree, just budding green, caught with rags of plastic, beyond it a wall with drain pipes, stains and small blank windows. Odd clothes are strewn about the room, a sock, a bra, magazines, a coffee mug full of fag ends, a comb with broken teeth. On her back on her mattress she stares at the ceiling, at a loop of dusty cobweb dangling from a torn paper lampshade.

She hugs a pillow, pulls her duvet over her, wishes for Alis to talk to. What would she think? She pictures her friend: coarse blonde hair, quick smile, narrow scoffing eyes. What does Marta know about her? They talked, but really it was only Marta who talked. She feels ashamed now; why didn't she ask Alis more about herself? But she didn't want to talk, she liked to listen, she said, and oh the sweet, painful relief of talking freely after home where Tata had thought their flat was bugged. Maybe he was right. He was so careful, so strict about what they said, even inside their own walls, and about how they behaved, who they mixed with. He forbade her from seeing Virgil. Behind her eyelids she tries to conjure up Virgil's face, green speckled eyes, a wolfish smile, but he's a blur. The stupid game they used to play in the wrecked car, his fingers on the steering wheel. What a child she was.

After that they began to fight, she and Tata. Always, she'd been his good girl, his favourite, but she could no longer bear to be in the same room as him. One day, she saw them on the bridge, Tata and Virgil together. She was rushing through pelting rain, hurrying to queue for bread. She stopped surprised; she didn't know they knew each other. They were too far away to tell, but she got the impression they were arguing. Next day Virgil didn't show up. And a few days later Tata too went missing. Nobody would say a thing, even Mama, though her face shrunk as if she'd lived five years in one night.

'He'll be back,' was all she'd say with a bright and desperate look in her eyes. Milya got a slap on her leg for asking and asking where her Tata was, the only time Marta ever saw Mama hit her.

Tata and Virgil both disappeared and a few weeks later came the news that twenty men and boys had been taken to the forest and shot. And later they learned that they had been part of a cell organising defection. Maybe Tata had been planning to bring them out of Romania? That's why he'd been teaching her English. Maybe he'd been working to make things better for them all?

Stop thinking it; stop thinking it.

Only a few months later Ceaușescu was shot.

And Tata missed it. Tata missed it.

That evil peasant man who starved and froze and murdered his own people, he and his wife were shot like dogs. Right there on the TV. It was a feast for the eyes. The puff of smoke and then the sight of the crumpling figures. Nicolae falling back, knees folding beneath him, a dark snake of blood slithering from his wife's head.

But Tata was not there to see.

She pulls herself out of the memories, sits up and rubs her eyes, eyes that have stayed dry. At last her crying habit is broken. She will be like Alis; Alis never cries.

At the top of the stairs she stands and listens. All quiet now. Maybe the men have gone? Maybe Ratman has gone? Dario? Maybe everyone? She takes her bag from its hiding place under the mattress and goes downstairs. Beads clack on their strings as she pushes through into the lounge. On the table an overflowing ashtray, nubs of gum stuck in the rims of coke bottles. She goes through into reception, rattles the door. Locked of course; she pushes and wrenches the handle, gives up, begins to investigate the window catch.

Dario appears, bare chested and shivery. On his chest and abdomen the skin is milky and hairless as a baby's.

'Go up.' He jerks his chin towards the stairs. In the bleak light she can see a rash of spots at the corners of his mouth, spindly black hairs on his upper lip.

'What's happening?'

He blinks at her, peels a bit of gum off the top of a Coke bottle and puts it in his mouth.

'Tell me, Dario.'

He stretches the gum between his teeth and chews.

'You gave Ratman the pastels, didn't you?'

His eyes are as blank as the TV screen.

'You told him about crazy Norwegian? Did you go to his house?'

He blows a grey bubble and she can see his tongue waggling inside it.

'You are a true shit,' she says.

He draws in the bubble. 'Everyone is shit,' he says. 'Shit, shit, shit, then dead.'

She stares at his teenage skin, his pretty nose, his eyes that might as well be dead already, and hate won't come; only a wash of tiredness.

'Let me out, Dario,' she says. Probably he'll go straight to Ratman and tell him this too. 'Please,' she says, 'please. Just let me go.'

A truck, maybe collecting rubbish clatters outside, rattling the windows.

'Go up,' he says.

'Please.'

He only chews, looking at the stairs and she gives up, passes him, climbs right up to the sleep room and lies down. No tears, but like beads tumbling from a necklace onto a shiny floor, her heartbeat scatters.

Mats

H E GETS THE last seat on the late plane, which turns out to be by the window over the wing so that his long legs are cramped unbearably. The woman beside him, in the aisle seat, prefers not to swap.

'Get panicked if I'm hemmed in, me,' she says, taking out of her bag an enormous piece of crochet. Expertly, she begins to waggle a hook through the dense hairy wool. 'For my father,' she says, 'ninety-one tomorrow.'

Smiling politely, Mats turns away his head. No chat. Please. Rain streams down the window. He shuts his eyes, listens to the steward going through the lifebelt and oxygen procedures, the brace position. As if the brace position would save you if the plane went down.

If only it would go down.

No.

But think of all the trouble it would save. No more worry about money or Marta or anything else ever again. What would they say about him? How disappointing his life would have turned out to be. Imagining his weeping mother, Nina, the disgusted face of his father, all in a row at his funeral, he finds his eyes filling, sniffs back the tears, straightens his shoulders. Man up.

If only he could stretch his legs.

Lucky it's the weekend. He'll fly back on Sunday night or early on Monday, go straight to the office. When the lie that Far was ill slid so smoothly from his tongue, Vivienne was helpful, sympathetic almost. No, not almost but *actually* sympathetic, *genuinely*, he must be fair to her. Maybe she really is getting better? Getting back to the self that he must once have loved, since he married her. He gives such a long, audible sigh that Crochet Woman notices and touches his arm.

'All right, lovey?' she says.

He smiles tightly. 'Lots on my mind.'

'Want to talk it over?' She peers over the top of miniature reading specs. She has wildly grizzled hair and a kind, deeply grooved face. 'Talking to someone who's not involved, it really can help.'

'Thanks anyway,' he says.

She laughs gruffly. 'Well you know where I'll be for the next ninety minutes.'

He nods, peers out of the window at the bridges spanning the tea-coloured Forth before the plane banks and all he can see is heaped grey cloud. Rain starts, running horizontally across the glass like wavering thoughts; but he must think in straight lines now.

What can he say to his folks? What possible reason can there be for needing that sum of money, immediately? Gambling debts? But Far would be almost as shocked by that as by the real reason. Vivienne needs an operation? What's wrong with the famous NHS – he can hear those words in his father's mouth. And anyway, how could he keep up such a lie? Investment opportunity? Far might go for that, especially if there was a profit in it for him. His standards are so high. Fiercely Christian, fiercely moral, he made his fortune through business, through going without, through never wasting a single penny. He'd never lend money for an investment without knowing every detail, of course he wouldn't. Mats fidgets his legs, restrains himself from another sigh.

He flexes his toes within his shoes, moving his feet up and down, his legs scream to be straightened. Tries closing his eyes. If only he could just rest his mind, worn thin and grainy with repetitive thoughts. At intervals spurts of adrenalin rush his veins. Relax? Who's he kidding? Thoughts flock and squeal through his brains.

The mortgage on the house is huge, no question of extending it, he's only just making the payments as it is. Should not have bought the expensive house in the expensive suburb, got carried away with the idea of being a family man. Of providing. Can't borrow fifty grand, not at short notice; the interest would be impossible.

He tugs his earlobe, pinching and pulling, a childhood habit that has made one lobe longer than the other. He hates the slightly frailer feeling of that flesh between his fingers, a ragged sensation that reminds him of how afraid of his father he used to be. Still is.

The trolley's in the aisle and his companion nudges him. He accepts a paper cup of cool, dreadful coffee and two wrapped biscuits.

'Can't stomach coffee,' says the crochet woman. 'Sends me berserk.' Instead she has a little plastic pot of orange juice. She pierces the lid with her crochet hook.

'Fly often?' she says. 'Me, I visit once a month.'

'Where do you live?' Mats gives in and learns about her extensive family, spread between Norway, Scotland and London, her husband's obsession with golf, her eldest grandson's staggering musical talent, her daughter's dreams of starting an alpaca farm.

'Have you seen their eyelashes?' She flicks her fingers up to mime them, giving a goofy alpaca grin.

He smiles. Wouldn't it be nice to be able to laugh without this dread that feels like concrete lodged in his gut? He can't remember how it feels to be light-hearted. This crochet woman might have sorrows in her life, she might have trials but she isn't racked with guilt, he would place a bet on that. If he was a betting man, which he is not, but then he's not a man who visits prostitutes either, not a man who cheats and lies and puts his family in danger.

He fakes a yawn. 'Going to try and sleep before we land.'

'Sure,' the woman nods cozily. 'Me, I never sleep on a plane. Sort of a superstition. I shut my eyes, the plane drops from the sky!'

Smiling, he shuts his eyes. He'll go mad if he can't stretch his legs out, but if he asks her to get up it'll lead to more chat. Imagine her reaction if he tells her he's slept with a Romanian prostitute, got into this *situation* with a pimp, needs £50,000 right now. What would she say to that?

There is one person he can tell, of course. For sure, she'll be crisp, sarcastic, practical. But she'll know what he should do. This thought both soothes and excites him. Nina can be relied upon to find a solution; Nina of the cool head. Prematurely he begins to feel relief in the thought. He'll find time to see her. It will be so *good* to see her. Tomorrow he'll arrange it. No need to mention the loan to his folks, not until he's talked to Nina.

Behind his eyelids, which he feels obliged to keep closed, he begins to drift, picturing her long neck, her white-blonde hair piled high, soft tendrils tumbling, little ears . . . and then he thinks of Marta, her tender neck, her mass of dark curls, the fear in her eyes. Her neck on the line because of *him*. As if someone has pumped their foot on the gas, he's flooded with adrenalin again.

He finds himself panting now, hyperventilating. Is this a panic attack? 'Excuse me,' he says to Crochet Woman, undoing his seatbelt. She rolls up her work with maddening slowness, winds the wool round the ball, pokes the hook into it, stows it all in her bag. And then she heaves up her bulky body so he can squeeze past into the aisle. A shudder of turbulence causes him to lurch, the seat belt signs ping back on, but he makes his way to the toilet, stretching out the backs of his knees. He can't get his breath. Sweat beads his brow. He feels he could punch someone or scream. A stewardess asks him to go back to his seat but he ignores her, locks himself into the toilet, stands with his forehead pressed against its plastic interior.

He breathes and breathes, easing the sickly scented toilet air down into his lungs until he's got a grip. Hunches to stare at himself in the curiously vague mirror, looks into his own eyes and makes this vow: once all this is over I will be a good and faithful family man.

He has a pee, flushes, squeezes a slime of pink soap into his hands, wipes the washbasin as requested and comes out to face the glare of the stewardess.

'Sorry,' he says, and her eyes soften.

'Sit down and fasten your seatbelt.' She's got a pretty curl to her top lip, that playful bossiness, like Christine, probably a grateful husband at home, yes, there's a ring. Mats hopes the man appreciates her. Crochet Woman struggles up again and he folds himself up to get back in his seat just as the plane begins its descent. He fastens his seatbelt and listens to Crochet Woman, who takes this last opportunity to pour out problems with her daughter, who has children by three different men, all different colours – a 'rainbow family' she calls it – and would do better to think about making a stable home for them, rather than worrying about stables for alpacas.

'Thank you,' she says, when they have landed and are awaiting the seatbelt sign. 'It really helps to have a stranger's ear.' She touches his arm and he looks down at the back of her shiny worn and freckled hand. 'Good luck,' she says, 'good luck with whatever it is that's on your mind.'

Mats

H E ACCELERATES DOWN the road between the silver trunks of birches, the heaps of decaying snow at the road's edges, enjoying the power of his father's Jag. Of course, Far had been reluctant to lend it, but Mor stepped in, shamed him for being mean.

Mats can hardly believe he's actually driving to the cabin to see Nina – and of course Lars, her new husband. He'd rung her almost as soon as he'd got up, as soon as he decently could after drinking coffee and eating the cinnamon cookies his mother had baked specially for him, so that the house, when he'd opened the door in the middle of the night, had enveloped him in a scent so childishly welcoming he'd almost wept. Breakfast of cookies, a childhood treat.

First, Nina said she couldn't see him this weekend, that she and Lars would be at the cabin decorating. She apologized, her voice, clipped, even, so familiar it made him ache. But then, thirty minutes later, she rang back to invite him down for Saturday lunch. Hell of a long way to drive for lunch, but there was no question.

For years, he and Nina had done all the maintenance on the cabin together, weather-proofing, painting, bramble-clearing, wearing themselves out before evenings of wine and firelight and that deep soft bed. Summers, they could be naked, no one else for kilometers, they'd swim in the lake, barbecue fresh-caught trout, hike in the late sun. The cabin belonged to Nina's parents but they gave up going there years ago, planned to sell it until Nina persuaded them not to and she and Mats took on the responsibility of its upkeep. Nina and Mats. And now Nina and Lars.

How thoroughly you can be replaced.

The road unspools like the memories it brings, the Roadhouse at the intersection, that steep bend, that tumbledown house, that massive oak tree and finally the long bumpy track, a right turn through a gate under the deep shade of old pines, over the bridge, until the peaked roof comes into sight, shining silver with frost, pocked with golden leaves. The car outside is unfamiliar – of course, why should she have the same car? A sporty black Audi – he can picture her in it.

He pulls in beside it, gathering himself to face her again, and to meet the husband. As he looks at the door it opens and she steps out, pale and smaller than he remembers, a huge white shirt over jeans, the old yellow clogs that live in the cabin between visits. He gets out of the car and goes to her, hands her the bottle of wine his mother pressed on him before he left. He hugs her, feeling her piled up hair tickling his nose, smelling just the same, tickling just the same.

'Welcome back,' she says, grinning almost shyly. The shirt is splattered with pale blue paint. 'Come in.'

He takes off his shoes and follows her into the room, which seems smaller too, bright with the grey light that spills in through the windows. Oh it smells so familiar – he inhales old wood, smoke, candle wax. One wall is part painted and a stepladder with a tin of paint, brush balanced on the top, stands waiting. He looks round for Lars.

'Lars is not here,' Nina says. 'I suppose I should wash my brush and get lunch.' She looks him up and down. 'You look like shit,' she adds.

'Thanks! You look great.'

'Put the slippers on,' she says. The slippers are an old pair of her father's leather moccasins worn black and shiny inside. He supposes Lars must also wear them when he's here.

'Why no Lars?'

'Something came up,' she says vaguely. 'Last minute thing.' Is she avoiding his eyes?

'I could finish painting that wall while you get the lunch,' he offers.

She nods approvingly. He takes off his coat, hangs it on the hook, there's a scarf there he recognizes, his own scarf left there years ago, soft striped wool. He'll take that when he goes.

'Put this on.' She pulls the enormous shirt over her head – he notices the wisps of transparent underarm hair – and stands before him slim as ever in her pale jeans and black vest. She goes into the kitchen area and opens the fridge; he pulls the shirt over his own, picks up the brush, begins to smooth paint onto the wooden slats. They have been well sanded; it's pleasant work and soothing. How long since last he painted this wall: ten years?

'How are your folks?' she calls, running something under the tap. 'Haven't seen your Mor lately. Oh, she showed me pictures of your son. Thomas, isn't it? Your image!' They talk easily as he paints. This really could be his life, a parallel life, the other a dream, lately a nightmare. He would swap it all in an instant except, of course for Thomas. And he feels a tug of guilt for not thinking immediately of Arthur, who he does love, really loves, though it is not *quite* the same. To recompense he tells Nina about his stepson, how well they've bonded, what a good big brother he is to Thomas.

By the time he's finished the wall, the table is set with bread, salad, cheese, *sild*, wine glasses and the open bottle. She's already sipping. He takes the brush outside to rinse it, goes into the damp and chilly outdoor bathroom to wash his hands, gazes at his face in the ancient spotted mirror. Does he really look so bad?

When he comes back in she hands him his glass. '*Skol*,' she says. It's a white burgundy, both oily and dry and the merest sip piques his appetite immediately.

'This is so strange,' he says, as he sits down. 'I mean, it's so familiar to be here with you, yet . . .'

'*Yet*,' she agrees, smiling warmly, meeting his eyes.

She tells him about her parents, who are both in poor health, her brother who works in Dubai and has three children now. She says little about Lars, he notices, and he says equally little about Vivienne. She describes her three nieces, shows him a photo – like a posy of pink and white flowers.

'What about you and Lars?' he asks.

She puts a slice of pale Gouda on her black bread and takes a neat bite, chews, sips her wine. 'This is good,' she remarks, holding up her glass. 'From your far's cellar?'

He admits it and she laughs. 'Good old Jan.' And then her face turns serious. 'The marriage is good,' she says, 'but we've been trying for a baby and it seems there is a problem.'

He hooks a curl of herring, stuck with strands of vinegared onion onto his plate. Cuts a tomato in half, though his appetite has gone. You didn't want a baby with *me*, he wants to say.

'It's not my fault,' she goes on. 'Lars' sperm are immotile.'

Ha! He butters a slice of bread. 'I'm sorry,' he says.

'That's why he's not here,' she adds.

'Because of his sperm?' Mats frowns, spears a morsel of fish and puts it in his mouth and chews the soft, sweet flesh, catches the tang of juniper.

'Because this is my fertile time.' She looks at him over her glass. 'We know *your* sperm is motile,' she says.

He stops chewing. The fish is mush between his teeth.

'It makes sense,' she says, then smiles, incongruously flirtatious, 'and it would be nice, no?'

With difficulty he swallows his mouthful. 'I'm married,' he says.

'Of course. That has nothing to do with it. But you can help me out, help out me and Lars.'

'Did you talk this over with him?' Mats stares in some bemusement at her serious face.

Her delicate shoulders rise in a suggestion of a shrug. 'He wants a child.'

'But did you say . . .'

'When I'm pregnant he won't ask questions.' She sips her wine. 'He wants no one knowing his problem. This way everyone is happy. He is tall and dark like you,' she adds.

Mats knows this; his mother sent him a photo of the wedding and he was struck by how much he and Lars share the same physical type. Except of course that Mats is no Olympic champion. He's even started to get a belly from all the drinking after work. The room is warm, the stove belting out heat; her arms are slim, the shape of her small breasts, their upturned nipples – under her thin vest she's clearly braless. He's tempted, very tempted; the wine is in his blood and even stronger than that there's the sense of being home almost, back in a world he understands.

'Vivienne has no need to know – unless you choose to tell her,' she says.

That name in Nina's mouth jolts him off track. *Vivienne.*

He's here to sort out one problem, not give himself another.

'What is it?' She looks at him curiously. 'I have a problem and this is a solution. It makes sense, no?'

'You didn't want a baby with *me*,' he says. He gets up from the table, carries his wine over to the sofa by the stove, and sits. The same old multi-coloured Afghan knitted by some ancestor, the same faded rag rug, singed here and there by sparks. Above the stove is a dark and primitive portrait of a woman – no one knows who she was – pine cones and wooden ornaments decorate the shelves along with books, candlesticks and oil lamps. All so familiar, the smell and feel, even the creaks in the floorboards.

He's been happier in this cabin than anywhere else in his life.

'That was then and this is now,' she says, coming to join him. 'It's a different circumstance.' She chooses to sit not on the sofa beside him but on the floor, knees drawn up to her chest. 'But OK. No problem. There's another guy I can ask.'

Mats looks at his watch. He should stop drinking; make coffee. In an hour or so it will be time to return to his parents' – he promised to be back for supper. And he must spend time with them before his flight on Sunday night. The whole trip has been a waste of time; simply more expense.

Her head is close to his knee and he leans forward to stroke the bundled hair. His fingers itch to touch the nape of neck. 'It's not that I wouldn't like to go to bed with you,' he says. 'Of course I would.'

She turns, eagerly, and catches his finger. 'Think of it like that then. Just sex between old friends. No strings.'

'You seem very sure that it would work,' he says.

'It would, of course,' she says.

He snorts. She is so clear and logical and certain, so different

164

from Vivienne, and even from himself. And she's probably right too.

'OK. And if it did work, you think I could just forget I had another child?'

'You wouldn't have a child,' she says simply, 'it would be mine and Lars''.

He takes his hand back, finishes his wine. 'I'll make coffee,' he says, but doesn't move, not quite yet. He didn't sleep well last night, or at least he fell asleep easily in his old bedroom, but woke after an hour or so with his predicament raging. And now here was Nina expecting him to solve *her* problem – and in such a way!

She gets up, fills the kettle and sits it on top of the black iron stove. It will take ages to boil, he knows. She opens the stove door and pokes the fire. A swarm of sparks flees up the chimney before she angles in another log and closes the door again.

'So,' she says, turning, folding her arms, gazing down at him. 'You said you want to talk over a problem with me?'

Wearily, he shakes his head. 'Doesn't matter.'

She sits beside him, puts her hand on his knee, waiting.

How long since I was here? he wonders, two years? Feels like ten. And feels like yesterday.

'Mats?'

Through the window he sees that the sky is tinged with apricot. He should not wait for coffee. He turns his head to scan the wall he painted. A good colour. Nina has excellent taste.

'Mats?' she says again. 'You come all this way to ask me something and now you will not ask? What is the sense in that?'

He groans and shakes his head.

'Go on.'

And after all, he might as well tell her. It can't do any harm. It's still possible that she'll have an idea. She never likes to be defeated.

'I've got into a situation where I need a lot of money fast,' he says.

'OK?' She waits for him to elaborate.

'That's it,' he decides, with a ripple of relief. 'That's it. In a nutshell.'

'But you aren't short of money,' she says.

'I've nothing spare. Not this much.'

'But Jan . . .' she starts and stops, knowing his father well enough to see the problem. 'What for?' she says, widening her eyes. 'Something illegal? *Really*, Mats.'

He says nothing. The kettle is fidgeting towards a boil.

'How much?'

'About sixty million krone.'

She makes an incredulous noise, jumps up and goes to the door. He hears her kicking off her clogs and pushing her feet into boots, pulling a jacket off a peg. The outer door bangs, frosty air gusts into the room and there's the familiar squeak of the bathroom door. It doesn't matter how much oil you put on, it will always squeak. Not his problem any more. He gets up to find the coffee pot and mugs; his hands remembering where everything is, new mugs he notices, feeling a bit affronted.

As she comes back in she says, 'OK. This is what we do.'

'We?'

She sheds her jacket, kicks off her boots, pushes her feet back into the clogs. The cold has rosied up her cheeks. There's a little wine left in the bottle. She tips it into her glass, swigs it back and regards him with clear, bright eyes.

'I've got money,' she says. She takes her coffee and says not another word until they are side by side on the sofa, mugs in their hands, feet up on the low wooden coffee table, a position they have sat in so many times before. He can't help but be aware of her body, the slim arms with their glint of hair, the light lemony scent of her. He's prickling to know more, but she's quiet.

'You can't have that much,' he says, 'and even if you do I couldn't—'

She blows on her coffee and sips. Time has flown. The room is darkening; it's almost time to light the lamps. Outside the window the sky is hectic red and saffron streaks. He should drink the coffee very fast and go. Fly home. Put an end to this nonsense. Maybe he will go to the police. He could move the family to Norway first to get them out of danger. Or go and confess to his father and beg cravenly for a loan . . . His mind races, rearing against every idea.

'Lars is loaded,' she's saying. 'I have my own bank account, he doesn't even look.'

Hope is a small bright bubble that he swallows down.

'You know my granny died last year? She left me her house. I just sold it. I have the money. I could lend it to you.'

Mats turns to her; he puts down his mug, grabs her arm. 'Mind,' she says as her coffee slops onto her jeans. 'Ouch.'

She jumps up and goes to sponge the denim.

'Sorry,' he says.

She settles back beside him on the sofa.

'*Really?*' he says.

She nods, a little frown denting her forehead. She has fine lines round her eyes, the beginnings of corrugations on her forehead. She's nearly forty, he realizes with a jolt, a few months older than he. Not a young woman though he still thinks of her as such. Thinks of himself as a young man. She's five years older than Vivienne and as for . . .no, do not let the other into your mind. 'I could go to the bank on Monday morning, have it transferred.'

Inhaling deeply he closes his eyes. Can he possibly accept?

Can he? Don't rush this. Think, think hard. His lobe is sore from tugging, he folds his fingers together so tight the knuckles crack.

If it could be true? If it could be this easy?

Once this is sorted out he will never stray again in any way. He will be a loyal, faithful husband, a hard worker, a family man.

He will. He will accept this loan, this lifeline, this safe hand reaching out to save him.

Though God knows how he'll ever pay her back.

'Thank you,' he says, voice muted with gratitude and shame. He kisses her cheek. 'Thank you,' he says again.

'It's a sensible solution,' she says with a little shrug.

'Of course I'll pay interest,' he says. 'Whatever you'd be getting from the bank. Though it might take me a while.'

They both pick up their coffee and settle side by side again.

'One condition,' she says. 'You must tell me what it's for. It's only fair.'

She's right, of course and anyway with the loosening of tension comes a sudden yearning to come clean, to let it out into the light. It helps to talk to someone not involved said Crochet Woman. But if Nina lends him the money, perhaps he *is* involving her?

But anyway, he tells her the whole sad and sordid story.

She listens silently, her face passive, then she turns to him. 'So, you went to a prostitute. Then you felt bad about it so you screwed everything up, put yourself, the girl, your family in danger?'

Shutting his eyes, he nods.

'Nice work, Mats.' She springs up, strikes matches to light the three oil lamps. Now the room is lit the sky disappears, there's only the shine of the room reflected on the windows.

'*You* Mats, *you* with a prostitute,' she says.

He puts his hands over his face. Yet it feels weirdly good to be chastised. It's true after all.

'And not even a willing prostitute. Sounds to me like she's been trafficked.'

'I didn't know,' he mumbles through his fingers. 'If I'd know I'd never . . .'

She's wandering round now, clogs silent on the rug, clopping on the floorboards. Her reflection flits across the windows. He watches her twirl her fingers through tendrils of her tumbling down hair, a habit he'd forgotten.

'You know,' she says, 'I always thought you couldn't surprise me.' She gives a disbelieving laugh.

Myself too, he thinks, but doesn't say.

'When people say all men are rapists—'

'It wasn't rape!'

'Or all men would do anything for sex, pay for sex, then I always thought that you were an exception. You were sort of . . . tame.'

He stares.

'You were so good, so upright, so *straight*.'

'Is that a bad thing?'

'Decent,' she continues. 'I always though that you were *decent*.'

He says nothing.

She comes back to the sofa, kicks off her clogs. 'A bit . . . boring, to tell the truth,' she adds.

'Boring?!' He stares at her grinning, lamplit face. He, *Mats*, boring? *She* was always the sensible one. Wasn't she? He sips his coffee, cold now. He frowns back over the years to their time together, their routines, all the socializing with his parents – maybe that *was* boring? But he thought she'd liked it. He feels a flicker of anger. All the things he's done for her. The person he became for her. No, no, the person she moulded him into.

He thinks of the night she told him to take the job in

Edinburgh. Not a sacrifice for her at all it seems but her first move away from boring. Maybe Lars was already on the scene. Maybe it was a relief that he moved away.

No way is he staying to be insulted. He heaves himself up. 'If you lend me the money I'll pay you back of course. With interest.' Trying to rid his voice of its stiffness, 'It is amazingly kind of you,' he makes himself add.

'Sit down, Mats,' she says as if she'd talking to a child, or a dog. She pats the sofa.

'I have to go.'

'You can go later.'

'No, I want to go. I must phone Vivienne.'

'Listen.' She pulls the coloured Afghan from the back of the sofa and wraps it round her knees and bare feet.

Puffing his irritation he consents to sit again, perches on the edge of the sofa. His parents will be expecting him back for supper – already he'll be late. Far will want to see his car. When it's returned he always walks round it searching for scratches as if it's a hire car.

'You *could* pay me back, with interest,' she says. One of her bare feet works its way under his thigh, he can feel the cold branching of her toes. 'Or,' she adds, 'maybe we can fix up some other kind of deal.'

Her expression is curious; her fair lashes glint, her mouth is small, the lips prettily modelled. 'Makes perfect sense,' she says. 'A simple bargain. I have what you need – money. You have what I need – motile sperm.'

An angry and unexpected laugh erupts from him. Could that be the least seductive line ever uttered?

Unsmiling now she quirks her eyebrows.

'So we sleep together and the loan is interest-free?' he says.

'More than that,' she says. 'I get pregnant you can forget the debt. Think of it as a fee. A stud fee.'

'A stud fee!' He pulls away, angry and aroused. Confused. 'Does Lars know I'm here?'

'Forget Lars.'

He focuses on a bulbous flame in the sooty glass chimney of a lamp. Soft peachy light pools round it, illuminating a wooden bowl of fir cones, the chess set in its wooden box (he knows a white pawn is missing) a toppled over birthday card. Black out there now, chilly black night.

'Mats?'

'But would you tell him? Would you let him think it was his?'

She gives a light shrug as if this is really not important. 'He will know it can't be his but . . . he has a public profile, an image to keep up. He doesn't want anyone to know about his problem. If I get pregnant, you can be sure no questions will be asked.' She says all this as if it's perfectly logical and reasonable.

And maybe it is.

'What if you didn't get pregnant?'

'I will,' she says simply. Her fingers press her side. 'I am ovulating right now.'

Another line that very far from turns him on.

'You can drive to the Roadhouse and ring your wife, ring your parents, say you're staying the night.'

'What will they think?'

'That is not my problem.' She folds herself up from the sofa and comes over to him. 'They know we're old friends. Maybe you're helping me, or trouble with the car, or a glass of wine too many? Say anything you like.' As she speaks she puts a finger on his chest and smiles. 'Let me open another bottle of wine,' she says. 'I have plenty of food. A nice evening together and lots of sex. We were always good,' she says. Her pupils have dilated and her eyes glow at him. 'Remember all those times in that bed?' she nods towards the platform and her finger bumps over his shirt buttons, tracing down towards his groin.

'Well, when you put it like that . . .' he says.

When he returns, with his arrangements – a pack of lies – all made, he's welcomed into the cabin by a smell of roasting meat. He spies a bottle of red warming by the stove, but can't see Nina and then he knows. He climbs the wooden ladder to the sleeping platform and there she is in the deep soft bed, face shadowy, hair flickering in the lamplight. 'Come on in,' she says and lifts the quilt to reveal her slim, white, naked body.

Vivienne

click

OK, IT'S SUNDAY afternoon and Mats is away. We were meant to be doing something as a family, Deep Sea World maybe. But that didn't happen. Poor Mats came home from work in shock. His dad suddenly taken ill; he looked so *scared*. I just wanted to hold him but no time for that. I said I'd go with him, but he said no. He booked himself on a plane, called a taxi and went. Just like that.

So the whole weekend stretched out with nothing. I rang Rita, hadn't seen her for a while which in itself was strange. She said she'd come on Saturday afternoon and stay for dinner, which cheered me up. I mean, I might have a drink on my own sometimes though it's a bit sad, but if a friend's round, well you have to, don't you?

Saturday was sunny, thank God, but still cold. We took the kids to the park, went for a coffee, looked in the toy shop and before I could stop her she was buying a book for Artie, a fluffy rabbit for Tommy.

She was kind of pent up like she had a secret, but I didn't ask, I mean it was up to her if she wanted to tell me.

She made dippy egg for Artie's tea while I had a bubble bath and shaved my legs. Once the kids were down, we phoned for pizzas and opened the wine and then she got this massive box of truffles out of her bag. Charbonnel et Walker, must have cost her an arm and two legs.

'Had a raise?' I said.

'Tell you later,' she went. She'd her hair cut in a new way like a leprechaun or a lesbian. Suited her though.

We watched *Stars in Their Eyes*. It was like the old days, before I even met Mats, when she used to come round to my flat – still miss that flat – and we used to talk about dating and stuff. We got through the first bottle pretty fast and I said, 'Shall I open another,' and she said 'Not for me,' but she did have some when it was open. People are always the same, pretending they don't want to drink, when really they do.

'Can we put it off?' she said when *Stars in Your Eyes* was over. She was curled up in a corner of the sofa, sipping her wine. She'd left half her pizza so I started eating it for her; she was making me nervous because she seemed nervous.

'It's not a raise,' she said in the end, 'but I'm leaving work.'

'Why?' I said.

'Well.' She put down her glass. 'I've got a new job.'

'Fab,' I said. 'Doing what?'

Her pizza was ham and pineapple and I was removing the pineapple, I mean it seems sort of unholy doesn't it, wet squares of fruit on a pizza? She picked up a Lego car, and span the wheels, red and yellow.

'Same sort of thing,' she said and then all in a rush went, 'only it's in Toronto.'

'Toronto in *Canada*?'

She slugged back her wine. 'I didn't say before in case I didn't get it. I mean I thought you might be upset.'

'Why would I be?' I said. 'Well done.'

There was this silence and my stomach felt too full. Spin, spin, spin went the Lego wheels.

'When are you going?' I said in the end.

'Wednesday,' she said and she kind of winced like she thought I might throw a wobbly.

But why should I? It's her life.

I wanted to watch 2.4 *Children*.

I wanted to throw up.

'You could have said before,' is all I said, not stroppy or anything. I mean she must have been planning it for weeks, and booking tickets and that. It was partly because of Eddie – an old boyfriend. Her first love. They were back in touch; he lived there.

'It's a bit of a risk, isn't it?' I said. I mean she hasn't seen him for twenty years and obviously it didn't work out then.

'If nothing else we'll be friends,' she said. 'And I can always come back.'

She showed me a photo of them together, when they were about sixteen. She's not tall but she's taller than him, he had one of those moon faces and a thick pale fringe like a slice of bread. I'm pleased for her, I really am.

I hope it works out.

click

After she'd gone I didn't know what to do. If I'd had more wine I would have opened it. I mean, wouldn't anyone? But there wasn't any in the house, Mats made sure of that. I thought he might ring but he didn't, which I took to mean that his Dad was OK. I mean if he'd died, surely he'd have rung?

Then he did ring. And it was quick and weird, from a public phone, he was at the hospital he said. His dad was out of danger, he'd tell me about it tomorrow. 'Is Tommy OK?' he asked and I said, 'Yes, why shouldn't he be?' And then his money ran out and he was gone.

I was too frustrated to sleep but I must have gone off because Tommy woke in the night and cried for ages before I remembered Mats wasn't there. When I went to him he was cranky, expecting to see his daddy. In the morning it was stormy, wet petals blowing off the cherry trees and sticking on the windows so it made me think of snow.

click

Waited and waited for Mats to ring again. He hadn't said when he'd be home. In the end I rang his mum who said he'd just left for the airport. I said, 'How's Jan?' and she said, 'OK,' sounding sort of surprised and careful. She asked about the boys. I didn't like to press about Jan. All I said when I rang off was, I hope he gets well soon and send him love from me and the boys.

After I rang off I got frightened. What if it was a lie? What if Mats had gone off for some other reason? Her voice sounded strange, fake. I opened the wine I'd bought to welcome him home.

click

Shouldn't have listened. All these little tapes sitting in a box, all full of my shitty voice. I was bored waiting for Mats, worrying if he'd lied to me. I decided to destroy them but listen first. I listened while I drank a bottle then I pulled the first tape off its little spools, all that tape tangled on the floor, sticky brown strings of my thoughts. I pushed it in the bin with peelings and nappies, then I pulled it out and snipped it up into tiny pieces, shiny pieces like brown confetti. Then I put it in a saucepan and boiled it. And that's what I'll do with this one when I come to the end. And record no more.

click

I want Mats; I want him. I want him to love me and stay with me and be a family. I am going to be better. I am already. I only got one bottle of wine today. I don't care if it was a lie about his dad. I don't want to know I won't even ask, just be nice. Just nice. Just make it work.

click

It's past midnight but I'm waiting up even if I have to wait all night. I'll make him a sandwich or whatever, coffee or whatever. I've got my silk nightie on. Maybe he'll want to make love. Men always . . .

That's him

click

Mats

IN DEPARTURES LATE on Sunday night, he spots Crochet Woman and ducks behind his newspaper. His mind is oddly blank, his body heavy yet buzzing, almost sore. He needs to shut his eyes, to do some processing. Or maybe to switch right off. No chat please. He waits till everyone has boarded before getting up. He's the last passenger on and as he makes his way up the aisle of the plane towards the back he sees Crochet Woman already embarking on a conversation with a startled-looking guy and feels a rush of fondness for her.

She catches his eye, gives a smile and a wave. 'Everything all right?' she mouths, raising her grizzled eyebrows.

He nods, feels his face stretch into a grin. Everything all right! If she knew the half of it! He secures a double seat to himself at the back – it's a quiet flight – swallows a whisky and manages to sleep.

Emerging groggily into post-midnight Arrivals he sees Crochet Woman being bear-hugged by a bald and beaming man. Probably the husband. Love there, he recognizes with a lonely pang: proper, simple *love*.

'Good weekend?' he asks, as he passes them by.

'Super,' she replies. 'You?'

He nods.

'Good luck,' she says. 'This nice man . . .' she begins telling her husband about him.

'Got to go, lift waiting.' As he leaves, Mats thinks how nice to be greeted with a hug, a smile, a lack of complication. How nice to face life with that openness. Now he's turned off that straight-forward path and the ways forward seem shady, *possible* maybe, but oh so complex.

There's no lift waiting for him, of course; he gets a taxi, sits cold in the back, shivering, disorientated. He recognizes a hot tight feeling in the back of his throat – a cold coming on, that's all he needs.

Expecting all to be dark at home, his heart sinks when he sees light glowing through the curtains. She should be in bed by now, asleep by now; he was counting on it. But maybe there's a problem with Thomas – this feels like something he might have earned. Fingers fumbling, he pays the driver and hurries inside.

Unusually, Vivienne comes out to greet him in the hall. She's dressed in one of her vintage negligees, and when she kisses him he's enveloped in a warm waft of perfume. She tastes of lipstick and wine and his heart sinks further.

'Poor Mats, you must be knackered,' she says. 'Come and sit down. Nightcap?'

He shakes his head.

'Go on,' she says. 'Warm you up.'

'OK,' he says, 'but I'm going straight up. Thomas all right?'

'They're both fine. Out for the count. But how about Jan?'

Mats fakes a laugh. 'Oh fine! False alarm. They thought it was a heart attack but it was only indigestion.'

'But they still kept him in hospital?'

'Just till he got the all clear.'

She gazes at him for an unnervingly long moment, head on

179

one side. 'What a palaver,' she says at last. 'You go up, I'll bring the drinks.'

His legs pull him up the stairs. In the boys' room he bends over the cot to inhale the scent of sleeping Thomas, tucks the cover over his legs – he always kicks it off– glances at Arthur, notices he's still wearing his specs, gently removes them and folds them on the beside table.

In the bathroom he pees and splashes his face. Definitely a cold coming on. Maybe she won't want sex. How can he after . . . ? He takes as long as he feasibly can flossing and gargling, but when he gets into the bedroom she's standing by the mirror, negligee off now, revealing an ivory silk slip.

'You look nice,' he says. She does. But at one remove from him. Objectively, she looks lovely.

'Glad you think so.' She tilts her hip at him, light-hearted, flirtatious, like she used to be.

'But I'm getting a cold,' he says. 'You don't want it.'

'I'll risk it.' She hands him his whisky and he drinks. She's got a glass of red on the go. He doesn't approve of drinking in bed. It seems irresponsible for parents with little ones sleeping close by, but still, he takes the glass and knocks the whisky back in one before he turns away to strip, awkwardly, feeling her eyes on him.

'I'm done in,' he says as he slides into bed and gives an exaggerated yawn, but still she snuggles silkily against him. He can't not make love to his wife because of Nina. That would be despicable. He rolls over, kisses her, smelling wine and hairspray and waiting for her to . . . yes she does it, to sigh luxuriously and stretch out on her back, to lie passive, like a plate of perfumed meat, waiting for him to take her. This is how it always is. At first he'd found it alluring, old-fashioned, unexpectedly modest even, after Nina's matter-of-fact approach; he'd found it moving. But now . . . if she only would be the first to make a move, to suggest, to do anything rather than just lie there. A bolt of guilt shoots through him as he takes her in his arms, feels the solidity that seems somehow innocent, remembering Nina's lithe body, so much fun to make love to, you knew where you were with her, she always said what she wanted, let you know if you made a wrong move.

Last night, in the cabin they'd made love for hours, stopping only to eat and return to bed, waking in the night to do it again, all so wet and sloppy and smelly that it was verging on disgusting, but funny too, and they had fucked and laughed and of course he knew she was deliberately filling herself with sperm, getting as much as she could while she could, and that was OK, made him feel virile, potent, valued.

And maybe, afterwards, a little bit used. Particularly in the morning – *this morning* he thinks with a shock – when he woke to find her already up, showered, ready to strip the sheets from the bed, ready to go and utterly unsentimental. So tidy in her black clothes, hair still damp, tied strictly back, face pale. Sunday, she must get back to Lars, they were lunching with his parents. Do you like them as much as mine? he'd wanted, childishly, to ask.

He forces away the thought of Nina, and runs his hands over Vivienne's waiting body, a hot tickle in the back of his throat.

Oh Christ but he needs to sleep.

Mats

TUESDAY NIGHT. THROAT sore, head solid with cold, he walks towards the King's Arms; it's like the city itself is infected. Gutters stream, clogged with a slime of rotting leaves, rain pours down. He should be in bed with a Lemsip and a fat airport novel instead of walking towards a rendezvous, a wad of money in his briefcase, like some character from a fat airport novel.

Nina had to argue with the bank manager, she told him when she rang, to arrange the transfer of such a sum, so swiftly – but her father has influence. At lunchtime Mats went, sweating, into HSBC to withdraw the money. Hearing the sum, the startled teller called the manager and Mats was led into a private office to tell his rehearsed story: he was after a rare Ferrari Coupe. Only chance, crucial to secure the deal today, great investment, discount for cash. Nina's bank manager had to be called to verify the transaction. Mats sank lower and lower in his seat, waiting for the scheme to fall apart. But, amazingly, it did not. Of course not; if Nina says a thing will work, it works. What about his sperm swimming up inside her? Will they work too? It only takes one she'd reminded him, at some point in the night, when millions were already in there and there were billions more to come.

Somehow in the stuffy manager's office, he managed not to pass out. Somehow he acted his own amazement at himself for this impulsive, indulgent purchase. Midlife crisis, he joked. And he went rather over the top, confessing to an obsession with vintage cars, leading to a tricky discussion of rare models, about which he knew very little.

Maybe his cold had helped, the manager regarded his sopping Kleenex warily, and though this sort of speed of transfer was 'highly irregular' he was satisfied that it was 'all kosher'. He wished Mats good luck, and finally handed the neat wads of £20 notes in a tight paper parcel.

'Shall I call a taxi?' The manager was nervous about his client walking out with that sort of cash, but Mats assured him his wife was waiting in her car. 'Little does she know!' he said, patting the bag and snorting an accidental bubble from his nose.

And now walking down the dark and rushing road he feels the money glowing through the leather of his briefcase. His hand is moulded round the handle like something plastic, the tension screaming up his arm.

Reaching the pub, he does not allow hesitation, swings open the door and enters. It's busy, men standing at the bar, a table of noisy women huddled round an ice bucket of sparkling wine. Heart kicking like a great boot, he glances around expecting some reaction to his entrance but there's nothing. He goes straight through the bar, down a corridor and into a cubicle in the Gents where he slides the lock across and stands with his head resting against the cold paint of the door waiting for his heart to slow. Then he stands straight, looks at his watch. Ten minutes. There's a poster warning of HIV, graffiti carved into the wall, a spurting cock and balls scrawled in magic marker. Closing the toilet seat, he sits down, rests his throbbing head in his hands.

When this is over it is the quiet life for him. Vivienne will be his life, Vivienne and the boys. Any excitement can come from books and films – excitement is overrated. He's afraid his heart will not take this stress, that at this rate it will soon stop kicking, stumble, stop.

He opens his briefcase and takes out the money, parcelled in white paper. There's a folded Tesco bag in there – he went in earlier to buy the Lemsip, and flowers for Christine, who's been so patient through all his oddness. She even gave him a little pot of Vick to rub on his chest tonight. He wishes she'd tuck him into bed, rub on the Vick.

Not that he'd want more from her than that.

Should he take the money out of the parcel, so that the separate wads of notes are more evident? Packed like this it could be anything, a ream of paper, a child's toy in its box. He does so, sliding his fingers inside and quietly tearing the paper. Each wad is neatly strapped together with paper tape. Someone comes in. He freezes, listening to the *zzzp* of a zip, a sigh, a splatter of pee, the sluice of the urinal, the re-zipping, the swing of the door. He exhales, looks at his watch again, he's been here five minutes. Briefly he regards the cash. What the hell is he doing? Who even *is* he at this minute? He could keep one of two of these bundles, take Vivienne and the kids away, or get the new curtains she wants for the sitting room.

But no.

This is for Marta, who will be here very soon. And then what is he going to do with her? What? That far he has not thought. Something. Put her in a hotel for the night maybe, he doesn't know, don't think about that now; get on with it. Get it over with. Get home and into bed and put your head under the pillow. Steam it under a towel, as Christine recommended.

He tips all the money into the carrier bag. Notices the till receipt inside and removes it, starting to think like a criminal;

might it be incriminating if the police get hold of the bag? Do they have CCTV in Tesco? He goes out, pinning the Tesco bag tight against his side with his elbow.

Back in the bar he scans the clientele but still no one takes any notice of him. Self-consciously, since someone must be watching, he goes to the end of the bar and waits, orders the drinks, the pint of McEwan's, the vodka and lime. The guy behind the bar barely glances at him. But there is a man standing near, a tall man in a Tweed suit with specs. Him? And a guy in a leather jacket who looks twitchy. Him? There's someone behind him but he can't turn and look. Follow instructions, take the drinks and sit down.

He goes to sit on the low leather banquette, puts the drinks on the table, settles his briefcase beside him and props the carrier bag against the table leg. Is it visible enough? Did Chapman mean under the table, or should he prop it against his leg? Or did he say put it next to you? Did he say on the floor? It would be better on the bench by his hip where he can keep an eye on it without looking suspicious. Does it looks suspicious to keep peering down at a carrier bag? Is anyone watching? The instruction was to put it on the floor – he's pretty sure – but it's shadowy down there and with his stuffed up sinuses it seems miles away to Mats.

So now he only has to wait. He has done his bit. He hardly dares to look round, sits with his eyes on his knees. Someone has left a newspaper folded to the crossword, half complete. He slides it over and looks, gets a pen from his inside pocket, dares to dart his eyes around as he makes this movement. The bag has slithered into the shadow of the table, but he can still see it. It could be someone's shopping, or a book; it could be anything. He nudges it with his foot as a reassurance.

Someone has tried out an anagram on the margin of the news-paper. Mats pretends to focus on the puzzle but can't think at all.

His heart is beating in his eyes now and in his brain, his sinuses throb in time with it. He blows his nose. The beer tastes all wrong, a Scotch would have been better for his cold, but Chapman said a pint of McEwen's and he has to follow instructions. To the letter.

A girl sits down beside him; he sees thin knees, tight jeans. His head jerks up, but no. OK. OK. This girl is blonde, all wrong, nothing like Marta. She's draped her coat across a chair so that it obscures the bag. What's he supposed to do? Could he ask her to move the coat? Or should he shift the bag to his other side? Chapman never specified whether he should put it to his right or to his left, now he thinks of it. Why did he put it by his left foot? He's about to shift it, when a woman takes the seat to his right, and he straightens up again.

'Stair rods out there, eh?' she says.

'Sorry?'

'The rain?'

It must be an expression. Mats nods and smiles. The woman has a clear drink with ice and lemon. Maybe G&T. She's thin, unglamorous, her grey hair cropped short, her wire rimmed glasses speckled with rain. She wedges her dripping umbrella between the table and her feet, takes off her specs and reaches for her drink.

A young guy comes to sit beside the blonde girl, puts two pints of beer on the table, reaches to cup her face, to kiss her on the mouth. 'Happy Birthday,' he says and hands her a gold-wrapped gift.

Mats focuses on the newspaper, pretends to fill in a crossword clue. Five letter word; he can't think of a single one, puts xxxxx. He's tempted to sip the vodka and lime, some Vitamin C in that at least. He angles his head to get a reassuring glimpse of the bag. Still there. A crowd at the bar now, mostly men; is anyone looking his way?

The girl has unwrapped a woolly ethnic looking hat and is laughing as she models it for her boyfriend. Mats flicks a glance towards the gin woman and notices her dabbing her eyes. Oh no. He pretends not to notice, but watches obliquely the way she has to force her lips against the glass, lips turning down with misery. Sipping his own drink, he feels for her.

'I don't usually do this,' she says, sensing his attention. 'I mean go into pubs, buy myself drinks, it's not my kind of thing but . . .' and then a tear breaks free and flows down her cheek and Mats is helpless. What can he do? He looks at the men at the bar as if to ask this question; whoever it is will be able to see his dilemma, surely? He can't ignore her.

'Sorry,' she says, 'it's just . . . oh,' and she buries her face in her hands.

He swigs his beer, puts it down and fishes in his pocket. 'Kleenex?' He holds out the little packet. She nods gratefully, plucks one out and blows her nose.

'Would you like to talk about it?' he says, thinking of Crochet Woman. If only she were here.

With the tissue pressed to her nose she regards him for a moment; her eyes are small and brown, serious.

'That's nice of you. I'm Sally.' She holds out a damp hand.

'Mats,' Mats says, sending his eyes around the bar. He bends to scratch his ankle, giving himself a chance to check the bag; still there.

'But talking won't make any difference.' Sally sniffs bravely and smiles. 'Oh God, this isn't like me at all.'

OK, Mats thinks and begins to turn away but she continues, 'See I just had my cat put down. Pickles. He was old and . . .' Her lips quiver and she presses them together before she continues, 'He used to be my Mum's, it was the last bit of her I had.'

'So sorry,' he says.

'He lost control of his bowels,' she says, 'and you can't have that, can you? Not with wall-to-wall carpet. But oh I feel like such a traitor. His little face,' and she buries her own face in her hands and sobs. Awkwardly Mats puts his arm round her and she leans against his shoulder and lets herself go.

'OK, OK,' he says. She smells of rain and cat and a faded flowery perfume, old fashioned – though she's probably not much older than he is. The young couple get up to go, the girl in her birthday hat beaming at Mats, amused by his plight. He can't lean down to see the bag without disturbing Sally. A couple of old guys come and settle there now, deep in conversation in accents so strong, Mats can barely make out a word.

At last Sally pulls herself away and sits up straight. 'God. Sorry about that,' she says. 'But thank you.' She dries her eyes. There's no make up to smudge, and when she puts her glasses back on, she looks quite recovered. She takes a tin of Vaseline from her bag and smears some on her lips. 'You must think I'm bonkers.'

'Not at all.'

'You a cat person?'

Mats shakes his head.

'Me neither,' she says and smiles. There's a lovely gap between her front teeth. 'I'm never getting another one.' She notices the untouched vodka and lime.

'Been stood up?'

Mats shakes his head.

She waits but he says no more. 'Oh nearly forgot! I get through that many umbrellas!' She bends down to retrieve it. 'Look, let me get you a drink – to say thanks.'

'No need.'

'I insist.' She stands blocking his view of the bar.

'A Scotch then, thanks,' he says.

As soon as she's gone he bends down to look, but the bag isn't there. Is it? His head begins to swim but then he sees a tag of white that could be the handle, under the table of the two old guys. Could have got kicked there. He just needs to reach under, would that seem weird? The two of them might be in on it for all he knows. He rests his eyes on them, waiting for some kind of communication but they seem oblivious of him.

It's way past 9. It was all supposed to happen at 8.

'There you go, got you a double. Highland Park, that OK?' Sally says, putting the drink down in front of him.

'Great. Thanks.'

'Now I must brave the elements.' She grins at him as she leaves.

He finishes his pint and downs the whisky.

Where is Marta?

He picks up the crossword and writes her name inside a 5-letter space, then scribbles it out. Would that be evidence? He doesn't know, doesn't know anything, feels his brain is going to explode, has to blow his nose, it's getting sore. Every time the door opens he looks up, and then down again. He must not appear obvious. Is anyone watching him? He keeps his eyes down, begins to fill in the squares with black, obliterating every letter of her name.

The old men make no move, voices getting louder, accents thicker. He watches them rolling their smokes. He reads, without taking in a word. Each time the door swings open with its gush of cold air his heart leaps but it's never Marta. He should have eaten something before he came, now he needs another drink. He swallows the sticky sweetness of the vodka and lime, which only makes him thirsty for another pint. He waits till it's quiet before he gets up to go to the bar. He tries to thread between his table and that of the old men, hoping to get to the bag, kick it back into proper view, perhaps, but they don't budge and there's clearly room for him to go the other way. At the bar, he scans the remaining customers and buys a pint and two doubles to keep him going.

It's closing time before the old men get up.

'Time sir,' says the barman, as Mats lingers, fussing with his coat, slowly putting on his gloves, stowing the newspaper in his briefcase, waiting till no one's looking before he kneels to reach under the table for the bag. It's lighter. It's not a Tesco bag but a Morrison's. As he stands again, steadying himself on the table, his heart lurches. This is a sign, he thinks, surely it must be, in the bag there will be a message. To tell him the whereabouts of Marta.

'OK sir?' The barman is giving Mats the sort of look he might give a drunk. Maybe I am a drunk, he reflects.

'OK sir,' the barman holds open the door eager to close up. Mats goes outside. The rain has stopped at least though cars swoosh through deep puddles in the gutters. He stands scanning the street, maybe she's out here? He stands under a street lamp to peer inside the bag. There's a crumple of gold wrapping paper, an empty Ribena carton, a banana skin.

No message, nothing else.

A bag of trash, that's all.

He stands in the wet glitter of the night, the bag dangling from his hand.

Mats

IN FRONT OF a litter bin he takes each item out of the bag, examines it, turns the bag inside out. There is no clue. He puts the lot in the bin. Head reeling, he sets off for home, the lighter briefcase bumping his leg. All that cash gone. Gone, just like that. *Vamoose.* He can't take it in. Rain starts to spit again and that's right, he deserves it, to be spat at.

A laugh rings out behind him, a loud jeer of a laugh, and he hunches over, walks fast. Of course they would laugh, of course they would jeer, why not? The laugh rings in his ears. He is a dupe. Walking shakes free this thought: Chapman is a crook and he a dupe and they are watching him and laughing. Faster he walks, head down, a bitter taste rising to his mouth. A hard feeling wires through his bones. Anger. What has he done? He is a fool, he is a fool, he is total fucking fool. And drunk to top it all. He walks fast but not quite straight, his legs not quite obeying. Face burning hot, the cold raindrops almost a relief. What can he do? He stops, looks round, is there anyone watching, laughing, is anyone following?

He can't go home like this. Can't leave it. Go back to the club then? Confront Chapman? Traffic swishes in the wet, a siren, lights flashing blue in the stripes of rain. The laugh is there behind it all, like a metallic taste. The sticky vodka-lime still on his teeth, mixing in his gut with Scotch. Go in there, face the boy with the smooth and spooky face, face the man. What can do they to him?

And maybe anyway this what they expect, that he will go there and Marta will be waiting?

Not that he wants her.

Only to know that she's safe and free.

And to know he's not a total dupe.

Not a total fucking fool.

The police then?

But that would mean admitting what a sucker he is. The police might find it funny that anyone could be such a mug. They might laugh. How can he stagger drunk into a police station with this story? Of course they would laugh.

Such a total fucking fool.

And even if he could bear the laughter, if he got involved with the police Vivienne would find out. And his folks. He groans at the thought of their *disappointment*. And Nina, Christ that doesn't even bear thinking about. He's just lost all her money. And Vivienne will want a divorce – that would almost be OK if it were not for Thomas, and Arthur. Poor Arthur who was made to eat a bowl of godawful cauliflower cheese last night, and bravely forced it down, tears standing in his eyes.

He has let everyone down. And himself. His gloved hands clench into fists. *It's not my fault!* He wants to roar it. Not home. Not the police. The Club then? Does he have the balls, to go in there, confront Chapman? If he does nothing he will not be a man. Whatever a man is. Nina's voice starts to come to him, *a real man is not afraid to be weak; a real man doesn't have to prove his masculinity.*

And Vivienne's voice: *Man up.*

What do you do? How do you win?

They can both shut the fuck up.

The laugh seems to ring in his ears, to reverberate through

his teeth as he walks and he is wired with anger, driven along by the primitive force of it. Is it the alcohol? He doesn't care. Not a civilized feeling; it's animal; it tastes of blood and musk. He's shivering, whether with fever or emotion, he doesn't know. It's unfamiliar, almost thrilling; it is another Mats. Now he can choose. He can go to the club or he can be a total weakling and go back home and forget it. He's spent his whole life trying to please, pleasing his father, pleasing Nina, pleasing Vivienne – and they are not even fucking pleased!

He shouts out a laugh of his own.

And stops, presses a his fist in its damp woollen glove against his chin, and turns, decisive now, scans the road. If anyone is watching let them watch. If anyone wants to laugh, let them.

Turning off the main street, he goes down the narrow slope, past kebab shops, off-licences, betting shops, to City Massage. But it's dark. No pink light. The place looks shut. Have they gone? Have they scammed him of his money and gone? There's a car parked, a BMW, a skulking cat, the bass boom of music from somewhere but no other person on the street. His blood picks up the rhythm and beats in his ears.

On the door someone has pasted a notice. Squinting in the poor light he reads it. A compulsory purchase order, this block is up for demolition with planning permission for twenty-nine dwellings. He peers closer, reading it over and over as if it can reveal any more information, as if it can help him.

His skin burns; his eyes are hot as embers in their sockets.

He tries the door, stumbling, heart lurching as it opens easily with its blatant jangle. The reception is dark, towels gone. He trips on a fallen chair. He flicks a light switch but the power is off. The lounge is cold and fusty smelling; he can just make out the sofas, the desk, the gleam of a Coke bottle. Weak light is coming from somewhere deeper in the building. He follows it through the bead curtain, past the stairs, to where a door stands open.

'Smith?' calls a distant voice, Chapman's, he's pretty sure and Mats stops. Each tooth in his jaw feels large and heated.

'Smith, you there?' comes the voice again, muffled, faraway, sounds as if it's coming from below.

Mats goes through into the back of the building, a room with broken furniture, a stained mattress leaning on the wall. On the floor a car lamp shines on a cardboard box – he lifts the flap; it's full of cacti, fat and spiny. On one of them a flower is coming, a waxy pointed bud of pink. There's a trapdoor open in the floor. A light is moving down below, the jump and slide of a torch beam.

'Let's get shot of her and get out of here,' comes the voice.

A foul smell floats up from this cellar, even with his blocked nose Mats catches it. He peers down into the trapdoor. The top of Chapman's hat is visible, a trilby, beaded with rain, a thin shine of torchlight on an earth floor.

Get shot of her? Get shot of her?

Marta?

He retreats to the shadow as the floor creaks and Chapman comes up the ladder, looking round. 'Smith?' Chapman climbs over the sill of the trapdoor, stands, dapper in overcoat and black trilby, brushing something off his coat with a leather-sheathed hand. His shadow cast upwards by the car lamp looms across the ceiling. 'Smith?' he calls, though his voice is less certain now.

Mats steps forward.

'Where is she?' he says.

Chapman's head whips round. 'Christ!' His hand goes to his chest.

'Where?' Mats steps closer, so much taller and bigger and

stronger and drunker, rising through drunkeness to a hard bright clarity. He doesn't know himself.

Chapman, clears his throat, smooths his beard.

'What's down there?' Mats steps towards Chapman and the man retreats, shaking his head. 'Who's down there?' Mats takes another step forward, heat in his veins, a fizzing in his fists, a fog rising up in front of his eyes; that *smell*.

'Think you can fuck with me?'

Chapman begins to speak but Mats pulls back his fist and hits him with all the force he has, all his anger fused and forged into a hard fast fist. He socks Chapman in the breastbone and the man's mouth opens, his eyes stretch wide as he topples backwards, cracks his head on the edge of the trapdoor, collapses into the folds of his coat, down into the cellar. The ceiling suddenly lights up in the lack of his shadow.

How long Mats stands there, panting and cradling his throbbing fist, he does not know. There's no noise except for the thudding of his heart and his own ragged breath. The hat lies beside his foot. Eventually he finds it within himself to move, bends to pick up the car lamp and shine it down the trapdoor. Chapman is splayed on his back, blood spreading behind his head, his mouth, his eyes, wide open with surprise.

A noise comes from Mats' mouth, one he's never made before and one that shocks him. A rough groan of satisfaction. He flashes the beam around until he finds what he has feared, another body on the floor, a human shape bundled up in something.

Marta.

He switches off the lamp and flings it down to land on Chapman's chest. With his foot he nudges the hat through the trapdoor and flips it shut.

The BMW is still parked outside; music still thumps from a

window; rain still falls. He tilts his head up to see the shine of lights behind glass in the tenement opposite. People at home on a Tuesday night, cleaning their teeth, going to their beds. Marta is dead. Little Marta. Of course he will grieve but not yet, nothing is happening inside him yet. He has killed a man. Killed a man. And the night is just the same.

Is it over then?

When he arrives back on the main road, he peels off his gloves and shoves them into a bin. Isn't that what murderers do? He's murdered a man and the world is just the same.

And now he will go home to his wife.

Marta

LAST NIGHT THERE were noises downstairs, doors banging. Dario came into the sleep room where Marta and Lily lay in the dark – electricity off – shut the door, told them to hush, not to move. He stayed in the room with them through the night, curled up on a mattress by the door.

But now it's a bright morning, Dario has gone and all is quiet. No electricity so no coffee, no shower. There are only crisps and biscuits to eat, salt and vinegar, custard creams. Lily sits stiffly at the kitchen table, like a school child waiting to be fetched. Marta finds a book, stained and dog-eared: *Love's Pursuit*, and devours it bitterly. After days of streaming rain, hot sun flows through the windows. Marta goes to sit on the rusty balcony, reading the book again, sun on her skin. With a mug of water to sip, some stale crisps to nibble, she tries to feel relaxed; she tries to tempt Lily out onto the balcony, but the girl won't budge from the kitchen where she sits, fiddling with the ends of her hair, or picking away at a scabs on the wooden table, making clean white spaces with her nails.

Next morning the rain is back. Dario comes up into the kitchen, early. 'Quick is time to go.' He's jittering from foot to foot, wearing shoes, Marta sees with a start, smart new trainers with a yellow flash. He keeps his face down, hair flopping forward, but when he moves she notices bruises, one cheek swollen, a black eye.

'What happened?' she says.

He blows a bubble and lets it pop, picks the residue from his lips and chin. 'Quick. Mr Smith, he wait.'

'Mr Smith?'

One nod.

'What about Ratman? Who hit you?'

No answer.

'Where are we going?'

'You need coat,' Dario says. But what happened to her coat? She follows him down the stairs. In the lounge stands Lily, clutching a carrier bag, ready to go. Lily's startled eyes seek Marta's, and she attempts a reassuring smile.

Dario shoves a jacket into her hands and her heart contracts, her knees soften because it's Alis' coat, not seen since they were driven up from London, shiny red plastic with a fur lining and a hood. Too big for Marta. In the pocket is a tissue stuck to an old sweet, a pill of some sort, a lidless stub of lipstick. Mr Smith opens the door. His eyes travel over the three of them. Still the dark glasses, still the hat, but he hasn't shaved; he looks rough and there's a smell of stale alcohol coming off him.

He beckons them outside.

'Bye Rosa,' Dario says, but she won't look at him. In the wet street petals from a blossom tree make a candy-pink scatter on the road. A car is waiting. The girls sit in the back though there's no front passenger.

Dario taps on the driver's window and he let it down. 'Boss say no funny business,' he says. 'Not to open door till you are there.'

The driver nods, the window rolls up. The radio is on - songs - weather - news - and heat blasts from the vents. The driver says nothing. As soon as the drive begins, Lily falls asleep, head bumping against Marta's arm. They drive through a grey, drizzly dawn. Beside the roads the trees are still bare or streaked with new green. The windscreen wipers squeak rhythmically like bed springs.

Marta looks at the back of the driver's head, his face in profile as he turns his head. He's young with dark stubble, wearing a woollen hat that someone must have knitted him. His fingers drum on the steering wheel, bitten nails. They make her think of Virgil's hands. Maybe he is nervous.

'Where are we going?' she tries.

'Can't say.'

'What's your name?'

'Connor.' But he will say no more.

Adverts on the radio, a talk show about problem pets, warnings about weather and traffic hold-ups. They are on the M1 heading south – to London, she supposes.

After a couple of hours Connor pulls into a service station. 'Need a slash,' he says. He leaves them locked in. When he gets back he throws them bags of crisps and Twix bars.

'I need the toilet,' Marta says.

'Sorry,' he says, 'no one's to get out. You'll have to cross your legs.'

'It's my period.'

He starts the engine, backs out of the parking space. Lily opens her crisps, begins crunching. The thin vinegary smell makes Marta feel sick.

'Then I will bleed on the seat,' she says.

'Oh shit.' He stops, pulls back into the space, sits motionless for a moment before he turns to look at her. 'Quick then,' he says.

He gets out, unlocks her door and lets her out. He locks the car again. Marta tries to catch Lily's eye, to smile, but she's looking down.

Connor escorts Marta to the Ladies. 'I'll wait here,' he says. 'Two minutes.'

She goes inside. All clean and empty. *1992 Service Station Convenience of the Year, Highly Commended* reads a sign. Beside the basins, pink tulips flop in a pink vase. The toilet doors are painted to match. She takes her time, thinking; there's a vending machine from which you can buy tampons, sanitary towels and condoms. She goes out again. Connor is shifting nervously from foot to foot.

'Feel like a right tit standing here,' he says.

'Sorry, but I need money for tampons,' she says, smiling into his eyes. 'I need one fifty in change.'

'Fucking hell, you don't want much do you?' But he grins – quite a sweet smile; he's younger than she thought. He puts his hand in his pocket, counts out coins – she holds her breath, hoping, hoping and her hope is rewarded. He doesn't have enough change. 'Need some fags anyway. Come on.' He leads her into the shop. She waits until his back is turned and then she runs. She runs past the parked car across a massive car park, crosses a slip road to a garage, bag bumping her leg, rain soaking, tarmac pounding up through the soles of her pumps. There's a sign indicating toilets behind the garage; she follows it, lets herself in to a tiny cubicle with wet paper all over the floor. She locks the door and waits, doubled over, panting, holding her hand against her leaping heart and then she flips down the lid, sits on it, waiting for whatever comes next.

This toilet, smelling of shit and petrol, would win no prizes.

If he comes what can he do? He can't break down the door without being stopped. He can't call the police. He's just a young guy hired to drive. He'll be in trouble with Mr Smith and Ratman, she's sorry for that but no time to think of others now. Not Lily. Not even her family; don't think of them now.

How long she's there, she doesn't know. Once her breathing returns to normal and her heart slows, she begins to shiver. The tap drips rhythmically, one, two, three and then a pause and then a trickle, one two three, pause, trickle. Graffiti everywhere, initials in hearts with arrows, something written very small in biro, she squints to read it: Jason is a lying shit.

Cold. Thank God for Alis' coat. The smell of her friend in the lining. Alis would be proud if she could see. She peels the sweet off the tissue and puts it in her mouth, getting comfort from the taste of licorice. It's as if Alis is there just for a moment in that taste.

A banging on the door; she pulls her feet up, clasps her hands round her shins, buries her head in her knees. After a while the banging stops and someone swears. Twice more, people attempt to get in and fail. And time goes by. Can't stay here forever. A banging and a rattling.

'Anyone in there?' demands a voice. 'Are you all right?'

She keeps quiet, eyes screwed shut, breath hot and moist against the fabric of her trousers.

'If you don't open up I'm calling the police, love. Are you OK? Do you need a doctor?' It's woman's voice. Sounds kind but you can't tell.

'I'm OK,' she manages.

'I need you to come out, love,' says the woman. 'I'll give you a minute, then if you don't come out like, I'll have to call someone. OK love?'

What if Connor called Ratman, or Geordie? What if *he's* there? If he is, what? He won't be, but if? but if?

He can't grab her in front of the woman.

She lowers her feet onto the wet squelch of toilet paper and flushes the toilet, as if that will make things seem more normal. She tries to turn on the tap but its fittings are loose and it only lolls and drips harder. Fingers trembling, she slides open the lock, takes a breath, clutches her satchel close to her side.

'Here she comes.'

She stands in the doorway eyes darting, scanning for Connor but there's no face she knows. Only a wide woman in a kaftan with red and grey streaked hair, and another fidgeting behind her. As soon as Marta steps out the second one darts in and slams the door.

'What's up with you, love?' the wide woman says. 'You've been in there hours.'

'I'm sick. Sorry,' Marta says.

The woman takes in Marta, the state of her. 'Are you with someone?'

'Just me.'

'Got a car parked up?'

Marta shakes her head.

'How did you get here?'

'A lift.' Marta shivers, snuggling into the thin coat.

'Well I better get back behind the till,' the woman says. 'Come in for a warm. You look perished.'

Marta follows her into the bright interior of the garage shop. There's a customer waiting to be served. Marta wanders round looking at comics, papers, racks of sweets and groceries, toys and oil, sponges and sprays of antifreeze. Beside a drinks vending machine sits a box of flapjacks and her mouth floods with saliva. One of those would be just the size of her pocket – she reaches out as the woman looks over, beaming. Marta drops her hand.

'Come and sit down.' The woman beckons her round behind the counter where there's a stool. Marta perches on it, her dirty, damp pumps dangling. 'Where you off to then?' the woman asks, noticing the state of them.

'Not sure.'

'Not sure? No car? No lift?' The woman regards her dubiously, then holds out a hand. Surprised, Marta takes it. It feels so *warm*. 'I'm Evie by the way,' the woman says.

'Marta,' Marta mumbles.

Not Rosa. *Marta*. Not Rosa ever again.

'Coffee love?'

'Please, *yes*.' Evie goes to the machine, presses buttons, asks, 'Sugar? Milk?' and Marta nods and shakes.

Evie comes back with two plastic cups of coffee and a flapjack. 'Look like you could do with it,' she says, with a curious smile. 'Get it down you.'

A customer comes in to pay for petrol and a newspaper. The coffee is weak but washes down the flapjack, sweet and crumbly, she means to save a bit for later but can't. Soon she's licking the cellophane, while Evie eyes her, amused. Is she expecting her to pay?

'I have no money, sorry,' Marta says, looking at her knees.

'Don't worry about it,' said Evie.

A queue of customers builds and Marta wanders round the shop, stopping to look at the glossy magazines. She picks one up, flicks through, so many shiny pages, so many shiny things to buy. One page is folded at the corner with a perfume sample under it. She rubs her wrist against it and sniffs; it smells of Auntie Deirdre. She puts the magazine back, and her eyes catch a photo on the front page of a newspaper. And she stares and stares. Could it be him? Evie's busy serving someone. Marta tears the front page from the paper, folds it and puts it in her bag. Her scalp feels stiff with goose pimples, yet sweaty too. She goes back to the counter and sits beside Evie.

In comes a man with two bunches of carnations from the

buckets outside. 'Someone's gonna get lucky tonight,' Evie jokes as he grabs a couple of boxes of chocolates. He shakes his head and gives a hollow laugh. 'Dangling by a thread, me,' he said, adding, 'two threads if I'm honest, like.'

Marta shivers. His way of speaking, it's like Geordie's.

'Good luck,' Evie jokes as he leaves. 'Men!' she says. 'It'd take more than cheap carnations and Ferrero Rocher to get round me!'

She opens a packet of Polo mints and offers one to Marta. 'So,' she says. 'What's your story?'

'No story,' Marta says.

Evie puts her elbow on the counter, and regards her frankly. 'We've *all* got a story, love.'

'I jumped out of somebody's car and hid,' Marta says.

Evie laughs. 'Good for you! Nasty type was he?'

Marta nods, thinking about Connor, not nasty at all. What will happen to him, for losing her? What will happen to Lily?

'You're better off without him. My ex – God you wouldn't credit it if I told you. Given up on the lot of them, me.'

'Me too,' Marta says.

Evie laughs, a white ring of Polo flashing on her tongue. 'You're a bit young to be giving up. Me, I've been round the block a few times too many.'

A woman comes in to pay for petrol, buy milk and a bag of wine gums. Evie chats to her and Marta watches, listens. How easy Evie finds it to chat, to be warm and pleasant. Marta puts her hand in the bag. She wants to read the newspaper page, look closer at the photo.

'So, what are we going to do with you?' Evie asks.

Marta looks at the payphone, searches for Mr Brunborg's card in the lining of her bag.

'If I could make a phone call?'

'Go ahead love,' she indicates the phone.

'But I have no money.'

'None at all? How come?'

'I dropped it in the car.'

Crossing her arms, Evie regards her for a long moment. 'Tell you what, you can have a go with my mobile one,' she says. 'Just got it. Have a look. Everyone's getting them. Thought I'd treat myself.' She takes a black phone from her bag. Ratman has one like it. Marta takes the card from her bag and puts it on her knee. There are two numbers, which to ring? She tries one but nothing happens, the same with the other.

'You haven't switched it on!' Evie says. 'You're as bad as me!'

Evie takes the phone from her, presses a button, waits till it bleeps and passes it over. This time there's a ringing and then a woman's voice, not friendly. 'Yes?' In the background, a baby's crying. Panicked, Marta rings off. Someone's paying for petrol and buying cigarettes, a red haired man. Marta's heart thumps, though it's not Ratman, he's big and fat, nothing like Ratman.

She tries the other number and this time a bright voice, says, 'DFI and G Enterprises; Mr Brunborg's line, how can I help you?'

Taking a deep breath, Marta says. 'Can I speak to him, please?'

'He's about to go into a meeting, I can take a message.'

'I . . .' Marta does not know what to say.

'Who is it please?'

'I . . .'

'He could ring you back before the end of the day.'

'But I must speak to him now.'

A pause.

'Who is this?'

'Tell him Marta,' she says.

Mats

CHRISTINE PUTS THE call through, raising her eyebrows and looping her finger in the air, indicating either that he should hurry or that there's a lunatic on the line. The others are already gathering in the boardroom. Surprising she put the call through at all, so desperate is she to get him into this long overdue meeting.

'Yes?' he says, though already a premonitory feeling is creeping over him.

A small, hesitant, accented voice: 'Mr Brunborg?'

As if yanked upwards by the roots of his hair he stands.

'Who is this?'

Silence, a small sigh. 'I have run away, I am in a place, I don't know . . .'

Before his knees can buckle, he sits down again, pressing his fingertips hard between his eyes. Christine's concern engulfs him; he turns his head away.

'Mr Brunborg is it?' cuts in another, older, female voice. The phone is threatening to slip from his grasp, he tightens his grip as he sags over his desk, listening. 'Poor lass was taken poorly. Can you come and fetch her? Garage at the Scotch Corner services, Junction 55. Know it? I'm only here till lunch like, best get her away before Jonno starts his shift.'

'Yes,' Mats says. 'I understand. Of course.' He lets go of the phone and sits staring at it.

What?

'Come on Mats,' Christine says. 'Are you OK? Need a Lemsip?'

Christine's phone rings and she picks it up. 'Yes, he's here. Right away.' She turns to him. 'They're all set. Coming?'

He shakes himself out of it. 'I've got to go.'

Marta alive? What did he see in the cellar then?

'But you *can't*.'

'Emergency.'

'But *Mats* . . .' Her voice is almost a wail.

He forces his mind into gear. 'Can you reschedule for later?'

'No, Fergus is—'

'Tomorrow morning then, first thing?'

'But—'

'A breakfast meeting. Apologise. I'll be in before 8.'

'But you can't keep . . .' She windmills her arms.

'*Please* Chrissie.' He sniffs, brings out a Kleenex to dab his nose.

'But what am I going to say?'

'You'll think of something.'

She stares at him. 'Ferg's been patient up to now but . . .' she tails off into a sigh. 'Anyway it's meant to be my late morning tomorrow,' she adds.

She always visits her mother on Wednesdays. Of course, she does. Part of her flexitime deal.

'But can you do it?' He lifts his lips into a smile, and steps closer, looking down at her, right into her eyes. '*Please* Chrissie,' he says, 'and look, take this afternoon off instead.'

'Fergus'll have kittens, I'm warning you.'

'Go on Chrissie.'

She flushes, runs her hand through her hair. She's lost weight lately he notices, the bones of her collarbone stand out above the neck of her silky blue top. Her throat, encircled by a fine gold chain from which dangles a golden C, is mottled with a blush.

'Och, just for you then,' she says, with her caving-in smile.

'You're a marvel.' He hooks his coat from the stand by the door. 'Don't know what I'd do without you,' he says and walks away fast, before anyone emerges from conference room.

Outside it's raining, as it's done almost all spring so far. He hails a cab home and creeps in for the car keys. He can hear the television on in the sitting room; it's the Easter holidays and Artie's watching cartoons. Vivienne's upstairs with Tom. Silently he lifts the car key from its hook and closes the door. The car's parked a few spaces along the road – she'll never notice it's gone.

꧂

It is Marta. Her small white face behind the counter jerks his heart. The old hippy woman kind and curious, openly tries to weigh him up: father or what? It's hardly an affectionate reunion, though he would like to hug Marta's small shivering body. Here she is in front of him, alive. *Alive.*

And his responsibility.

He thanks the woman and leads Marta out to the car. The sky is clearing; rain filtered by sharp sunshine lights her face strangely, making her seem to glow like a little icon, but she is live, warm, flesh and blood. What to do? What to do? Take her somewhere safe . . . but where?

She climbs into the car, clicks the seatbelt, remains silent, staring at the windscreen. For what must be several minutes they share this silence. Once she turns to him and opens her mouth as if to speak, but changes her mind.

Eventually, he starts the engine, pulls out onto the slip road. On their slowest setting the windscreen wipers squeak and jerk; she appears hypnotised by them.

'I thought you were dead,' he says at last.

Her head whips round at that. '*Me?* Why?'

He is incapable of an immediate answer, but at last says: 'How did you get here? Did he – Chapman let you go?'

'No.'

'But I paid him to let you go,' he says.

Her face clouds with disbelief, frown lines cutting deep between her eyes.

'I ran,' she says.

'When?'

'Early. They, Dario and Mr Smith, they put us in a car. Not Ratman,'

'Ratman?'

'Mr Chapman. He was not there today.'

Mats flexes his bruised knuckles on the steering wheel, says nothing. The traffic is heavy, juggernauts, coaches, vans. Water sluices up from a passing lorry, visibility is bad. He increases the wipers' speed, concentrates on driving, pulling out into the fast lane. There are blossom petals stuck to the windscreen where the wipers don't reach, like pale fingertips pressed against the glass. He coughs, cupping his hand over his mouth. A police siren sounds and he pulls back into the slow lane between two towering juggernauts, till the police car has raced past, blue light flashing on the wet glass and on her little face.

They sit in their own thoughts for a while and then she turns to him, eyes huge. 'We were going to London, I think. Or somewhere. I got out and ran. I left Lily.'

'A friend?'

She's quiet for a moment. 'Not really.'

He glances in his wing mirror and pulls out again, digesting this.

'You did not *really* give Ratman money for me?' she says, almost a smile in her voice.

Is he going to look foolish in the eyes of this girl now, after everything?

'I thought you were dead,' he says again.

'Why?'

He opens his mouth but doubts every possible word and doubts what he saw or thought he saw. What *did* he see? Doubts even his memory; what did he do?

'How much did you pay?' she asks.

If you can read this you are too close, he reads on the back of a van and eases his foot off the accelerator.

'Where's the money now?'

'I have no idea,' he says. And finds he doesn't care. The thought could almost make him laugh. Fifty thousand pounds gone like snow on the water and he doesn't care! It feels like nothing. I'm a murderer, he thinks. I have killed a man. This fact is still not real; thinking about it feels like probing a dental cavity still numb from the anaesthetic. He switches on the Radio, *You and Yours*, a cosy woman talking about the price of pet insurance.

As they approach Edinburgh he struggles to get his mind to work straight. 'Have you got anywhere to go?' he asks with little hope.

Sunlight on her skin is rippled by raindrops through glass. 'I have nowhere,' she says in a small voice. 'I want to go home.'

He nods.

'But I am illegal immigrant. I have no passport, no money for ticket.'

His nose is starting to run. He overtakes a coach, pulls out a tissue. 'I'll find out how to deal with that,' he says. 'Did, *does*, he have your passport, Mr . . . Ratman?'

She tells him in small halting bursts almost too quiet to hear above the sound of the engine, the swish of the wet road, about how she was smuggled and forced to work, how she was owned by Chapman or maybe by a man called Smith. As she speaks he glances at the swollen knuckles on his right hand and catches the hard edge of an idea: even if Marta *is* alive, Chapman deserved what he got.

'I'll get you home,' he says.

'I don't know what I will say. Why did I send no money all that time? Only one letter – it is letter you posted,' she adds. 'Thank you.'

He feels the lightness of her hand on his knee, just briefly. He flicks the indicator and they turn down a slip road to the roundabout, the City Bypass; home soon, what is he going to do?

'There will be a way,' he says, feigning confidence.

'You think?'

Such a detonation of hope in her eyes, he nods though he has no idea. 'For sure.' He dawdles to let the traffic lights go green and makes the only decision he can make. 'Till then, you'll have to come home with me.'

She sends him an uneasy glance.

He parks round the corner from home, but can't bring himself to get out yet. If only he could just close his eyes. He could, he thinks, actually sleep now. After all the whirling in his brain, there's a sudden vacuum, as if he's shocked himself senseless. He massages his fingers, almost forgetting Marta's there, stares at an old woman being pulled by two terriers on a double lead, watches their ten stiff legs turn the corner into his road. That lady lives only two doors down, though they've never spoken.

'So,' he says at last. 'This is how it'll go. I'll tell my wife you were working for a friend, as a cleaner maybe? And she didn't like you. Maybe she accused you of stealing? Threw you out, you've nowhere to go.'

'Yes?' she sounds doubtful. 'She will believe this?'

'She'll have to.'

Vivienne

click

THE DAY WAS a snotty mess but I drank *nothing*.

That's really good.

And then the door opened early, about 2 o'clock, and there was Mats.

'What are you doing home?' I said.

Tommy crowed and waved his arms from his bouncer and Mats scooped him up.

'I've catched a cold, Dad,' Arthur said, 'and I didn't even try.'

'That was *Daddy's* germs,' I said.

'I've brought someone to help,' Mats said, almost *ducking* as he spoke – I don't like surprises, he knows that. Then, get this, he brings in a tiny girl, tangled hair, filthy gym shoes, hideous plastic coat red as a stop sign.

Rosie? I thought, dumbstruck by the nerve of him, but no.

'This is Marta,' he said, pulling a face behind her, meaning, *please don't go off on one.*

'Help?' I said. 'What do you mean?'

She was looking at the floor.

'Help me build a space station?' Artie said.

The girl peeped up at Mats as if for permission, great big, dark brown eyes with starry lashes. The way she looked at him! My kind and handsome husband holding his baby. How *wonderful* he must look to her. How sweet and pliable she must look to him. How petite. How young.

But still, the *state* of her . . .

'This is Arthur,' Mats went, 'and this is Thomas.'

The girl looked up at Tommy's face, high on Mats shoulder.

'And this is my wife, Vivienne,' went Mats.

'Hi,' I said, maybe a bit shortly. I mean! He could at least have started with me.

The girl was already kneeling on the floor with Artie.

Mats took my arm and steered me out into the sitting room where the curtains were still shut from last night. Artie had been watching telly and it was still showing a noisy cartoon. He put Tommy down on the rug.

'She is homeless,' he said before I could get a word in.

'You must be fucking joking!'

There was a long pause. Mats sat down on the sofa. He clasped his fingers and bent them back till they clicked. I hate that. I watched his face, but I couldn't tell anything.

'Is this *her*?'

He looked up at me.

'The girl. When that guy came round he said something about a girl.'

He shook his head. 'Don't know what that was about.'

Hmmm.

I watched Tommy struggling to roll over.

'She can stay in the attic, can't she?' he said. 'Just for a day or two.'

'What?'

I *mean*!

'I'll sort it out,' he said, fiddling with his ear now, really bloody irritating habit, 'do the sheets and everything.'

'But *Mats?*' I was giving him an incredulous look, but he wouldn't receive it. 'Who even *is* she?'

He sighed – as if this was an unreasonable question!

Come on!

'Look, *she* needs somewhere to stay. *You* – *we* – need some help about the place. I thought it would be a good solution.'

'No, I don't need help.'

He looked meaningfully round the room, which OK was a mess.

'Is there something dodgy going on?' I said.

He gave me a level look, like shame on me for even thinking such a thing.

'Where did you find her?' I went at last.

Tommy was waving his arms and legs, eyes fixed on the cartoon, shrieking at the colours.

'God's sake.' Mats retrieved the remote from between the sofa cushions and switched off the telly; Tommy continued to stare at the screen, expectant, baffled. 'Someone at work.'

'She's not a stray cat!'

'All I know, she's had a really bad life. We can't leave her out on the streets.'

'Why not? What's she to us?'

'She's a human being who needs help,' he said. I wanted to slap him for sounding so . . . whatever the word is.

Tommy had rolled over and found a crayon to chomp on now, and I leant forward to flick the spitty yellow wax from his gums.

'There must be people to deal with people like her,' I said. 'Can't you take her to a hostel or something?'

'She'll help. Won't cost anything.'

I said nothing. He *knows* I hate people in my home. Sanctimonious, that's the word.

'OK.' He put his head in his hands for moment then looked up at me almost pleadingly. 'Just a few nights, till I sort something out? It would be so kind.' He gave me a small hopeful smile, caught my eyes with his. His look, I thought, was loving, almost like it used to be. He took my hand and squeezed.

'Where's she even from?' I said. He hadn't held my hand for such a long time. It felt nice.

'Romania.'

To be honest, I wasn't even sure where that was.

'How old is she?'

He squeezed my hand. 'I don't know,' he said. 'Just for a few days?'

He knew I'd been dreading keeping Artie busy in the shool holidays. I thought a bit before I nodded. I wasn't sure though. I'd seen the way she'd looked up him with her big dark shiny eyes.

But when she took off her jacket I saw she was wearing the crappiest of crappy clothes. She had nothing with her but a broken plastic satchel. Her feet were bare under the plimsolls, skinny mud-splashed ankles. Now sorry, but that is not what you'd expect your husband to be having an affair with. And anyway, if he *was*, why would he bring her home? Maybe she really was a stray, a refugee even? I would show him I could be kind. It was lovely, the way he'd looked at me, the way he'd held my hand.

While Mats made tea I took the girl upstairs, showed her the attic. He'd have to move things, make up the bed. I dug out some old clothes. I had a couple of stretch-velvet tracksuits - one pink, one navy, from when I used to be thinner - waiting to go to a charity shop. When I gave them to her, she stroked the material and looked about to burst into tears.

'You are a kind lady,' she said.

And I did feel kind. I handed her a towel and pointed her at the bathroom.

click

So Marta stayed for a few days, that turned into a week, that turned into a month, and I actually started to like her being around. At first I didn't. Well, it was pretty weird, wasn't it? But she was great with the kids, and had an efficient way of tidying that made it seem like nothing at all. It was like having a helpful friend, well like Rita, I suppose.

Was I using her as a stand-in? Never thought that before. No, I don't think so.

But she was someone to talk to. We had to organise childcare for when I went back to work – and hey presto! She could be the nanny! Perfect!

One nice thing about her, she was there when I wanted her, but she also knew when to keep a low profile – like evenings she left me and Mats alone, went up to the attic where she had a portable telly. She was sensitive like that.

Something's up with Mats, seems like he's been squashed or hollowed out. I keep asking him, *What's up? What's up?* But he only says it's hell at work, but you don't need a medical degree to tell he's depressed. I said to go to the doctor. He keeps having nightmares, sitting bolt upright in the middle of the night, covered in sweat. Why not go to a counsellor like I did? I said. No shame in seeking help, I said, look at me. But he won't. Just like a man. He's clammed up and taken to the bottle, drinking whisky at night, which I can't stand, so it's no danger for me having it around. I feel protective of him and it makes me love him more in a way. It's like for the first time he really *needs* me. Our sex life's back on track, well in an old married couple way, i.e. reliable but not all that often. (Suits me!)

click

This day came when we were watching afternoon TV, Marta and me. *Neighbours* had finished and Delia came on and she was making a simnel cake. Tommy was lying on the floor sucking his toes. It was nearly time to fetch Artie from school. Marta was happy to do that. I'd got her some clothes and a pair of trainers from C&A so she had decent stuff to go out in.

'Do you have this cake?' Marta said. 'Is it a UK tradition?'

'I've never had it,' I said.

'Maybe we could do it?' She sat up, smiling – her smile was pretty like a flower coming out. 'Maybe I could make a cake to say thank you?'

Delia was waxing lyrical about homemade marzipan.

'Don't bother,' I said, 'I'm not that fussed about cake.'

She looked disappointed. 'Maybe Mats likes cake?' she went.

I didn't answer, realized I didn't really know. How could I not know!

'He's more a savoury man,' I said.

Tommy began to fret and Marta picked him up. He cuddled against her, twisting a strand of her hair round his finger. I did feel a pang, I mean I am his mum, but then she was only temporary and it was giving me a rest. Soon I'd be at work anyway and it was nice to know he was happy with her. Mind you, I had to look away from the blissed out expression on his face.

The cookery programme finished and the local news came on. Headlines: two decomposed bodies found in the basement of a building in Edinburgh. I never saw such a look of shock on any-one's face. Marta went white as a . . . well whiter than any sheets in our house (they're taupe). I stared at her. Tommy had his hand tangled in her hair and she pulled it out, you could hear the rip of hairs, and he was left with them snarled round his fingers.

'What's up?' I said.

She shook her head. 'Is sad,' is all she'd say. She went out then to pick up Artie and when she came back was distracted, waiting for more news.

I put two and two together then and maybe I made nine? I don't know. I couldn't wait for Mats to get home to—

click

Is this still working? The thing's going round . . . so quick, quick before the tape's finished.

Anyway. Suspicious about this murder, why was it was such a big deal to Marta? Bodies were a young woman and a mid-dle-aged man, police treating the deaths as suspicious. Well that was obvious, I mean, two people don't just drop dead in a cellar for nothing, do they?

Not that I ever thought it was *her*. But she might know something.

Later, I was upstairs with Artie, when I got this sudden feeling, like a prickle. I went halfway down the stairs and I could hear Mats and Marta talking in the kitchen, sort of quiet and urgent. I called her upstairs and went down.

'What's going on?' I said to Mats.

He was shaking oven chips onto a baking tray. 'Crispy pancakes or fish fingers?' he said.

'What were you two on about?' I went.

But Tommy started up then and I had to go. Later I opened a bottle of wine, though it was Tuesday, and he said nothing. He poured himself a giant Scotch, sat staring at the telly with no expression through *East Enders* and a documentary about birds. When the news came on I watched him. There was no expression on his face at all. If you could iron a face, that would have been his.

'I wonder who they are,' I said.

He shrugged, emptied his glass.

I continued to stare till he turned and said, 'What?' and he seemed normal and puzzled and gorgeous. Of course it was nothing to do with Mats! What was I thinking? That he'd turned into a murderer, or she had done it? Tiny little Marta! I let it drop, decided to go upstairs and shower, get out my lovely vintage nightie, give him a treat.

click

OK. Tiny bit of tape left. A few days later Marta playing with Tommy on the floor. Dye on my roots, waiting for rinse time. When the news came on Marta's head twisted round so fast I could hear the vertebrae crack in her neck. Headline news: the Toll Cross murders. They showed a picture of the dead local businessman, nice looking little guy, arm round his wife and daughter – such a shame; and an artist's impression of the girl. Marta stood up, fists clenched—

click

Marta

MARTA LIES ON her back, fists crammed into her mouth. The pain that is the loss of Alis is too huge. It presses the air from her lungs, the air from the room.

That horrible picture, drawing of a dead face. Dead Alis. Alis dead.

What can she do?

What can she do?

Noises from the house go on beneath her. Ordinary noises.

But Vivienne, she knows something's wrong.

Cracks in the sloping ceiling, the blind with its rows of poppies stuck down, broken.

It makes her think of a room where she and Alis lay when they first met. A cover with bright flowers, were they poppies too?

She clenches her stomach like a fist. She bore the death of Tata. She must bear this.

Her teeth grind till she can taste particles of enamel.

But no tears. Alis taught her not to cry.

What should she do? Go to the police?

And Ratman dead too.

Well that one is good.

From under her pillow, she takes the torn bit of newspaper that she's studied so many times. A story about a corruption trial. Though the men were guilty the sheriff gave only a short sentence.

Then he retired. That is the story. But what gets her is the picture of the sheriff. It's not big or clear but it looks like Geordie. Exactly like Geordie.

She hears the little feet of Arthur on the stairs. In he comes and sits beside her on the bed. 'Are you OK?' he says, patting her knee. The little boy is sensitive, more sensitive than his mother knows, to the feelings in the house.

Marta sits up, smooths her expression into a smile, even her eyes. Don't make a fake smile for a child. And he really does make her smile, this earnest, little boy.

'I'm OK my darling,' she says.

'Shall we do a story and feel better?' he says.

His glasses are smeary, his hair, which never wants to lie flat, sticks up in tufts, there is orange round his mouth from spaghetti hoops.

'It would be so kind,' she says.

'Wait.' He jumps up and charges down the stairs. She leans over and peers at her face in the mirror, shuts her eyes quickly before the Alis image can replace it. She puts on a red jumper that Vivienne bought her, one that crackles when she pulls it over her head, brushes her hair, sips water. She switches on the bedside light and waits for Arthur to bring back his favourite book, *Where the Wild Things Are*, and as she reads it, she feels comforted by his warm, bony little body snuggling beside her.

'There, are you betterer now?'

She smiles, yes, a real smile that hurts. 'Much better,' she says.

'Again?' He turns eagerly back to the first page, but there's the sound of more feet on the very creaky stairs, and Vivienne comes in. She hardly ever comes up here. Marta's spine stiffens.

'Artie,' Vivienne says. 'Daddy wants you.'

Artie pulls himself away.

'Everything all right?' she sits beside Marta on the crumpled bed. 'You could do with better light in here, couldn't you?'

Marta nods. 'I'm fine,' she says. 'You want me to do something?'

Vivienne shakes her head. And then, startlingly, she takes Marta's hand. Hers feels greasy with hand cream and there's the smell of Atrixo. 'We'd like to take you on as a nanny,' she says. 'What do you think?'

Marta swallows.

'Well?' Vivienne looks at her brightly, as if she expects delight, but Marta can't pretend, she tries, she tries, but Alis is dead and despite her determination not to cry, the tears come.

Vivienne's arm comes round Marta, and they sit awkwardly on the narrow bed. 'There, there,' Vivienne says. 'Let me get you . . .' She reaches for the box of tissues on the floor. Marta plucks a handful and buries her face in them.

'Vivienne?' calls Mats. 'Vivienne?'

'Up here,' she calls.

'Everything OK?'

'Down in a minute.'

'Want me to . . .'

'I've got this.'

Marta can hear Mats' heavy feet on the stairs, hesitating before they retreat. She can hear Tom shrieking and Mats giving up, going all the way down to the kitchen. Vivienne is being kind, but the weight of her arm is a pressure. Marta pulls away, blows her nose.

'Sorry,' she says. 'Only I am homesick.' Her voice wobbles and she clears her throat.

'Poor you.' Vivienne pats her leg. 'Look, how about this? You think about it. Staying. Maybe go home for a holiday – we could give you an advance. And then come back. The boys would love it.' She clears her throat, touches Marta's arm. 'I would love it.'

'I will think,' Marta whispers.

'Shall I bring you a cup of tea?'

This is so strange. Vivienne has never brought anything to Marta up here, never been so kind, but of course it is because she wants something. She wants Marta to say yes.

'Is OK,' Marta says. She wills Vivienne to leave now, leave her alone to think, to crawl under the duvet and turn to stone.

But though Vivienne stands, she doesn't leave. 'I forgot about the blind,' she says, fingering the cord. 'We'll get you a new one. You can choose it yourself. And a lampshade. How about a shopping trip?'

Marta nods, dumbly.

'We can decorate the room up for you, any way you like.' Vivienne hesitates, clears her throat. 'By the way,' she says, 'I was wondering about those murders.' She sits down again, puts her hand on Marta's knee. 'I mean, you seemed very upset about them.'

Marta hides her face in her hair, waits till she can control her voice. 'Is just a shock,' she says. 'Makes me think, so many murders in my country, my Tata.' The tremble in her voice is real. 'And this dead girl, she looks like a friend of mine.' *Where the Wild Things Are* is on the floor. Artie might want it. She could get up to take it down to him. Get out of this.

But Vivienne is nodding thoughtfully; Marta can feel the burn of her eyes. 'Is that all?'

Marta stares at her lap. Go, she thinks, go, go.

'I didn't know about your Tata, Dad is that? Sorry.'

Go, go.

'Don't know much about Romania to be honest. That was the Ceauşescu one wasn't it?'

Marta nods, staring at Vivienne's hand with its gold wedding ring, its nails painted deep pink but scratched and chipped, the bones faintly branched under the white skin. She wills her to remove it, the weight enormous on her leg.

'Must have been awful.'

'Please,' Marta says. 'I want to go home.'

They sit in silence. Downstairs there is the sound of Artie laughing, the growl of Mats' voice.

'You don't just mean a holiday do you?'

At last Vivienne lifts her hand and Marta feels released from something. She shakes her head.

'OK.' Vivienne's voice is flat with disappointment. 'I understand. Maybe once you're home you'll reconsider?'

Marta can say nothing.

'How about we pay for your ticket, no strings, you go home and think it over?'

'But I have no passport.'

'How come?' Vivienne shifts away to look at her better. 'How did you get here then?'

'I . . .'

'You lost it?'

Marta nods, then shakes. She might as well be honest now, or honest in part, at least. She tells Vivienne how she was smuggled into the country.

'What?' Vivienne stares at her wide-eyed. 'Oh my God! Does Mats know this? Oh my God!'

'So I have no papers. I have nothing. Only what you have given me. You are kind.'

'My God! *Does* Mats know? What does Mats know?'

Marta shakes her head.

Vivienne gives a tense little laugh. 'I had no idea! This is crazy.' She gets up, walks the few paces between the top of the stairs and the bed, fiddles with the blind cord, sits down again. 'Smuggled!' She puts the tips of both thumbs in her mouth, scrapes the nail with her teeth. 'How do you mean?'

Marta twists her hair around her fingers, tugs.

'Well, we must get this sorted,' Vivienne says at last. 'I'll phone the police.'

'Please no,' says Marta quickly. 'I do not want the police . . .'

Vivienne frowns at her, eyes sharp and busy. What is she thinking? What is she guessing?

Marta shrinks in her own skin, waiting for what next.

'There must be a way to sort this out,' Vivienne says. 'Don't worry, I'll speak to Mats. We'll get you home.'

Once Vivienne has gone downstairs, Marta sits numbly, listening to downstairs: the TV, the children, the sound of Mats and Vivienne talking, quietly at first but growing louder, growing sharper, growing into a row. She reaches down and picks up the book, flicks through its pages. 'Let the wild rumpus start,' she reads. This is the bit Artie loves the best.

Mats

THE DOOR SLAMS on Vivienne. Mats stands looking at its blank face, hears a groan as she hits the bed. Alcohol has fuelled her anger all evening; but he's stayed calm and numb. He treads carefully towards Marta's stairs. It's dark up there. He goes up one step at a time, wincing at each creak. At the top he lightly taps the door and, stooping through the low door frame, puts his head inside. He can see the shape of Marta curled up under the duvet. The TV is on, but muted, an old film. A woman smiles and beckons, light flickers on the wall.

'Marta,' he whispers.

She sits up, reaches for the lamp, cheek creased, hair a dark storm round her face.

'We have to go,' Mats whispers. He picks up the TV remote and switches off.

'Now?'

'Now.'

'I heard you fighting,' she says. 'It is my fault?'

'Come on.'

She rubs her eyes, pushes back her hair. 'Your wife is throwing me out?'

'Bring your things.'

He creaks back down the stairs. The bedroom door is still closed. He uses the bathroom, splashes his face, rinses his mouth, the Listerine reacting so aggressively with the taste of Scotch it makes him retch. He listens at the boys' doors, silence from both, thank God. Did they hear Vivienne shouting?

Downstairs he puts on his coat, waits in the hall, keys in hand. Marta follows a few moments later, a fat carrier bag in her hand. He hands her her red jacket and watches as she pushes her bare feet into a pair of trainers, tiny like kids' shoes. He remembers Vivienne and Marta coming back from their shopping trip, the girl so thrilled with the pink and white plastic shoes, taking them out of their box as if they were treasure as Vivienne glowed with beneficence.

He opens the front door and she steps out first. It's a cold, clear night; the air smells fresh and raw. In silence they walk down the road and get into the car. Before they speak he starts the engine. As they pass the house, he peers up to see the corner of the bedroom curtain lift, the silhouette of Vivienne's head. She will think, oh Jesus knows; let her think what she will think. Later he will sort it out. He drives for only five minutes, finds a space and parks.

'So,' he begins, but it takes him a moment to continue. Magnolia blossoms reach over a garden wall towards them like cupped hands, glowing waxy white.

'So?' she says.

'I'm taking you to the police.'

'No!' She begins to scrabble with the door; he leans across and catches her hand. He presses her back into the seat. She shrinks away from him, eyes huge in a shaft of street light, gives a little moan of fear.

'Marta!' He's shocked. Surely she isn't afraid of him? 'Will you listen?'

She contracts further down into the seat; the plastic jacket shines as if it's wet. He can't see her face, only the massy hair. He can smell apples from the shampoo Vivienne uses on the boys.

'British police are not like Romanian police. They will help.' As he speaks he cringes at the sound of himself.

'But—'

'Shhh. I'm going to take you near the police station and leave you there. You walk in and say you were held prisoner by Mr Chapman and you ran away.'

'But my family!' Her voice is shrill with panic. 'If I go to the police they'll be in danger.'

'Trust me, Marta, they'll be OK. Do you believe me?'

No answer.

'Do you know the name of the man in Romania?'

A tiny nod.

'Of course, it may not be his real name,' Mats says, 'but it might help. You must tell the police everything. About everyone who is involved. Nobody will hurt you or your family. I promise,' he adds.

She peeks sideways at him; he hears the scrabble of her teeth on her fingernails. 'How you, how do you know?'

They sit in silence. A couple lurch by, arm in arm, she's laughing up into his face, a bright bag swinging at her hip. Of course, he doesn't know for sure, but at least Chapman is no longer a danger.

'Think of the other girls,' he says, and is startled by a thin animal whimper. He puts out a hand to comfort her, but she recoils from it. 'Be brave,' he says.

She might nod, give a tiny sound of assent, he can't be sure, but he starts the engine again and begins the drive into town. He parks a five-minute walk from the Police Station.

'I do not like police,' she says. 'I am an illegal immigrant.'

'Ask for a female officer,' he says, wondering if it's naïve of him, after all he knows of women, to think this might mean more sympathy, a gentler handling.

'You've done nothing wrong,' he says. 'Remember that.'

She puts her hand into her bag and brings out a piece of newspaper. She unfolds it and hands it to him. He has to click the interior light on to see. *Sheriff Resigns after Judicial Leniency Questioned* reads the headline.

'What?' he says.

'This man.' She points at a photo. 'This man, I think he is a bad man who knows . . .' She stops and he can hear the gritting of her teeth. 'I think he knew Ratman. I think he is the man who hurt me. Maybe he hurt my friend. Maybe even he killed her. I think so.'

Mats peers harder at the photo: an elderly bearded man in a suit. He looks harmless, but who ever can tell?

'Are you sure?'

She shakes her head. 'But I think it. Shall I show them this?' She takes back the tatty scrap, folds it carefully and puts it in her pocket.

'I don't know,' he says. 'Marta, I really don't know.'

He listens to her breath, shallow and fast. 'I'm scared,' she says. He turns away from her, tightens his hands round the steering wheel to prevent himself from taking her in his arms.

'Be brave,' he says, 'for other girls. For your little sister,' he adds, feeling a tug of unworthiness. He senses her stiffen. She was only telling them about her sister the other day; a girl who can sing and dance, turn one-handed cartwheels.

'OK,' she whispers.

'Yes?'

'Yes.'

'Good girl.' So condescending, some women would slap him,

yet she flicks him a quick look, pleased, fearful. 'Marta,' he says. 'I have no right to ask this, but I'd be so,' he swallows hard, 'so incredibly grateful if you didn't mention me.'

She shakes her head. Does that mean yes or no?

'It's just with the kids and—'

'Of course I will not mention you.' Her voice has firmed up. 'You are *sure* my family will be safe?' she says. 'You promise?'

'As sure as I can be. Safer if they catch the man that brought you here, don't you think?'

She regards him with her head on one side. 'OK,' she decides. She unclicks her seatbelt and reaches to the door.

'Straight up the main road.' He points towards the building.

She gets out and slams the door. He watches her walk along, a tiny figure with a bulky carrier bag, hair like choppy waves. There she goes. Of course, she might reveal his name. And if so, it will all unravel, the messy tangle his life's become; it will unravel and he'll lose everything. Maybe go down for murder.

He watches her small figure approach the police station, watches her swallowed by the light.

Marta

Marta pushes open the door. The light is flat and white and there's a sour smell of old coffee and smoke.

'Can I help you, love?' A policewoman speaks from behind a desk.

There's a biro mark on her cheek and smudges of mascara under both eyes. When she smiles her face crinkles tiredly.

Marta swallows, looks over her shoulder at the door. Could she still run?

'What can I do for you?' The policewoman tilts her head. 'Are you OK, love. You look a bit—'

Marta forces a breath in. 'I am illegal immigrant,' she says, too loudly. 'An illegal immigrant and I have been forced to be prostitute and I know the girl who is dead.'

'Whoa!' The policewoman's mouth has fallen open but she gathers herself quickly. 'OK,' she says. 'You'll need to see the duty officer. She pushes a list of names and a pen towards Marta. 'Put your name here and I'll take you through.'

With a sweaty hand, Marta signs her name, her own full name, with a pen tied to a string, a pen that has nearly run out and writes in blots.

'This way.' The woman leads her into a small room with red plastic chairs. 'You sit your wee self down.'

Obediently, Marta sits. The chair is sticky; she moves to

another. On the walls are posters about drugs and numbers to ring for help. The grey floor tiles are swirled like marble but are not marble; some of them are broken with dirt seamed in-between. Marta bites her thumb till it hurts.

The room has a window down one side looking out onto a corridor with doors. A couple of policemen walk past, hats under their arms; they glance in without interest.

One of the doors opens and man steps out, no uniform, a man she . . . She snatches her thumb from her mouth as their eyes meet and electricity shoots through her. Her heart is sudden thunder.

It's Mr Smith. Is it?

He closes his door. The policewoman puts her head in. 'Sorry for the wait,' she says. ' Shouldn't be long. Cup of tea?'

Marta shakes her head. Through the glass she watches the man's door open again. He steps out, walks along the corridor and comes into the room behind her. Marta stands, chair scraping the floor.

'What have we here?' he says. 'I'll see to this Tina.'

'But I was going to get Steve—'

'No problem. Come with me Miss . . .' Mr Smith beckons and Marta stands. He leads her back along the corridor to his office. On the door it says CHIEF INSPECTOR MALCOLM ROLLINSON. As he ushers her into his room, she hears him say, 'Don't worry, I know this poor unfortunate lassie, she's a bit . . .' and maybe he mouths something or makes a gesture. Marta can't see.

He shuts the door, asks her to sit. Drawing up a chair, he settles in front of the desk, so close to her that their knees are almost touching. Big solid knees under thick navy-blue cloth. His hands are rough and bony; his wedding band shines.

'Mr Smith,' she mutters.

'Sorry?' He cups his hand against his ear as if he hasn't heard.

233

'Mr Smith,' she says again.

'Ha!' He sounds amused. 'Mr *Smith?*'

She looks up into his face. His mouth is like a pencil line drawn on wood. His chin is square. His eyes are narrow and the colour of mud. On his nose are shiny red dents where glasses have been. Now she's staring right at him she isn't so sure.

'So what's the problem?' he says. 'What brings you here?'

Her mouth opens dryly.

'Go on,' he says. 'Haven't got all night.'

Is it him? He always wore a hat and shades before. His chin is the same, his mouth. She never heard his voice.

Watching his face, she speaks slowly, telling him everything, finding her English slipping under his scrutiny. She doesn't mention Mats. And she doesn't mention the man called Mr Smith. And she doesn't cry when she talks about Alis. As he listens his expression betrays nothing. She brings out the newspaper scrap with the picture of the sheriff to show him. By the time she's finished the cuticle on her thumb is bleeding where she's been picking and picking.

He goes to the window and stands with his back to her. Stares out at she can't see what for a long time. Then he pulls a string to close the blinds and turns. 'I expect you'd like a cup of tea after all that?'

Her mouth is so dry now, that yes, she does need a drink.

He leaves the room to give the order she supposes, and returns to sit behind his desk, steepling his hands under his chin and gazing at her in a way that makes her sweat. The mouth is surely the same? The chin? The more she looks, the more uncertain she becomes.

The policewoman brings in a tray with two red mugs. The tea is grey. 'Sugar?' she asks Marta. Marta nods and watches her spoon one in, three please, she wants to say, but doesn't.

'Sure you don't want me to call Steve, er DC Brennan?' the policewoman says. She seems surprised that the man's prepared to talk to Marta himself.

'I've got this.' Mr Smith or Chief Inspector Rollinson gives her a look that combines exasperation and amusement, a look that drops away as soon as she's gone.

'Drink your tea,' he says. He's silent for several moments before he clears his throat. 'Now listen,' he says. 'This can go in one of two ways.' He picks up his own mug, looks at it, puts it down.

Marta's hand shakes so that tea slops onto her jeans. When she sips it tastes of sweet metal. She puts it down and waits.

He clears his throat. 'Option one: you make a formal statement, recording all that you've told me. I must warn you, this might put you in danger. If you repeat these allegations – which sound like hysterical tosh to me – we'll be obliged to investigate. You realize that you're accusing a sheriff of – ha! – almost everything in the book including *murder*.' He gives a mirthless laugh and shakes his head. 'That, my dear, is enormous and enormously dangerous. To you personally.' He's not even looking at her as he speaks, but at somewhere beyond her shoulder. 'Let me see that.' He holds out his hand for the newspaper clipping, takes it, has a closer look, snorts, screws it into a ball and tosses it into a bin.

'Apart from all that,' he continues after a moment's thought, 'the trial could take months, even years. You'd be called upon to give evidence in court. If the court finds against you, you'll be in for some serious grief and debt. And of course,' he adds, 'we haven't even addressed the question of your illegal citizenship.'

Marta's heart thuds coldly between his words.

'Or the second option.' Now he does look at her. 'You forget this whole silly nonsense and I can have you home in a few days.'

'Home?' she says, though the word comes out silently.

He nods.

'I apologise for the tea.' He gives a sudden smile, thin brown lips stretched tight. 'Institutional gnats' piss.' He stands and comes round his desk, leans himself back against it, legs stretched out and crossed. He's too close to her, the thick trouser material too near her face. 'So, which is it to be?'

She thinks of Mats, of his trust in the British police, and a laugh the size, the colour, the bitterness, of a lemon grows in her chest and lodges there, unlaughed.

Chief Inspector Rollinson or Mr Smith folds his arms, gazes down at her with murky eyes.

'How about a night in a cell to make up your mind?'

She thinks of Alis. She thinks of the other girls she could maybe save. Be brave, Mats said. But *he's* not brave.

And she's so tired. And the longing inside her is far too strong.

'Home,' she says and she hears him breathe out long and slow.

17 Arcola St, London E8 6FE
June 28th '92

Hi Rita,

Thanks for your card. Toronto looks <u>amazing</u>, will definitely come and visit. How's it going with Eddie? Hope it works out. Would ring but Mats has gone weird about money, can't wait to be earning my own again.

Anyway, big news!!! Notice the address? We've moved to London (your card just got forwarded, sorry for delay in replying.) You're not the only one who can suddenly up sticks! It's only a rented flat till we find something more permanent. Love being down south again, more at home with the voices and everything and hope to track down some old mates. Plus it's warmer!!!

After you left we had a <u>really</u> weird time. You will <u>not</u> believe it but Mats suddenly waltzed in with a Romanian girl, an illegal immigrant, just like she ws a stray cat.

I wish you were here because I want to ask you this. Do you think Mats would ever go to a prostitute? Nobody said she <u>was</u> one, they said she was a cleaner, but I'm not stupid. I saw a Panorama about sex trafficking. There's been loads of it from Eastern Europe since communism went tits up. Mats watched it too and he never moved a muscle just sat there with his whisky in his hand and a kind of weird glare on his face.

Oh and another thing, don't know if you get British news

there? We had some murders in Tollcross about the same time: a girl and man. So <u>close</u>. To think a murderer was walking about so close to me, the kids. We might have passed him in the street. Makes you shiver to think it.

Having Marta – that's her name – around was OK, actually quite nice, like having a teenage daughter, but it still felt odd. Then one night Mats and me had a massive row. See, if Marta had been trafficked I thought he . . . But can you imagine <u>Mats</u> with a sex slave????!!!!! We had such a humongous row, I actually thought it was over between us. He went off with her, but then he came back. He'd taken her to the police. I don't know where she is now. Romania or what. Don't dare ask.

I actually miss her. I thought she might send a card or something. But no. And Artie is pining for her. And for you.

Anyway, straight after that Mats comes home and says his job has moved to London. Just like that. So we pack a few things and leave. All the rest of our stuff's in storage till we have our own place.

I'm applying for jobs, can't wait to get back to normal life.

Must go, trying to sort out Artie's new school.

Write soon, a longer letter this time!

Love Viv xxxx

P.S. Meant to say before you went, I hope you'll be happy.

P.P.S. Also thank you for . . . well helping out and everything. I know I was a bit of a pain for a while there. xxxx

P.P.P.S. Maybe <u>any</u> man would secretly like a sex slave? What about your Eddie?

P.P.P.S But <u>Mats?</u> No. Don't believe it.

17 Arcola St, London E8 6FE
July 20th '92

Dear Rita,

Thanks for your letter. Wow and congratulations! Were you trying or was it a slip up? So quick! But I guess the clock was ticking. Wish you were here so we could do baby stuff together. I'm putting off job hunting till September now. Started Legs, Bums and Tums to get in shape for it.

All fine here. I found a school for Artie. Tommy's running around like mad now and says car and juice. Mats is a bit down though, the doctor's put him on pills. He's not like his old self and every time you look at him he's got a new grey hair. But he's OK really.

We went to Oslo for a long weekend. The Brunsborgs spoiled the kids rotten and were nice enough to me. At least they'd taken down the picture of Mats and his ex, replaced it with one of Tommy. At one point Mats' mum beckoned me into the kitchen and asked if Mats was OK. I said he was fine, just a bit stressed out by work and the move and everything. I mean that _is_ all it is, I think.

Oh but get this, on the Sunday morning Nina (Mats ex) comes over with her new husband, Lars, who is <u>gorgeous</u> like a movie star (and actually is an Olympic ski champion) for drinks. Not very awkward! So anyway, we're having a drink and then Nina suddenly announces she's pregnant.

So we all toast Nina and Lars and then they go off but the mood has changed. I got the feeling that Mats' mum would rather he was still with Nina and it was his baby she was expecting. Mats said I was being paranoid and got all moody and drank too much. You could see his parents were worried. But what can I do?

So anyway, write again soon. When's your first scan?

As soon as I get a job I'll be saving up to come and visit, just me!

Loads of love Viv xxxxx

P.S Mats says congratulations.

P.P.S. Forget what I said about Mats and sex slaves.

Vxxxx

PART 3

JULY 2005

Mats

THE SEAT BELT sign pings off and the Captain announces the altitude, the estimated flight time, the weather at their destination. Mats watches his son remain oblivious, gazing out at the shining clouds, head nodding along to music on his new iPod. At least *that* pleased him, the surprise gift. Nice still to be able to please the boy, to elicit a grin, when usually he's so slouched and monosyllabic these days.

Soon lunch is delivered on its plastic trays. An icy slice of quiche, a perfunctory salad, a roll of bread with butter, a plastic posy of cutlery, serviette, wet wipe.

'Drink?' the stewardess offers.

'Scotch,' says Mats.

'Beer?' Tom says hopefully, one earphone dangling.

'And a Coke.' Mats grimaces at the woman who is smiling at his handsome son.

'Coke it is,' she says. 'Ice?'

Tom plugs himself back in, but Mats nudges him. 'Speak to me.'

'What?' long-sufferingly, Tom removes the earphones.

'Can we have a conversation? Just while we eat.'

'What about?'

'Well . . .' Mats unscrews the bottle, pours the whisky into his plastic cup and glugs. Good. But gone. 'How about school? Got your books with you?'

'Dad, that's crap.' Tom pulls a face, snaps open his mini Coke.

Mats cuts the quiche and spears a tomato. The plastic prongs prick his tongue and his teeth ache with the sudden chill of the food.

'Well, tell me something else then. What were you listening to?'

'Snow Patrol.'

'Good? Perhaps I'll have a listen?'

Tom grunts.

'What kind of music is it? House? Indie? Hippity-Hop?'

Tom gives him a withering look.

'Heard from Artie lately?'

'Not since he went back to Uni. Why?'

'Just wondered if you'd been . . . *talking*.'

'You mean crying on each others' shoulders?' Tom rips his bread roll with his teeth and crams it in his mouth.

Mats picks at a limp flap of cucumber. 'You'll get used to it,' he says at last. 'Lots of your friends' parents are divorced, aren't they? I know Sam's are.'

'That makes it all right then,' Tom says.

Mats can't make up his mind whether Tom's really as hurt as he's making out, or if it's an act. It's a great way to get things, that's for sure. The iPod for a start. And this holiday, though he didn't jump at it. It took a bit of persuasion to get him away from his PlayStation, where he's deeply involved with something called *Final Fantasy*. Mats tries to take an interest in this virtual world, but his interest isn't welcome any more. He used to take the boys to football, cricket, fishing, everything Vivienne liked to call 'boys' stuff'; the three of them every weekend on some sort of outing, until first Artie peeled away into his own interests, and now Tom.

It's just a phase, he knows it is, and Tom's a great kid, everyone says so. He'll come through the other side in a year or two, come back to himself. They've always had a special bond, secret in Mats' case, he couldn't admit to Vivienne or Artie that he loved Tom more than anyone, more than his own life, and *liked* him too. In his effort not to let there be any favouritism he might sometimes even have erred in Artie's favour.

He shifts to ease his back that always aches when he's stuck in one position for too long.

Of course Tom's disappointed that this holiday isn't to any of the places he requested, but to Romania. *Romania? What the hell?* But he can't be allowed his own way every time. Like a ball thrown regularly against a wall, Mats' heart thuds when he thinks of the reason for the trip. Methodically he chomps through the rest of the food, a square of sweet mush, some kind of 'gateau', and then he screws up his serviette and turns back to his son.

'Tom,' he says.

'Mmm?' The boy is restlessly jiggling his long legs. He's as tall as Mats, 6'2" already, though he's only 14.

Mats puts a hand on his son's thin knee. 'Try and sit still,' he says. 'I maybe should have told you this before. The town we're going tonight, we're going there so I can catch up with someone.'

Tom stops mid-chew and raises an eyebrow. He looks so much like Mats' father that it takes Mats aback sometimes. He resembles Mats too, of course, so everyone says, but that particular sceptical mannerism is pure Far.

'I didn't know you knew anyone in Romania.' Tom's interest is caught. 'Who?'

'Someone you've already met, actually.' Mats cranes his neck to look down the aisle, calculating how long before the drinks trolley comes back.

'Someone I know?'

'You won't remember her.'

'A woman?' Tom snorts. 'I get it.'

Mats finds he's pulling his ear, knits his knuckles together in an effort to stop it. 'It's nothing like that.'

'Who then?'

'She stayed with us for a while when you were a baby, a sort of *au pair.*'

Raising his eyebrows, Tom runs his finger round the plastic space where the dessert was, licks his finger.

'So you kept in touch?'

'Well no, actually. But I found her on the internet. I remembered the town she comes from and her surname of course. Turns out she's working at a college. So I . . . The internet's wonderful, isn't it?'

'Same as Mum,' Tom said.

Mats sighs. Back to this. The separation was precipitated by Vivienne contacting an old flame on Friend's Reunited. The plan had been to stick with the marriage till Tom was at university, but Vivienne had fallen in love. 'Proper love,' she'd said meaningfully, narrowing her eyes.

'No, not like that,' Mats says.

'Tit for tat?'

'Nothing like that. This is purely, this is just . . . some loose ends I need to tie up.'

Tom crushes his Coke can between his hands. 'That's cool, Dad. Mind if I read now?'

He produces a battered *Animal Farm.*

Revision. Good.

Mats fishes a copy of the in-flight magazine from the seat pocket in front, flicks though its glossy pages, registering nothing. When they return to London in five days, the house will be empty. Vivienne's moving in with her new man – Brian – in Chelmsford.

Tom will stay with Mats during the week and with her at week-ends, though he's already rebelling against this idea. How's he supposed to see his mates? What about football? Mats wonders what Vivienne will leave behind and what she'll take. What the hell does it matter? At last the trolley rattles back past, he orders a couple of Scotches, knocks them back and shuts his eyes.

Tom

DAD'S IN THE bathroom – the door's like cardboard –
can hear every detail of his piss, fart, shower, shave, teeth
brushing, spitting, nose blowing.

'Rise and shine,' he says when he's ready. 'Shall we go and see
what's for breakfast?'

'See you down there,' I say.

'It's straight down the stairs, ask at reception if you can't—'

'I'll find it,' I say.

What am I, ten?

He snorts and nods and faffs about looking for his wallet and
cleaning his glasses and finally leaves the room. When he suggested a holiday, just the two of us, I thought he meant somewhere
cool like New York maybe or Greece or Italy. Or Oslo, even,
where I know my way about. We could have gone there, hooked
up with Else, who's so cool and an actual approachable human –
even though she's a girl. She's Dad's ex-wife's daughter, also his
god-daughter – but she's more like a cousin or something. We
even look alike. We are *sympatico*.

But *Romania?!*

So I get dressed and go down to survey the 'brekfast bufet':
yogurt, a bucket of soggy cereal, hard-boiled eggs and gherkins.
Gherkins! Also some tiny cold croissanty things wrapped in
cellophane.

Dad's got his cheerful face on, his holiday face, but it doesn't fool me. His eyes are kind of bleak and yearning. Can't bear to look at them when they're like that. 'What would you like to do today?' he says.

'What is there?' I tear open one of the croissants with my teeth. Nice, chewy and sweet but minuscule. I could eat about thirty.

Dad's got a leaflet in his hand. 'Plenty of things,' he says, 'Museum, park . . .' He's running out pretty fast. 'There's a river walk, see here's a map, the red dots . . .' He waves the leaflet at me. 'That takes you all round town. Let's start with that shall we?'

This town isn't set up for tourists and though no one likes to think of themselves as a tourist, it's nice if there are *some* touristy things to do, isn't it? But this seems to be a place where people either work or beg, not somewhere you'd buy rock with its name down the middle or send a postcard from – if they even bother to *have* postcards.

I go over to the buffet to grab more croissants. I think that's the point of a buffet? But the waiter looks at me as if I'm a thief. He's got ratty hair and teeth like a criminal. If I had a hotel I'd never hire someone who looks like they'd slit your throat for taking a handful of pastries from a so-called 'bufet'.

'Tomorrow Bucharest.' Dad gestures for more coffee. The waiter comes with a brown pot and a murderous look.

'So you're meeting this *au pair* for lunch?' I say after he's gone.

'You too if you like.' Dad sips and shudders. 'Tell you what, I saw a Starbucks type place in the town square. Let's start there, shall we?'

Apart from American Pie, where I have a Mocha and a giant choc-chip cookie, it's a lame morning. We walk round battered, run-down streets while Dad reads out the names of pointless churches and other buildings and tries to make them sound interesting. But there are some actual bullet holes in a door – that *is* actually interesting. Dad reads to me from his pamphlet about the Revolution, which happened only a couple of years before I was born.

Where does history start? How long ago does something have to be before you call it history?

It starts to rain and we duck into the museum to shelter, and there, pinned up on boards and in glass cases, is the story of the Revolution. Mostly in Romanian with only a few bits translated into dodgy English. Once we leave the museum, I start noticing more bullet holes in walls, and pot holes in the road, made by actual bombs, maybe. Weird to be walking on roads where people were shot and blood ran between the cobbles. Weird and sad and I have to admit, pretty fucking cool.

Then it's time for the lunch date. We sit on a pair of sofas in the bar to wait. Dad's nervous as hell, breathing on his glasses to clean them, cracking his knuckles and cleaning his glasses again. I have a Coke and a burger and chips, but he wants to wait and eat with her. More polite, he reckons, but manners are the last thing on my mind. Dad sits there while I eat, tugging at his ear till it goes all pink and stretchy.

It starts to look like he's been stood up, which is actually a painful thought. But then he half stands, hand on his bad back, mouth hanging open. And he's looking at this small, ordinary woman with long hair tied back in a bun. Surely, it can't be her? But she clocks us and comes across. Dad introduces us and she smiles at me; surprised and sort of warm and pleased, and says she remembers me as a baby. There's a gap at one side of her mouth you can only see when she smiles. Close to she isn't all that old, just stressed out looking. Don't they have dentists in Romania? She's quite attractive in a way. Her eyes are twinkly anyway.

We all sit down – but the expression on Dad's face. I can't stand it; it's like he's seen an angel. But the feeling isn't reciprocated. She doesn't even smile at him. It's excruciating. I have to get out of there.

I find my way back to the museum and look though some old photos stashed in a loose-leaf file with newspaper cuttings too, enough from English and American papers to give me some kind of gist. Also photos of fighters, militia, the *Securitate*; of weeping women; of ordinary men and boys with terrified faces. Or blank faces. And pictures of shapes on the ground, dead bodies. And there's a screen that plays a video clip where you can actually watch Ceauşescu and his wife being shot on Christmas day 1989.

I can't stop watching.

Imagine if there was actually a revolution on your own street, and your own house where you are supposed to feel safe was being shot at, your windows smashed, your dad maybe, or your own brother, dragged out and shot in the street. Or you. It's awful and it's fucking brilliant. Not my family being shot, of course, but feeling it, imagining it, as if it's real. Well it *is* real. It's history now but it *was real* then and in this shit-hole of a town you can nearly still smell it. I'm glad Dad made me come here. If you only go to bright shiny places and visitor centres you don't get that smell of the past like this, it's all tidied up and made into visual displays and computerized reconstructions. It has no smell.

I always thought history was pointless. Artie does it at St Andrews and we've argued about it loads. The past is the past, get over it, I thought. But now I can see the point. Maybe I'll do history at uni instead of English. Though Artie'll crow his head off.

Last time I saw him was Easter, he'd come home to revise and get his Easter eggs. Mum cooked our favourite family dinner, roast chicken and trifle, and afterwards they sat us down to tell us they were getting divorced.

'It's nobody's fault,' Dad said. He reached out and held Mum's hand. They were sitting side by side on the sofa, which they never usually do. I never noticed them holding hands before either.

'That's cool,' Artie said, but his face had gone a pukish colour.

'Why?' I said.

'Mum's met someone else,' Dad said.

She snatched her hand away. 'That's a symptom, not the cause,' she said, 'as you well know.'

She's gone blonde and lost weight, looks younger – so wrong in a mother. Her eyes were skidding about everywhere and Dad just had this awful resigned, hang-dog look.

'There's no hard feelings,' he said with a dreadful smile. 'These things happen. We both love both of you just the same.'

Artie said nothing but stomped upstairs to pack. He was going back to uni next day.

And now here we are in Romania and Dad's lunching with an *au pair* and talking about history – excuse me but there's obviously some sort of history between them. And back at home Mum's packing up and moving out.

I watch the Ceauşescus falling to the ground over and over and over on a grainy loop.

Marta

MARTA STOPS OUTSIDE the Bucaresti. Still the smartest hotel in town, though shabbier surely that it used to be? Or maybe she's less easily impressed? A place to drink, to meet friends – but she hasn't been in since . . .

Now, watching a woman go up the steps to the hotel, she remembers herself in a tight, blue, borrowed dress, remembers being swallowed by those revolving doors – and feels giddy, as if she might be revolved back through the years to the naïve and credulous girl she was.

She gets a sudden flash of Pavel's thighs on the sofa beside her, sausages in tight grey skins. A taste in her throat of plum brandy and vanilla cake. Pavel Antonescu. He got his punishment. After she was taken, he was shot dead. Ant told her this when she returned, told her with a sharp, proud grin on his face. Maybe he didn't pull the trigger, maybe he did; she doesn't want to know. But he was responsible, that's for sure. Maybe it's terrible, but she feels a little puff of pleasure, to know that her big brother, that Antoni, did this for her. How can she be sorry that that man is dead?

According to her watch she's ten minutes late. Why do this? Why not walk away? He won't know if she got his message; he's probably only half expecting her anyway. He might not be there at all. All this tension is causing her to sweat. There's less than an hour for lunch, then back to work, teaching a class of trainee call centre workers, her least favourite session of the week. They resent being taught by a woman, particularly a local woman, younger than some of them. English idioms, styles of phone conversation, pronunciation. There's a script they have to stick to, not her fault, privately she agrees that it's stupid, but it's Marta they blame.

She takes a breath. Oh. What is there to lose? Pushing through the doors, she waits for the swirl of years, but there's nothing. It's smaller, less overwhelming than she remembers. It's just a place. The walls are still mirrored, but now the floor is bare boards – she blinks, remembering the sinking of her feet on soft carpet – and there are mismatched sofas and tables. The lighting is too harsh and bright, draining the faces of the staff and customers, and the air smells of frying, smoke, beer. Her eyes skim the tables; he's not here, relief and disappointment, she will turn and walk straight out.

But then she sees black hair, Mats' profile – but it is a boy! So like . . . and then she sees the grey haired man beside him. Their eyes meet, he half rises. Thickened, a bit stooped, wearing square silver-framed glasses; but yes, it is Mats. His hair's still thick, but shorter. It occurs to her that she could still leave. Why put herself through this? Why *should* she want to see him? Crazy Norwegian guy. Once he brought her a gift – a box of pastels – she remembers how that almost killed her. To be given a gift as if she was a person who might have the time, the talent, the inclination to use them, as if she was a *person*.

She walks towards the table. 'Marta.' He envelops both her hands in his, a big man, with a belly now. Of course, he must be – she has no idea, but maybe fifty, fifty-five? He has not aged well.

'This is Tom,' he says.

Tom stands too, shakes her hand. He might as well be a clone of his father but so much younger, a beautiful, gangly, shy boy. The way he pushes back his hair; it is Mats.

'I remember you as a baby,' she says.

'You were our *au pair?*' Tom says. 'Dad said. When Mum was ill?'

She nods. What a devastatingly charming boy. Her eyes search his face for the baby she knew – and did love.

'OK,' he says. 'I'm going for a walk. Back in an hour, Dad.'

'Make sure you are.'

'Nice to meet you, Marta.' A flicker of smile and he has gone, threading lankily between the tables. They both watch until the doors have revolved him away.

'Sit, please,' Mats says, sinking back into his own chair.

She does sit. Her legs feel weak. The place is noisy, a waiter passes with plates balanced all down his arm.

'What will you have?'

'A Coke.'

'Nothing to eat? Sandwich? Cake?'

She shakes her head. 'I don't have much time.'

Mats beckons a waiter and orders coffee, a cheese and ham sandwich, a Coke. 'Sure you won't have anything?' he says and she shakes her head. Her eyes rest on the paunchy belly between the wings of his jacket.

'So,' she says, once he's sitting. 'What do you want?'

'To see you again,' he says. 'See what became of you, if you like.'

'What became of me,' she echoes.

'Tie up a few loose ends,' he adds, tugging at his earlobe, a gesture she dimly recalls. He waits, looking at her over the rim of his glasses, almost shyly.

'Well, this is it,' she says, voice light and brittle, sweeping a hand to indicate her entirety.

He nods, clears his throat. 'You teach, I understand?'

'English.'

'Of course, your English was always excellent. Married?'

'No.'

'Children?'

The waiter delivers their order, the bill in a smart little folder, embossed with gold, like a holy book. The Coke is in a towering glass with ice, a slice of lemon.

'Tom is very . . .' She almost says handsome but changes it to '. . . tall. How's Artie?'

'He's at University – just finishing his first year. History. Doing well.'

'Clever boy, I knew it.'

He stirs sugar into his coffee. The sandwich is huge and served with crisps. Her fingers itch to take one, but that might seem too familiar, might seem some kind of encouragement. But to what? What does he want? He takes a bite of the vast, dry looking sandwich and chews for ages; she can hear a clicking in his jaw.

When she lifts her glass the ice clunks against the sides. No need for lemon in Coke, she thinks, watching a pip spiral through the rising bubbles. With a teaspoon she flips the lemon out of the glass.

Behind Mats' head she sees a woman take a dress from a flashy carrier bag to show her friend, or maybe her mother, a vicious lime green thing, strappy and frothed with lace. Horrible. The woman arranges it on a chair, tweaking the skirt straight.

An awkward silence stretches before he says, 'Tell me about you.'

'What?'

'I don't know. Where do you live?'

'I have a flat, above ironmongers. *The* ironmongers. I live alone. It is fine.'

Her stomach growls. She should have said yes to a sandwich.

He asks about her work and she describes the various aspects of her job, the big workers' classes in the evenings, the private tuition. He asks about her homecoming, and she braces herself. Will not think back to that time. Although he did help her. Maybe it's natural of him to ask; but still. No. That time is over. Sealed up inside. Why would she ever want to think of it again?

She takes another sip, the bubbles scrambling through her empty stomach. 'Of course, my family were happy,' she says. She stops and scratches at a fleck on the table. He probably wants to hear that it was wonderful, wants her to fall at his feet in gratitude. It was good to be home, of course, and of course she was and always will be grateful for his help. But it was never the same; her family never looked at her the same way. Never was she able to feel properly at home again.

She changes the subject, asks about his life, his work, but he won't say much, and what he does say is dull. The conversation is tiresome. She longs to check the time. What is she doing here with this dull middle-aged man, who, she realizes hasn't mentioned his wife?

'How's Vivienne?' she says, remembering the troubled, suspicious woman. Maybe they'd had some warm moments together, watching soap operas and cookery shows, but Marta could never quite look her in the eye and Vivienne must have sensed that something was off. But she could be kind, gave her things, bought her things.

Mats shrugs unhappily, fills his mouth with sandwich. A waiter arrives at the women's table with a bottle of wine in an ice-bucket. Maybe it's a birthday and that's the party dress for later. Mother and daughter. They are both baked tan-bed brown with stiff sprayed hair. She thinks of her own poor Mama, feet swollen in her slippers, hardly able to walk now. But at least she doesn't have to work anymore. Milya lives in the same block so Mama sees her grandchildren every day, and Marta helps with the bills and visits at weekends. Milya married young, has two kids; her husband seems to be a good man. Milya and Sig are best friends now, neighbours, their children play together, and sometimes Marta feels left out. She feels replaced.

'Vivienne's fine,' Mats says at last. 'But we've gone our separate ways. Thought we'd wait till Tom had finished school, that was the plan, but well, she met someone and . . .' He shrugs.

'Shame,' she says, although she's more surprised they've stayed together all this time; there was never any true warmth between them that she could detect.

He's gazing at her intensely, and she stiffens. Surely he hasn't come here because of the break up? Surely he's not expecting something from her?

'Would you like these crisps?' he says. 'I'm supposed to be watching my weight.' He pats his stomach ruefully.

She would like to refuse but reaches out. The crisps are stale, but still she eats them, finishes her Coke. She takes out her phone look at the time.

'Well it was nice to meet you again.' She stands and extends her hand. 'Thanks for the drink.'

'You've got to go? Already?' As he stands to take her hand, he looks so stricken she almost laughs. Does he really want to prolong this deadly small talk?

'Look,' he says. 'Can I take you out to dinner?'

She slides her phone back into her bag.

'Tonight,' he adds. 'We're leaving tomorrow. Tom wants to see Bucharest.'

'Tonight?' she says.

'Just dinner,' he says.

She stares up at him. Just dinner! She cannot read his expression.

'What *are* you doing here?' she says.

'Seeing you.'

'Yes but – you did not come to my country just to see me!' She laughs, but he isn't laughing.

'Dinner?' he says and he gives her a little smile, *intimate, meaningful*, and she sees what he wants, stupid, old man, after all this time; in English they call it a wild goose chase, he is on a wild goose chase and she's filled with disdain. She stands up, takes a step away. 'You think you will buy me dinner and I will have sex with you?'

He takes off his glasses and blinks. 'No.' He attempts to take her hand. 'No, no, no, no, NO . . .' The no grows louder and people are looking.

'OK,' she says quickly. 'Sit down.'

'Sex is the last thing on my mind,' he says, much, much too loudly.

The two women and the empty party dress are riveted.

He is so earnest, the way he inclines himself towards her. 'You must believe me, Marta. That is not why I'm here.'

Marta sits down and he slumps back onto his chair. They sit in silence for a moment.

'What do you want?' she says, her jaw is clenched so tight she can hardly speak.

'To talk, there's something I need . . .'

A bitter fragment of laugh comes from her mouth. '*You* need?

Look, thank you for helping me back then. But there's *nothing* between us. OK?' Her voice is hard enough to strike sparks. 'OK?'

The eyebrows of the women rise, they grin and nudge each other, but she doesn't care.

Mats sits dumbly, slack faced, defeated, *sad*.

'How *dare* you come here and try to make me think about, about . . .' The choke of tears is in her throat but she won't cry; two waiters are making for the table, has her voice been raised so loud? She makes a dash for the Ladies where oh God it is familiar but dirtier than back then, paper towels overflowing from a bin and strewn across the floor. There was a rose she meant to steal for Mama, a tatty, cheap bit of shit. She locks herself in a cubicle in case they send someone in after her, but no one comes. She uses the toilet, washes her hands, stares in the mirror. Like a floater in her eye is the appalled sadness on Mats' face. Her anger fizzles out of her into the wet paper towels under her feet.

She'll be late if she doesn't go now. And someone will be sure to complain. Her job is not secure. So many people with good English now. She catches her eye in the mirror, her hair needs washing, her face looks pinched – a bit like Mama's. She touches her pale lips with her finger. What is she doing back here? If only she could leave and start again. But there is no chance of that, a waste of time to think it. Time is money, of course, it is; she must not keep the students waiting.

She straightens her expression and goes out through the door. Mats hasn't moved. He sits, hunched, hands dangling between his knees. He looks defeated, humiliated. The women are looking at him with pity, giggling and watching her now. What will happen next in this little show? She means to walk straight past, straight out, but she swerves back to him.

'OK.'

He looks up at her doubtfully.

'If you want.'

He clears his throat before he speaks. 'Thank you. Yes.'

'So now I will go to work.'

'Here? Eight?'

She shakes her head. 'I am not finished work then. Nine o'clock. And not here. There's another place. Premiera. By the way,' she says to the women who are rudely, openly listening, 'that is a shitty horrible dress.'

And she walks across the lobby, through the revolving doors and out into the street.

Mats

MATS STANDS UNDER the feeble shower. He puts his head back, lets water drench his face. The greyish soap is reluctant to lather, he rubs it against his chest hair, under his arms and with soapy hands washes his soft, slippery, unwanted genitals. When he thinks of tonight his stomach tightens as if a fist is in there, squeezing. Marta, she has grown so . . . he is afraid, awed by her. A child really, thirteen years ago, and now an assured woman, so stern. He felt an idiot at lunch under her level brown gaze. Didn't dare speak of the past at all, or hardly, and that is all there is between them, isn't it? The past. But tonight he will speak. It may be the only chance. He's waited thirteen years for this; for thirteen years the secret has gnawed inside him. No one in the world knows that he killed a man. All the strategies to make it right, to bargain with the universe, all the money to charity, all the patience with Vivienne, the determination to be a perfect husband and father, stepfather to Arthur, none of this has worked. He still knows. He still did it. He still killed a man.

And then, after all those years of trying to be a good husband, Vivienne fell in love with someone else! With his stiff back he can't easily reach his feet, knows the nails need clipping, rubs one sole on top of the other and staggers, leaning on the cold tiled wall. Not that he minds Vivienne going really, maybe it's even a relief? He can't imagine finding another wife. How can he move on with this secret lodged inside him? The only hope is to tell it. To go back in order to go forward. And the only one he can tell it to is Marta.

He switches off the shower and shudders as it trickles cold before the water stops. He dries himself, watching his own pink bulk in the steamy mirror. Of course, he would like another wife, someone to take care of, rub his back maybe, bring some fun into his life, some affection.

He sits on the toilet lid and grunts as he leans forward to dry his feet, the muscles dragging in his back. He can understand what Tom must think: that he is after Marta in that way. But no. Really no. What *is* it you want from her? he asks himself. *Absolution* comes the inane reply. Obviously no one can provide this. Not Marta, not a priest, not God, unless you believe in him, and even then?

He stands to rub deodorant under his arms, hairs catching in the roller ball. Besides, how can he offer a woman this stiff, bloated body? He thinks of Tom, the litheness, the effortlessly flat, muscular stomach, the gleam in the grain of his perfect young skin. Once Mats was like that. Christ, now even his father's in better shape than he is. He squirts shaving foam into his palms and rubs it over his cheeks and chin, begins to strafe the razor through, a sensation he finds comforting, a kind of shedding.

Once he's talked to Marta, told her the truth, once he's back home, then he will take control, cut out the booze, at least cut down, go on a diet, join a gym. With Vivienne there was no point. They stopped being physical years ago, she barely even looked at him. But he's not old. In a couple of years he'll be a different man. He could move back to Oslo now he's free – though no, he must stay close to Tom, to *both* boys, of course. After drying his face he pats it with a stinging aftershave that Vivienne always gives him for Christmas. He's not sure about it but supposes she likes it and thus that other women will.

Wrapping a towel around his waist he steps out into the room, where Tom is stretched on his bed, eyes shut, plugged into whatever the music is.

Tom

THE TV'S IN Romanian. My pizza hasn't turned up. He said this holiday was about *us* time, boy time. He never mentioned leaving me stuck in a hotel room while he dated an ex-*au pair*. He says it isn't a date but excuse me.

Anyway, tomorrow Bucharest.

I keep thinking about the revolution. In the museum it said eighty men and boys from this town were shot in a forest nearby. *Eighty.* Imagine me and Dad walking with a gun at our backs, walking with Artie and Ben and Si, to be shot. Ordinary men and boys like us walking on our own legs into the forest for that. Did they realise? What the hell was going on in their heads? Me, I would have run. Plenty of places to hide in the forest and you could live on berries and mushrooms and squirrels and stuff.

After lunch, we went to American Pie for doughnuts and Coke, though Dad only had coffee. We talked about massacre and war and he said I didn't know how lucky we were living in the UK, my generation; we hadn't had to go to war, not even national service.

'Mind if I leave you to your own devices this evening?' he said.

'Went well then?' I said.

He shrugged and began listing plans for Bucharest. There's the Palace of Parliament built by Ceaușescu, which is the third biggest building in the entire world. Yesterday I would have yawned, but now I'm actually interested. He kept reading information out of a guidebook, building a sort of fence of words so I couldn't ask him any questions. Not that I wanted to.

When we got back to the hotel I watched him getting ready for his date, slapping on the aftershave, trying not to look too keyed up for my sake. I could understand if she was some 'sexy babe' type, though the thought of Dad and a sexy babe . . . Don't go there. They would only be talking, he said. For old times' sake. She's got missing teeth and grey hairs! Not my idea of a good night out.

Now he's gone and where's my pizza? There's a match on TV so I watch the first half between two teams I'd never heard of, and still no pizza. There's a phone in the room but I don't know which number to call, or what to say if they answer in Romanian. Maybe if I just say, 'Pizza Room 12' they'll understand. *Pizza* is an international word, I think? I picked up the phone but there's only a beeping sound so I go down to reception. No one about except an old man asleep in a cupboard with his mouth hanging open and rows of keys behind him.

Outside the sun's still shining so I go out through the open door. Surprisingly at this time of night, the streets are crowded with people strolling, eating ice creams, pushing prams, walking dogs. Many more people than during the day. I walk along behind a family like ours used to be: dad, mum and two kids about the same distance apart as me and Artie. The parents are holding hands as if they actually *like* each other. I never heard Mum and Dad laughing together like these two. It's probably right that they're getting a divorce. Mum's happy with Brian (twat) as much as she ever could be; she's never been a very happy person, I see that now.

Marta

MARTA CUTS A small slice of veal, puts it in her mouth and chews. It's a little leathery, maybe, but good. She sips her wine. Mats has gone to the toilet and at last she can breathe, enjoy the food. It's still a mystery – if he really isn't after sex – what he wants from this awkward evening. OK, he wants to talk about the past, but that she will not allow, and he seems resigned to this.

She rushed straight from work, aware that she might not smell perfectly fresh, having had time to do nothing but drag a brush through her hair. Even so she was ten minutes late and found him already part way through a bottle of wine; he was smartly dressed, freshly shaved, as if this was an occasion, and she felt sorry about her crumpled skirt and blouse.

He stood, took her jacket and pulled back her chair before the waiter could get there and do his job. He poured her a glass of wine; she rarely drinks, but accepted this time, hoping it might relax her. She translated the menu for him, and he ordered the chef's special for both of them.

Now she nibbles a floppy green bean. Her head's aching as it usually does after work; all she really wants is to go home, stretch out on the sofa, eat bread and tomatoes, drink tea and watch television until her eyelids close as she does every night.

He returns from the toilet, speaks to the waiter on the

way, ordering more wine, maybe. And then he sits across from her looking at her almost expectantly, it seems, though the candle flame reflected in his glasseses makes it hard to read his eyes.

'Nice town,' he says.

She pulls a face. 'You think?'

'Tell me about your family,' he says. And OK, this is harmless, she tells him about Milya's children, the daughter, Anya – so like Milya herself – the son, Georg, who she privately thinks is rather slow. Milya doesn't know it yet, but Marta's saving money to send Anya to university. She's only nine but bright, serious and eager to learn, reminds Marta of herself at that age. She helps the girl with her English at the weekends – she can't wait to introduce her to *Jane Eyre*, a shiny new copy, she will order online and present for her tenth birthday, she's just about ready for it. This is Marta's new accomplishment, online shopping; you can get anything from the West now, as long as you can pay.

'Hey. You still there?' Smiling, Mats snaps his fingers.

Marta shakes herself out of a sleepy trance. 'Sorry.'

'How often do you see them?'

Can he really be interested in her small life? She takes a breath, tells him about her weekend visits, how she babysits on Saturday nights so Milya and Egor can go out dancing. How she cooks lunch for everyone at Mama's flat on Sundays, how even Antoni sometimes turns up with his spoilt son and his spiteful shiny wife. Mats appears interested, just as he did when she told him about her work. She stops to take a piece of potato.

'I should let you eat,' he says. 'More wine?'

'A very little. You speak now.'

And so he pours her wine and as she eats and sips, feeling the headache drain way as nourishment gets into her blood, she listens and watches. He tries to make his job sound interesting, but he's most animated when talking about the boys, particularly Tom. His face glows with love then, and in her chest she feels a softening towards him. An affection. He's buying her dinner, he's straining to be kind. He is kind. Maybe he wants nothing more than this? Is this possible? She watches his mouth, the teeth a little stained but still, good strong teeth. She questions him about Tom, about Artie, about Vivienne, asks him what happened to break them up.

'We stuck it out,' is how he puts it. 'It was a good enough marriage while it lasted.'

'Good enough?' she says.

He wipes his mouth with a napkin, frowns. 'You know . . . it was a stable home for the boys.'

The waiter comes to clear their plates. 'Dessert?' He issues them with menus.

'What do you like?' Mats asks.

She runs her finger down the laminated page. 'Ah, they have *lapte de pasăre*,' she says. 'This,' she explains to Mats, 'is clouds in custard.'

'Sounds good. Sounds light.'

'Is light,' she says, 'is delicious,' forgetting her pronouns but too tired to retrieve them. She smothers a yawn.

'Two of those, please,' he says to the waiter, who nods curtly. He's been eyeing Mats with suspicion all evening.

Marta gives him a hard stare.

'Of course, you're tired,' Mats says. 'I'm sorry.'

'It was the biggest treat when I was small,' she says, with a pang remembering her grandparents in the country, so many years ago, remembering the sweet, eggy taste of the dessert, served always in the best dishes, with their blue and gold design. 'I haven't had it for years.'

Maybe she'll make it on Sunday for her family. Anya and Georg will love it, as they love all sweet things.

Mats is quiet for a moment, pouring himself more wine, extending the bottle to her, but she's had enough.

'Sure?' he says. 'Won't go with the pudding. Needs to be finished.'

She shakes her head. She could almost swoon with tiredness, but at least she doesn't have to work in the morning, not till 5pm when the first workers' classes begin. Really, she should search for more work to fill Fridays, her quietest day of the week – but it is good to have a few hours to herself. Friday is her reading day. Right now she's working her way through Tolstoy again – and sometimes sits in American Pie, reading and drinking espresso and smoking, pretending she's in London or Paris or New York.

The *lapte de pasăre* arrive – white dishes with pale thin custard – so different from Grandma's, hers was always thick and yolky yellow; these clouds are dainty puffs, not the towering mounds of cumuli Grandma used to whip up. Marta's throat hollows with disappointment; but of course this is restaurant food, refined. With the hollowing of her throat, another yawn comes. So rude.

'Sorry,' she says, and smiles at Mats from behind her hand.

'They have this in Britain,' Mats says. 'Floating Islands. Also in Norway too, but with jam under the custard. Can't remember what we call that.' He puts in his spoon and scoops up a cloud. 'Mmm.'

They eat in silence. The custard is thin, cool, grainy with vanilla, the meringue melts in the mouth. It is delicious, but really mostly air, she thinks.

'Coffee?' the waiter is there, as soon as they've finished.

Mats raises his eyebrows at her and she nods, takes out her cigarettes and offers one to Mats, but he shakes his head.

'I wish. Given up. Doctor's orders.'

She lights up and breathes in the rough smoke, closes her eyes for a moment. Never will she give up this little pleasure.

The coffee comes and she tears the ends of two paper tubes of sugar, stirs it in.

'OK,' Mats says, nodding at her cigarette, 'since you insist. One won't hurt.'

She smiles as she passes him the packet and her lighter, watches his big fingers fumble. 'Oh,' he said as he takes his first drag. 'This takes me back.'

She stiffens, back is not the right direction.

They smoke and sip coffee with no conversation but she can sense him preparing to speak.

'If you could have one wish,' he says, 'what would it be?'

She snorts, half laughs, 'What?'

'A wish,' he repeats, 'one wish.' His expression is quite serious, interested.

What nonsense is this?

'Tell me,' he says.

She sighs. 'A million dollars,' she says sarcastically, 'world peace.'

But he is looking at her with such attention. She might as well indulge him, she can give him that much for the price of a meal. 'OK. One wish?' Oh but it is sore to think like this and a wish arrives swiftly like jab in the heart. 'That my Tata was still here.' She breathes in sharply, stiffens her shoulders and her face. 'Before Tata died I was so angry.' She twizzles her cigarette between her fingers, talks almost with her teeth clenched. 'He stopped me seeing a boy, Virgil. Now I understand. I would do the same. He wanted me to go to university,' she adds. She grinds out her cigarette in the ashtray. She will not cry.

'You wanted that?' Mats says. 'University?'

She can't speak now, but she nods; her throat seems turned to stone.

'Finished?' The waiter is back again. Wanting to get rid of them and close up, of course; they are the last diners.

'The bill, please,' Mats says. 'Don't go yet, Marta, I want to talk.'

She takes a deep breath and blows out smoke. 'We have talked.'

'I mean—'

'No,' she says, more sharply than she means. 'Sorry. Thank you for dinner. Very nice, very kind, but I am too tired for more talk.'

His face sags, but he nods. He pays the bill, leaves a tip so huge the waiter will be laughing; Marta feels protective on his behalf. 'Don't leave so much,' she says, taking up half of it and pressing it in his hand.

'Sure. Don't want to look mean.'

'You make yourself look a fool,' she says and sees him flinch. 'You're not mean,' she adds, touching his arm. There's warmth in her voice, and though she doesn't mean this as encouragement, he seems to take it as such.

'Can we meet tomorrow?' he asks, as soon as they are outside.

She looks up at him curiously, his face, tilting down at her, is in shadow. 'But you're leaving in the morning, you said? I live this way.' She throws down her cigarette stub, grinds it with her heel and starts to walk, Mats beside her.

'We don't *have* to leave tomorrow,' he says.

'Where are you staying?' she says.

'Casa Antiqua,' he says.

'OK. That's near me.'

They walk in silence for a while. A car goes past, loud music pumping from its windows. 'I hate that,' she says. 'Is showing off, stupid pricks.' As she says this she has a sudden memory of Alis. See, that is the trouble with this, with seeing him, with looking back. She must keep all that, *all* that, shut up, shut off.

'Tomorrow?' he says.

'I don't know.'

'Please.'

They walk behind the Church; a short cut. She is so tired, her legs could fold underneath her.

'Maybe,' she says at last, she's almost too tired to care what she does tomorrow, as long as she can get to bed now. She's shivery with exhaustion, though it's a warm night.

'Please,' he says, 'look, I'll bring Tom, we can do something together.'

'Is a short cut.' The path is rough and potholed, wet and smelly from a broken drain, and he stumbles. He's breathless, she realizes and slows her pace.

They stop outside the hotel. 'Meet us for coffee in the morning,' he says. 'Maybe we can go somewhere? An outing?'

Her quiet morning with *Anna Karenina* dissolves as she sighs, but OK. He is likeable, she did like him then and though she's struggling not to, she likes him now. She knows she should let go the part of her that has turned so bitter. Milya scolds her for being a bitch; she never used to be one. The bitterness, the bitchiness, is only disappointment about the smallness of her life, the let-down. But who does she think she is? It's a good enough life, isn't it? Many in the world are so much worse. She shivers.

'You're cold,' he says. 'Come here.' She lets him hold her, stands stiffly in his warmth.

'I won't have sex with you,' she mumbles into his chest.

'I know.' He holds onto her tighter. 'That's not what I want.'

He bends down and kisses her on the top of the head, more like a father than a lover. Maybe he is on the level after all? He's not a bad man, that's for sure. He's warm. And when was she last held? She sighs. 'OK. ten o'clock,' she says, 'American Pie.'

She misses that warmth as she hurries away, fumbling already for her key.

Tom

STRANGE TO BE out on my own in a strange town in a strange land. I get loads of looks, not sure if friendly or not. They don't smile all that much here. My feet ache. I don't know where I am. I go into a café, crowded with mostly men, drinking coffee or beer or some kind of shots. It's hot and full of smoke, shouts and laughs, music jangling out of a speaker, a TV screen showing the same match with no one watching except some sad old git scratching his balls.

Coca Cola is another international word, so I go to the bar and when I finally get noticed say, 'Coca Cola please?' And before I can even get my money out, a voice says: 'I pay.'

I turn to see a short woman with a round face and puffy orange hair. Her eyelids are blue and her lips bright red.

'English?' she says.

'Kind of,' I say. 'Actually half Norwegian and born in Scotland.'

'You help me practise English?' She picks up my Coke and carries it away, winking at the guy behind the counter and saying something foreign. We sit in a corner under the TV. Light comes through a dirty window and shines on the side of her face, all fluffy and powdery.

'What's your name English boy?' she says.

I tell her and she lights herself a cigarette, offering me the box.

I take one though I don't smoke. She lights it for me and I inhale and cough.

'Maria,' she says, breathing out smoke. 'How old are you?'

When I say sixteen she pulls a doubtful face. 'Nearly,' I say and it's true. Fourteen is nearly fifteen, which is nearly sixteen.

'What are you doing here?' she asks. I tell her we're off to Bucharest tomorrow then I find myself telling her that Dad and Mum are getting divorced. I don't know why, words just keep on coming out.

'Ah poor Tom,' she says and squeezes my hand.

'S'OK,' I say.

She nods, peers at me with her eyelashes all squished together. I don't know if it's mascara or actual false lashes, but they're massive and sticky looking. You could trap flies with them. Her tits are massive too, that does not escape me. They're fighting to get out of her dress, all crammed in in a way that looks cruel. Between them's a dark powdery crease and when she sees me looking it seems to deepen as if she's pushing her tits together with her elbows. I look away quick but my face goes red. She laughs, hand to her mouth. Her nails are artificial with one missing.

I look away and sip my warm Coke. 'What bit of English do you want do learn?' I say, thinking she seems pretty good already.

'Talky English between friends,' she says. So we talk about weather and food and then she says. 'You have girlfriend?'

I tell her about Else. I make it sound as if we're together in that way; Else would kill me!

'You fuckyfuck with her?' she asks and my face goes beetroot.

'You want to practise?' she says. 'Only 600 krone.'

At first I don't get what she's saying, but then she puts her hand under the table and squeezes my knee, smoke drifting out through her lipstick.

'Or hand job is 300.'

I stand up so suddenly my chair falls over behind me and I run. Laughter chases after me, not just hers. I run and run, totally lost now, and it's nearly dark, the sky like a spill of Tango and Ribena. I can see factories and blocks of flats outlined against it in the distance. My heart hammers and I've got a hard-on so it's difficult to run. Horrible. I stop by a stinking river and sit on a wall, getting my breath back. She was so *old*. But she *was* a woman and I've never done it. Imagine telling Ben and Si I've done it with a Romanian prostitute. That would be so cool. Cooler even than seeing a bear. I can say both. Who'll know?

Takes me till proper dark to find the hotel again. There's a girl behind the desk now, a proper one, pretty and young with shining brown hair. I can't look her in the eye when I ask about the pizza. She apologizes and says she'll get it sent right up. I go upstairs hoping Dad might be back but no, the room's empty, the TV still on, just as I left it. I flick through the channels and find a dubbed version of *Friends* and it's kind of fun watching and trying to read their lips to see what they're actually saying. And at least they're familiar. Like actual friends. How sad is that? It's getting late. Where's Dad?

The more I try not to, the more I think about the prostitute and her eyelashes and tits, imagining being trapped in the crease between them and the horror of that makes me wonder if I'm gay? I have wondered before. I could have paid her to try it out. I had enough money in my pocket. Or paid a nicer one, younger like the one on the desk. But that would probably cost more. You get what you pay for in this world, Dad says. And then I realize: I am actually thinking about paying for sex! And that's so wrong. When

I do it I want it to be with an actual girlfriend (or boyfriend) who wants it too and not for money. Though maybe it would be worth practising first?

I try thinking about Else instead. I've seen her naked in the sauna at her home (seen her mother too and her dad) but it's not sexy it's just embarrassing. Though perfectly normal for Norwegians. I don't want to think of Else in a sexy way. Does that make me gay? I will never pay for sex though, whatever I am, I know that already. Dad would be so ashamed, disappointed if he knew I'd even *thought* about it. He's always told me to respect women, girls, not to look at porn and stuff.

There's a knocking on the door and when I open it there's the girl with a big red pizza box flat on her hand. 'Sorry for delay,' she says. I get a hard on again at the idea of her coming into the room. I take the pizza and hold it in front of myself, stand back, not sure whether to tip. In the end I just give her more money for the pizza than it is and say, 'Keep the change,' like Dad does.

The pizza is pure stodge and not much taste but I don't care, I'm ravenous. I munch my way through it, watching Ross and Joey and Monica and the rest with Romanian spouting out of their mouths not quite in synch with their lips.

It's late. Dad should be back. Every five minutes I look out of the window. What if he doesn't come back? What if something's happened? In a place like this, what would I do? There's a tree under the window and the street lamp flickers on and off and makes the leaves look purple. I keep the telly on, some old film now, and my music in my ears and try to read a bit more *Animal Farm* to use my time profitably, as Dad would say.

I make this rule. I have to read a page of book between each time I look out of the window. And after four more pages, there he is.

And she is. Don't see her at first, it's just him hunched over, the street light flickering leafy shadows on his on his grey hair and his humpy shoulders. And then I realise they're specially humpy because he's hugging someone and of course it's the *au pair*. They're partly hidden by a branch of the tree, but I can see enough. I drop the curtain, lie down on my bed with *Animal Farm* and wait, feeling all kind of sick and squirmy.

And soon, in he comes with his face all pink and strangely open like he's dropped an E or something. He takes off his glasses and looks at me with a naked dazzle in his eyes.

'You OK?' he says.

I nod.

'Have a good evening?'

'OK,' I say.

'Pizza nice?'

'Not particularly.'

He clears his throat. 'Er, I'm considering staying here for another day,' he says. 'No need to go haring off to Bucharest, is there? Bucharest will wait.'

'Why?' I say.

'Unfinished business.'

I refrain from comment.

'Would you mind?'

I look at his face. I want to say no, but how can I? 'It'll cost you,' I say.

The smile he gives me is like no smile I've ever seen before. It's so hot and pure it almost burns and I have to look away.

Mats

THE PATH IS steep, winding between trees. Mats is out of breath from trying to keep up. This could be a forest in Norway, or Scotland for that matter, a fringe of birch and rowan leading to stately areas of beech and the shadows between creaking pines. Tom and Marta have stopped to examine a great craggy toadstool allowing Mats to catch up. Tom pokes the fungus with his stick. 'Poisonous?' he asks, with relish.

'No, it is delicious, but this one is too old. See.' She takes Tom's stick and chops the flesh, to show that it is full of little squirming grubs.

'Shitting hell!' Tom jumps back.

Smiling, Marta shakes her head at Mats.

'Have *you* seen many bears?' Tom asks her.

'Not lately.' She pulls a face. 'You're more likely to see them at the rubbish tip than anywhere else.'

Regardless, Tom leaps on ahead, wielding a stick.

Marta grins over her shoulder at Mats as she follows. It's lovely the way her face lightens when she smiles like that. Back in Edinburgh he hardly remembers her smiling at all.

Tomorrow they leave for Bucharest, this is the deal with Tom: one extra day for an iPhone. He drives a hard bargain. Only one more day with Marta and later, she says, she must work. She was reluctant to come to the forest with them, suggesting other outings: a hunting lodge from communist times, where they hoarded their precious artworks and wines; a monastery, a castle. But Tom, London boy, had insisted on the real wild forest, on a bear hunt.

'I loved coming here when I was small.' Marta turns to Mats, rather sadly maybe. 'Tata used to bring us for a picnic in August every year, to pick mushrooms. Mama dried them to last the winter.'

Knuckles of root lift the path, make a gnarled stairway; he watches Marta's small sure feet, feels gross in comparison, plodding, out of breath. Last night he didn't get the chance to say what he's come to say, but today he will speak. It may be the only chance. He fixes his eyes on her slim back in its white T-shirt and dark jeans, the tumble of her hair, admires the way she walks, feet lifting neatly, surely.

He will tell her what he did to Mr Chapman. He must. That name in his mind causes a sensation like a fist thrusting upwards between his ribs, winding him, squashing his heart. An organ has grown there made of darkness, made of guilt, made of the thing never spoken, hardly admitted even to himself and if he doesn't speak this secret, he fears that it will kill him. It makes no sense to say it to anyone else. It wouldn't work to say it to anyone else.

'Hey,' shouts Tom, 'check it out!'

Marta follows his voice and Mats lumbers after her into a clearing in the wood, and in the clearing is a pool, almost circular, scattered with leaves, reflecting treetops and a vivid blue and white sky. White and yellow flowers, butterflies – blue and tawny – and a ridiculously gaudy circle of fly agarics, it's like a setting in a Disney film.

'Wicked,' Tom says, smashing a perfect toadstool with his stick. 'Loads of men were shot in this forest,' he adds. 'Did you know?'

Marta gives a single nod and turns her face away but not before Mats sees her expression. She moves away from Mats, trailing her fingers against the trunk of a knotty birch.

'Any fish in there?' Tom asks. Fly fishing was his last year's craze. 'Should have brought a rod.' He peers into the water.

'I do not like this spot,' says Marta, darting Mats a panicked look. 'Let's go back now.'

'But it's cool!' Tom edges round the pool, begins mucking about with sticks, trying to dam the little stream that trickles into the pool.

Marta comes to Mats; a finger brushes his sleeve. 'Please. We must go back,' she says. 'I have to work.'

'Give him five minutes.'

They stand side by side, faces reflected in the smooth green sheen of the water. Water skaters make tiny dimples on the meniscus. Behind their heads a cloud shape-shifts.

'A dog,' Marta says, her voice a sad scrape.

'Sorry?'

'The cloud, looks like dog. No it's changed now.'

'Into a sheep.' Mats remembers playing cloud pictures as a child and with his own kids too. 'A sheep with feathers.'

Abruptly he finds he can't breathe. The opportunity is draining away. If he doesn't tell her now, he never will. Tom clambers up a tree.

'Careful,' Mats calls.

In the water Marta's face is small, his own a heavy wedge, specs glinting. Tom sits on a branch, legs swinging. The wires of his headphones snake from his hoodie down to his iPod; his legs swing in time to his music.

Between Mats and Marta the silence stretches. A leaf drops onto the water rippling their reflections. She snatches her face away. When she meets his eyes he sees that hers are huge and black. 'This is where the men were shot, I think,' she says. 'See.' She leads him to the trees, points out thick scars, black against the silver bark. Mats glances at Tom high in the tree, he'll be thrilled to hear this.

But Marta is continuing, 'My Tata. And boyfriend, Virgil, and others. Maybe it was here. I don't know for sure.'

Mats looks at the ground, the lush grass where blood has maybe soaked, the knobs of fungus pushing up. Birds whistle, leaves whisper. The uneven rooty ground makes him think of bones.

'Sorry,' he mutters. So useless. Oh he wants to fold her in his arms. But he does not dare to even touch. Last night, when he held her, she was so stiff.

They must go. Soon it will be too late. Mats calls Tom but he doesn't hear, waves but he doesn't see. His eyes are closed, feet thrashing away to whatever music is pumping into his ears. Usually it would annoy Mats: listen to the birds! he'd say, but right now he's glad.

'I must go,' she says.

'One more minute?' Mats nods at the boy.

Marta sniffs and nods, hugs her arms around herself.

A couple of small brown birds, some kind of finch, flit down, peck at the ground; butterflies are like flying petals. The stiller you are, the more you see; a metal dragonfly flashes turquoise, flies buzz, wiry and sinuous. The fist is pushing up, squashing his heart, his lungs, till he really thinks he might collapse. Is he having a heart attack? He props himself against a tree, takes a deep breath.

'I want to tell you something. I need you to know,' he says in a rush. 'No one else knows.'

Her eyes widen as she waits for him to speak.

'Mr Chapman,' he begins.

She flinches, steps away. 'No.'

'Listen,' he says. 'Please.'

She turns her back on him but she can still hear.

'I killed him.' The three words come out just like that after all this time. Three bits of something breaking off. Her back stiffens but she is motionless, listening.

'I went that day to look for you. He was there in the Club, in the basement. And I saw down there . . . I saw a body.' Heart thudding now, hard and loud, as if it will bound right up his throat. Forcing it down, he says, 'I thought it was you.'

She turns, face parchment yellow, such deeply scored furrows on her forehead she has become almost ugly.

'So I killed him. I punched him and he fell backwards. He fell into the basement. I shut the trapdoor and left.'

The words are a jerky string and the whole world dangles from it, the whole world depends on what she says and what she does now. Or else it does not matter. At least he's said it. Legs weak, he leans back against the tree, a finger of sweat tracing down his temple. How can his heart withstand this?

She whispers something he doesn't catch.

'What?'

A fly scribbles between them.

'I thought it was you,' he says.

Tears well up in her eyes and roll over but she steps back when he reaches out. Tom is singing something along with his music. From high above a grinding sound – a plane. He glances up at the straight white vapour trail. Gasps in a breath.

'You murdered Ratman?' Her lashes are spiked, there's a thread of grey in her hair he notices and his poor heart stutters, blooms.

'I thought he'd killed you.'

She puts her hands in front of her face, looks at him, huge eyed over her finger tips.

'Maybe you saw Alis.' She swallows, scrubs her wet cheek with her fists. 'My friend.'

A branch cracks, startling making them both, and Tom jumps down. 'I'm starving,' he seems to yell. 'Can we get a burger?'

Mats looks down at Marta, arms hugged tight around herself. If only he could take his thumb and smooth out the lines on her brow. He aches for contact with her; it seems necessary to help him breathe.

'OK,' he says to his son.

'Cool!' Tom grabs his stick. Gives Marta an odd, almost mocking look, extends it to Mats, shrugs and jaunts off, shouting over his shoulder, 'Watch out for bears.'

Marta has remained motionless, hunched, staring at the ground.

'Hey, we'd better go,' Mats says unwillingly as the sounds of his son recede. Somewhere deep down fear stirs. What if there *are* bears?

'You murdered Ratman,' Marta says, looking straight into his face, and giving – no it can't be, but it is – a choke of *laughter*. '*You*,' she emphasises the word in a way he doesn't quite like. '*You* crazy Norwegian, *you* murdered Ratman?'

She stares up at him, her face a struggle of shock and amusement, shaking her head, tears brightening her eyes. 'And you got away with it.' She gives a whimpering, almost exalted moan, opens her mouth as if to say more, does not, turns her back on him to thread away between the trees.

'But wait . . .' Mats follows, heavy, tripping, clumsy, soon out of breath. His poor heart trudges laboriously. But at least it is still beating. He catches up with her.

'I didn't get away with it,' he says. 'Not here.' He screws his knuckles against his chest.

'Let it go,' she says, and turns away.

'What?'

'Let it go.'

He's halted in his tracks. She leaves the words behind between the leaves. *Let it go.* He carries on, following her, trying to breathe. He can't catch up. Maybe there is more room in his chest now that he has spoken? *Let it go.* These are simple words, beautiful words. Up ahead Tom is whooping about something; a bird sings, just like a blackbird at home. Mats stops and gazes up between the treetops to see the contrail dissolving into the blue.

'Let it go?' he says to the sky. 'Let it go?'

Not until they're at the forest fringes does he manage to catch Marta up again. She's leaning against a tree smoking a cigarette. When she holds the packet out to him, he shakes his head. Across a field he can see the hire car parked glinting blue in the sun. Tom is already there, a tiny figure, leaning against the bonnet. Quite safe; no bears.

She tilts her head back and breathes out smoke. On her cheeks are the smudges of dried tears. Her hair is stirring in the breeze, deep brown-black with those darling premature threads of grey.

'Let it go?' he says to her.

A warm bee blunders through the air between them and there is something honeyed in the sensation between his ribs, a sweet softening when she says, 'Yes. It is over. Let it go.' She throws down her cigarette and walks off. He puts it out with his sole; they don't want to start a forest fire.

They begin to walk, quite slowly, across a rutted weedy field strewn with flints and bits of broken pot. He feels the beginnings of a lightness; as if he might have left something behind in the forest, between the trees.

'About our conversation,' he dares. 'Last night.'

'Mmm?'

'You said you wanted to go to university.'

She shakes her head impatiently.

'You did.'

'Maybe once.'

He stumbles and rights himself. The sun is hot out here, he can feel a sting on his neck.

'You still could,' he says.

She snorts.

'Why not?'

'Is too late for me.' She bends to pick up a small mottled feather, smooths the filaments between her fingers.

'Rubbish,' Mats says.

She has turned towards him and the look on her face is almost startled.

'You could go to night school.' This plan began hatching in the long wakeful hours of night. A plan to do a good thing to try to make up for the bad.

'I work evenings,' she says. 'And I must earn money for my family.'

'Come to London,' Mats says tentatively, half expecting her to turn and walk away, or tell him to fuck off. 'Nothing like that,' he says hastily, 'just listen.'

She shrugs as if she doesn't care what he says, but he detects a sharpening of her attention.

'If you came to London, I could help you,' he says. 'You could earn more there. You could study.'

'How?'

'You could stay with me, or if you prefer, I could find you somewhere else, lend you money, you could sign on for evening classes, qualify for university in a couple of years. Plenty of mature students do that.'

'Mature students,' she repeats. Clearly, she likes the phrase. She throws the feather up and watches it twizzle down.

'Yes, you could be a mature student, part-time maybe so you could work too, send money home. I'd help you get set up.'

'What about a visa?'

'I'd help with that. Looks as if you'll be in the EU before too long, then you can come and go as you like.'

She bites her thumb staring at him.

'I can't,' she says, 'it's too much, how can I?'

They've reached the edge of the field.

'Hurry up!' calls Tom. 'I'm starving to death here.'

'What do you say?'

She stands for a moment, clenching and unclenching her fists, then, 'I'm hungry too,' she says, looking up at him. 'So much I could eat a horse!'

She looks so proud of the English idiom it makes him smile. He takes a breath, deeper than any he has managed for a long time. 'So?' he says.

She reaches out to take his hand. Her fingers are small but strong, cooler than his own. She doesn't answer, but squeezes tightly before she lets go. And as she turns away to cross the road he sees that her eyes are brimming, not with tears, but with light.

Acknowledgements

WITH THANKS TO Bill Hamilton, Jen Hamilton-Emery, Andrew Greig, Jane Rogers, Tracey Emerson, Ron Butlin and Regi Claire.

NEW BOOKS FROM SALT

XAN BROOKS
The Clocks in This House All Tell Different Times
(978-1-78463-093-5)

RON BUTLIN
Billionaires' Banquet (978-1-78463-100-0)

MICKEY J CORRIGAN
Project XX (978-1-78463-097-3)

MARIE GAMESON
The Giddy Career of Mr Gadd (deceased) (978-1-78463-118-5)

NAOMI HAMILL
How To Be a Kosovan Bride (978-1-78463-095-9)

CHRISTINA JAMES
Fair of Face (978-1-78463-108-6)

SIMON KINCH
Two Sketches of Disjointed Happiness (978-1-78463-110-9)

NEW BOOKS FROM SALT

STEFAN MOHAMED
Stanly's Ghost
(978-1-78463-076-8)

EMILY MORRIS
My Shitty Twenties
(978-1-78463-091-1)

SIMON OKOTIE
In the Absence of Absalon
(978-1-78463-102-4)

GUY WARE
Reconciliation
(978-1-78463-104-8)

TONY WILLIAMS
Nutcase
(978-1-78463-106-2)

MEIKE ZIERVOGEL
The Photographer
(978-1-78463-114-7)

This book has been typeset by
SALT PUBLISHING LIMITED
using Neacademia, a font designed by Sergei Egorov
for the Rosetta Type Foundry in the Czech Republic.
It is manufactured using Creamy 70gsm, a Forest
Stewardship Council™ certified paper from Stora Enso's
Anjala Mill in Finland. It was printed and bound by
Clays Limited in Bungay, Suffolk, Great Britain.

CROMER, NORFOLK
GREAT BRITAIN
MMXVII